PROLOGUE

Death. The word that passes our minds infrequently. How will it happen? Will it hurt when it does? Or occasionally, I'd think about the date. Knowing that I had already lived through the date I would die sixteen times. The eerie feeling of being right on the reaper's doorstep twenty-eight times is a feeling that would haunt me every year.

Only it doesn't have to anymore. Because that date has come.

Water engulfed me as I slid deeper and deeper in. Black. Dark. Empty and silent. No waves crashing, no screams. Everything is just so silent.

I opened my eyes, my long dusty brown hair floating around me. I can't breathe. I can't see past the murky waters.

This is it.

I'm going to die.

I'm no longer waiting for death to take hold of my languid soul, I'm there. Door wide open.

I sunk deeper and deeper into oblivion. The unknown. The darkness that holds no promises...

CROWNED BY FATE

AMO JONES

Crowned by Fate

Crowned Duet: Book Two

By Amo Jones

Copyright 2020 Amo Jones

Shout out to my team!

Cover design: Jay Aheer
Editing: My Brothers Editor
Content Editing: Petra Gleason
Proof-reading: Rosa Sharon
Beta readers: Sarah Sentz & Amy Halter

To you, my readers.

ONE

Not all truths should rise. Some should be doused in lies and remain buried. - Isa

To sin, you would need to believe, because evil cannot exist without the faith of good. I am not good. I am not well. I am something that has been caged inside of a dark cell for years. A cell that has no key, no access code, and no escape route. It lives within me, between the twisted knots of my brain.

I wake, shivering, my lips trembling and my teeth chattering. *Why is it cold?* It's so so cold. I stumble off the bed, fisting the clean white sheets with me and wrapping them around my body. My hand comes to my stomach, where there was once a swollen bump, it is now flat, with no evidence of me bearing a child. *What is this? What is my name?*

I scan the room. I'm so cold. There's a metal bed. A fireplace, stone and inbuilt into the silent echoes of white walls. Unlit. *It's so cold.* There is a load of logwood beside the front mantle, bark scaling off and scattered over the ground. I shiver again, goose bumps breaking out over my flesh. Under my toes is a plush red rug, the color of...

"Blood..." I whisper to myself, as memories crash into my brain at a hundred miles per hour.

My name is Isa Royal.

Bryant Saint Royal is my husband.

I didn't have to fear death, I am death. It follows me everywhere.

It's so cold. Air whooshes past me, and my body violently shivers with its embrace. The door creaks. Wooden, like a cabin. The windows, sealed with icicles, slip down the other side of the glass, melting away.

I'm in a cabin, but how and why? There's a double bed that I'm curled up in in the lounge room.

I tilt my head, confused. The front door swings open and a man enters, kicking it shut behind him.

"Oh, it's fucking cold out," he says casually. Too casually.

I squeeze the sheet, a scream slipping from my mouth. "Who the fuck are you?"

The man. He's large, broad, and hairy. His beard is long, but his eyes are pretty. They slant softly around the edges, but the color pierces me like a flying dagger, target: me.

"Quiet." He drops some logs down near the open fireplace, the flames licking through the air. I don't want to ask more questions. Confused and dazed, I crawl backward until my back hits the wall. Sweat coats the palm of my hands, a tightening in my chest that I can't loosen.

"Why?" I whisper, my hand coming to my head. My hair is brushed, curled in perfect curls and when my fingers touch my lips, I can feel the cream from the lipstick smudge off. "Where am I?"

The man doesn't answer.

He moves around the cabin, and I watch in pure fascination as he shuffles with precision despite his size. A wooden table, an outdated stone style kitchen, a two-seater fabric couch, and no TV. A large portrait painting hangs on the wall. A woman. Dark hair that drops over her slender shoulders and a collarbone that looks to be sharpened by a scalpel. Her face is a warped mess of oil colors stirred together to conceal her identity. I don't know why, but I resonate with the painting. Transfixed and entranced by the art, I reach out to touch the wilted canvas, needing to touch her face.

Movement catches me off guard, snapping me out of my trance. I spin around, the flames from the fire licking my back. "Do I know you?"

"No," he answers, clipped. Not a man of many words.

I swallow my nerves. "Where's the bathroom?"

He points a big finger over my shoulder. "Second door on the right. If you're not out in five minutes, I'm coming in." I slide past him, heading straight for the room he directed me to. I don't want him near me right now. Not until I know who he is.

I close the bathroom door and kick down the toilet seat. That's when what I'm wearing catches my eye. A white linen robe that cuts off at my upper thigh. I touch the soft texture, rubbing it between my thumb and index finger. What is this and how did I get here?

A loud bang on the door jolts me out of my daze. "Isa! Hurry up."

"Hang on a minute!" I call out, pushing the robe up higher and taking a seat on the toilet. Once I'm finished, I hit the tap on the basin and wash my hands. My eyes come up to the mirror in the bathroom and I freeze.

I look the same, only different. My hair is longer, a shade darker. My skin is pale, as if I've missed a whole season of summer, and my eyes have lines beneath them that I have never noticed before. There's another bang and I jump.

"Oh, alright!" I pull open the door to see the man—

"What's your name?" I ask, tilting my head. He's dressed in jeans and a dark shirt that hugs his muscles perfectly. He is big, burly and bearded, but there's a softness that lays beneath his eyes. Beneath the hard exterior. Or maybe I'm deluded. That could be it. Actually, that could be backed by facts.

"Max." His eyes drop down my body before traveling back up to meet mine. "I don't want to make this any more difficult on you, so just do as you're told." He turns his back and disappears into the sitting room where the open fireplace is now blazing like an inferno storm.

"What do you mean?" I ask, falling behind him. "I don't understand how I woke here. The last thing I remember is my wedding day." I gasp, my hand coming into view. Seeing my finger empty is like a bullet being shot through my heart. "Where's my ring?"

Max stabs at the fire with a long metal fork, obviously unwilling to answer my question.

"Hey!" I step closer, my hand coming to his back. "Where's my ring?"

His shoulders tighten beneath my grip. He slowly turns to face me. "What ring?"

"I'm married!" I yell, frustrated at myself that I can't remember anything. I slam my mouth shut as realization hits me like a race car with no destination. "Where's Bryant? Where's my daughter, Harper?"

My arms fly out as I hit him with the back of my hand. "Where are they!" I feel myself slowly slipping, losing control of what little power I had already. My bones soften, irritation digging its claws deeper and deeper into my skin.

His big hand snatches my arm and flings it away from him as his other squeezes around my other arm. His face comes close to mine. Nose to nose. "You. Aren't. Married."

I take four breaths.

One.

Two.

Three.

"What the fuck do you mean?" I fail on the fourth because I'm ready to punch him straight in the face and take my chances running. I need Bryant. I need my daughter. *Where am I?*

I fly backward when he releases me, my ass hitting the wall. Running his hand through his hair, he grips it at the ends. "You're not married. Not anymore." Before I can swear at him, he storms down the hallway and disappears through one of the doors.

I sink to the ground, bringing my legs closer to my chest, resting my head between them. "Not anymore." I squeeze my eyes closed. I want answers. I need them, but I'm afraid that if I sink deeper into my mind, I'll get lost. Unable to grasp onto what is real and what isn't, I am petrified that she'll take over and I'll never come back....

"Do you, Bryant, take Isa to be your..." I was standing at the altar. Bryant's hands wrapped in mine, his eyes searching mine eagerly. He wanted this just as much as I did. Our story wasn't easy by any means, but it was ours to write, and we scribbled it down in permanent ink.

"You alright?" he asked, his eyebrows knotting together.

What's happening? I never go this far in...

"Yes?" I cleared my throat. "Where's Harper?"

Bryant's arm hooked around my waist and he tugged me into him further, his nose running over mine. "She's fine. Look." He gestured with his head, where my family sat. There was Lydia, my father, Brianna, my sister, and Jess, Bryant's sister. Harper was curled in Brianna's arms. A smile stretched over my mouth when I saw how happy Harper was with my sister. There weren't that many people at the wedding. Close friends and little family. Devon was here, in the second row behind Lydia. "Nothing to worry about. Can you let us have our fairytale now? Or would you prefer I use force?"

I chuckled, shoving him playfully before we went back to our vows.

Suddenly my breathing slackened, and my limbs wilted. As if I recognized her energy entering the room. I turned my head sideways, my smile fading from my lips. My eyes locked onto hers and confusion warped my vision slightly.

"Brooke?" I whispered, confused. "What are you doing here? You are supposed to be dead!" Everyone turned to see who I was speaking to. Brooke was a friend I partied with when I was going through my party days, one of them when I met Bryant. She and I had caused mischief and chaos all over the country, going on benders. She occupied a chunk of a dark part of my life. When she took me and drugged me, I almost died. It was her or I.

"She can't have everything!" she roared, and it's that moment I took in what she was wearing. Worn rags and bloody arms. Her face looked sick, her eyes sunken in. She continued to walk down the aisle. Did she break out of a hospital?

"Brooke!" Bryant roared back. "Get the fuck away now before I put a bullet between your eyes."

Brooke laughed, her gaunt shoulders shaking beneath her worn shirt. "Fuck you, Bryant." She lifted the pistol in her hand and aimed it at Bryant. "I'm sorry, Isa. This isn't—"

I stepped in front of him instantly, my fight and determination to protect those I love kicking in. "No!" I screamed, closing my eyes.

Bang!

I flinched at the sudden crack of the bullet exiting the barrel. When I felt nothing, no pain, I slowly opened my eyes, my hands going to my stomach. Everything slowed as people started rushing around behind me. Bryant shoved me out of the way and ran to the front seating where Brianna sat.

Blood pooled around her feet as her curdling screams ripped through my mind. I took a step forward slowly, and that was the exact moment Bryant took Harper from her, turning to face me with tears pouring down his face.

My eyes fell to Harper in his arms.

Her body seemed limp.

Her blue eyes unfocused, was it just my paranoia or was her skin turning an unnatural shade of purple?

Blood fell from her blankie.

"Shit!" Brooke screamed. "That—no—no—"

My heart snapped, my vision peaked, and everything went black.

Max's hands are gripped around my shoulders, shaking me on the cold wood floor.

Tears streak down my face, but I swipe them away angrily. "Who are you?" I feel defeated. I remember everything from that day, and like some strange timer inside my brain, it's as though everything has clicked into place.

Brooke was my friend. I thought she was my friend. Until she kidnapped me. Parts of the kidnapping are still fuzzy, fuzzy and blank, but I know she kidnapped me.

Max sighs, leaning back against the wall near a window.

He runs his hands through his hair. "I'm Max Barrack. I was your doctor when you first came in." I remain silent, hoping it gives him the floor to speak. "I stepped out of line bringing you here, but I had to help you." He brings his brown eyes to mine. "You're not broken or sick, Isa. You've had horrible events happen to you." When he pauses, I bring my legs under my butt and tuck my hair behind my ear.

"You were my doctor? At the facility?"

His Adam's apple bobs past his swallow. "Yeah."

I lick my lips. "When was that? When did you bring me here?"

"Last week." He kicks up, and I quickly follow his lead as

he heads into the kitchen area. "I didn't exactly do it legally, but I needed to get you out of there."

"Why?" I ask, leaning my hip against the counter. "And how have I been asleep this long?"

"You haven't." He shakes his head, reaching above into the cupboard to take down a ceramic teapot that looks too out of date to be living in the year we are in. "You come and go, drifting back to sleep. You've never come to as clear as you are right now, but you have drifted in and out."

"God," I exhale, shaking my head. "I'm crazy."

"No!" Max snaps, turning to face me while holding two mugs. They're both made from stone, only fitting with the Viking-like feel this cabin exudes. "You are not, Isa. You need to understand—" He blows out a deep breath. "You're not crazy. People have been feeding you drugs for six months, since the wedding. These pills, they've made you *think* you're crazy. See things, hallucinations. You've been fed a cocktail mixture of pharmaceuticals that you most definitely should not have been fed." He turns back to continue his tea making. "Shit, that isn't even fucking legal."

My eyebrows cross as I warily make my way farther into the kitchen, slowly dropping down onto one of the bar stools. "I don't understand, Max. Can you tell me anything that will help me understand? I was used like a lab rat?"

He slides a mug over the counter toward me and I blow on the hot liquid until the condensation dissolves on the tip of my nose. "Yes. But I can only speak to you here. Anything else that happens outside of this cabin, cannot be talked about. Do you understand?"

I take a sip of the tea, sighing once the hot contents slip down my throat. "I understand." I don't, but I got the gist of it.

Don't talk outside this cabin.

His arms fold in front of his chest, pushing his muscles up

higher as they fight against his tight V-neck. "Your wedding day—"

I wince.

"Sorry," he apologizes before softening his tone. "Are you ready to talk about it?"

I think over his words. He said it has been six months since that day. Though I don't know when I will ever be ready to talk about it, I am aware that I need to.

"I am." I straighten my shoulders, hoping that it gives me some sort of strength, or at least creates the illusion of strength.

He nods. "Your fateful wedding day set off a chain reaction of events. Do you remember much of what happened after you fainted?"

I shake my head. "No. I actually only just remembered that part now. Usually, I only get to—"

"*I take thee, Bryant,*" Max whispers.

"Yes. How'd you know?"

Max takes a mouthful of his tea before bringing his eyes back to mine. "Because the drugs that your father has been trialing, work that way." He places his mug down. "Isa, you have been living the same events over and over again for the past six months."

The words float between us, but I can't seem to grasp onto them and let them sink in. "What?"

"You've lived yours and Bryant's love story over and over again for one year. From the very first page. It all starts with 'Isa, pick your chin up and smile. I taught you better than that.' And then... 'I'm twenty years old, Lydia, not fifteen. I know what I'm doing.'

I'm frozen to the spot. My heart turning to ice.

He leans forward, his fingers grabbing onto my chin to bring my eyes back to meet his. "You have lived through that entire ordeal, tormenting yourself, for one whole year. Right up until you see Bryant and Harper in the institute, when you're Brooke."

I stand from my chair, my feet moving back and forth. I begin pacing, frustration cutting me through the core. "So I didn't really see Harper and Bryant?"

Max's eyes turn somber. He shakes his head. "No. I'm sorry. Some parts you created, they weren't real. You would live through the same events, but there were very few times that some events were tweaked. Only slightly."

"So what was real?" I stop, pinning him with my stare. Confusion doesn't even cover how I'm feeling.

"All of the major events were real, except for the part where you thought Brooke was inside your head. She wasn't. She was very real. But after the incident at your wedding, and mixed with the drugs you were being fed, it's as though you turned Brooke into the villain in your head. You separated yourself and put all of your bad tendencies into Brooke and the good with Isa."

I still didn't understand. I was being filled to the brink with information.

I drop back onto the stool, massaging my temples.

"So I'm not crazy, in short, my daughter is—" I swallow past my swollen throat. "Brooke was real, my best friend did rape me, and my father has been feeding me drugs? Why?" I knew my father was capable of extreme things. He always put his presidency first before his own family—I knew that—but it still didn't make sense to me.

"Well," Max begins. "Devon didn't rape you. During that scene, it was just you and Brooke. If you think back over time, you will find where your mind was slipping in and out of reality. You'll eventually be able to recognize what part was real and what wasn't. After Bryant killed Brooke on your wedding day, your father needed a way to suppress what was happening, but when you came out of your daze and picked up the gun that Brooke used and emptied a whole clip into the head of her already deceased body, he could see you weren't going to hold it together. He was worried about what you might make him look like. When you were in the institution, before you would come to as Brooke or Isa, one of the other had to kill each other in your head. If Brooke killed you with the machete, then Brooke would come back. If you killed Brooke with the gun, you would come back."

I grind my teeth. "Not surprised about my father. So he had me locked up."

Max remains silent.

"And Bryant?" I ask, bringing my eyes to him. "Where the fuck is my so-called husband?"

"I don't know what his reasoning is, Isa. No one knows. He hasn't visited in months. He simply went about his routine. I do know that he and your father remain friends."

I can feel searing hot anger fueling my rage, threatening to spill over the edges. "He abandoned me." I exhale through my tears. "They all fucking abandoned me."

"Hey!" Max steps around the small counter. His fingers come to my chin. I find myself searching his face, focusing on his thick beard. The skin beneath his eyes and forehead is smooth and youthful, his brown eyes soft and trustworthy, yet intense enough to grasp onto my attention. He has brown hair that's shaved short on the sides and a little longer on the top, enough to slick back—which he does. He's not what I would expect from a doctor. He's something straight off the set of Vikings. His proximity moves closer, muscles flexing with his movement. "I won't."

My eyes fall to his soft lips. The perfect bow that dips in the middle.

"Eyes up here, trouble."

"Trouble?" I ask, tilting my head.

His hand drops from my chin, falling to either side of himself. "I called you that. You were a pain in my ass."

He gave me a nickname?

I sigh. "Why are you helping me? Forgive me for having trust issues, but the men who were supposed to be there for me were everywhere but where they were supposed to be."

"Simple." His eyes remain on mine, unflinching. "I'm a good fucking person, Isa, and when I found out what was really happening at the clinic, I shoved you into the bed of my pickup and drove us out here." He steps back, giving me some space. I'm appreciative of that. I feel as though oxygen isn't being ingested as quickly as I need it to.

"And you dressed me?"

He shrugs. "There are clothes here from someone who I knew you could fit."

I swallow. "So you're helping me because you're a good person? That's all?"

Max searches my eyes. "I realize how difficult it could be to grasp that, but it's true, Isa."

I rub my eyes, feeling my energy drain. The crackle from the open fireplace burns in the corner, setting off heatwaves around the small cabin. I haven't had time to look around yet, but it's small enough to explore in ten minutes.

"It is hard," I whisper, my eyes staying on the angry flames. "But I want to trust you."

"I won't hurt you."

My eyes shoot to his. "I want to believe you. I don't right now, but I want to. Is that okay?"

Max's burly shoulders relax beneath his shirt. "Yeah. Yeah, fuck it is."

Max gestures toward the hallway. "Come on. You must be tired. There's only one bedroom, but that's where I've kept you. You must have made your way onto my bed out here while I was out grabbing wood this morning."

I slide off the stool, offering him a smile. "Thank you, Max." I follow him to the bedroom and take in the area. Vertically placed logs make up the walls, and there's a large queen bed in the middle with two white bedside tables on either side. A window is on the other side of the room, hidden behind a white curtain. The bed is unmade, probably because of me. There are clothes piled up on top of the only dresser that's in here, all folded up neatly.

Max points. "More clothes if you need them. The bathroom is the door opposite this one, there's food in the cupboards, so have at it." My knees shake beneath my weight, the realization of my current circumstances beginning to weigh down on me.

"Well, yeah. Get some rest. We will talk more in the mornin'." He turns to leave, but my hand flies out and tightens around his thick forearm.

"Max?" I whisper, turning to face him.

He licks his lips. "Yeah?"

"Thank you."

The floor was unstable, as if it rocked against waves that threatened to tip it over. The smell of ocean and fish surrounded the small cabin of the boat and I blinked past my tears.

"Hello?" I called, banging on the only door that was in here. "Is anybody here? Help me! Please!" I'd bang. And bang. But no one would come. Not one person heard my cries for help. Finally, a blaring sun shone down from above me and I used my hands to shade over my eyes, blocking the violent assault.

"Who's that?"

TWO

Anger is the perfect weapon; if you can handle the kickback. - Isa

I woke this morning feeling just as bitter, if not more, than when I fell asleep. The dream I had of me on a boat didn't help either. I can feel all the ugly in me rising to the surface, but it's different this time.

I can feel it.

I can recognize it.

I can embrace the way it slithers through my veins, threatening to head upstairs and enter the crazy side of my brain.

"Hungry?" Max murmurs from behind the stovetop as I groggily make my way into the kitchen. It's an old one that requires a fire to be lit beneath the plates. The smell of sweet, crisp bacon and fluffy buttered scrambled eggs drifts through the air. My tummy grumbles.

"Starving. Thank you." I slip onto the bar stool and reach for the teapot. My eyes fly around the cabin again. "I take it no power?"

Max doesn't turn to face me. "No. We're completely off the grid out here." Interesting. I inwardly wonder why one might need a cabin off the grid, but I don't voice it.

Pouring myself a cup of the hot tea, I place the kettle back onto the stone counter. "It's beautiful, you know."

Max turns around with the pan in his hands, placing it straight onto the counter. Must be a perk to having it built from stone, not having to stress if you're burning the counter. "You think?" He begins dishing out the food onto a couple of plates. "Beautiful? Really? Haven't really thought of Fate like that."

I slide my plate closer to me and take hold of a knife and fork. "Fate?" I ask, biting into my sourdough toasted bread.

He takes a seat beside me, a piece of bacon hanging from his mouth. There's something very obvious that I have not stated. I'm not ready to admit it yet either, because it is beside the point. Max bites his bacon and chews. "That's what this cabin is called. Fate." Max is wearing a pair of dark jeans, military-style boots, and a white button-up flannel with a few buttons undone. Over the bacon and eggs, the smell of his fresh soap envelops my senses, while his thigh presses against mine.

I gulp, moving away from him instantly.

"Sorry," he mutters, turning to face me. "You okay?"

I bite into a piece of bacon. "Yes. I think I'm starting to feel a little more human. Well, Fate is beautiful." I don't think my transition into changing the subject was as smooth as I thought it was.

He grunts, reaching for his tea and taking a sip. "Not always." He pauses, and it took me a few seconds to catch his doubled-edged answer. "I can't imagine how you must be feeling. The drugs should be almost cleansed from your system."

"Don't take offense to this, but you don't strike me as a

doctor." I quickly shovel food into my gob so I don't say anything else that I might regret.

He chuckles for the first time ever, and I finally get a glimpse at his Colgate-white teeth that hide behind the beard. "I get that a lot when I'm not in my scrubs."

"I'm sorry that I don't remember you, Max." I wish I did. Then maybe I'd trust him a little more.

"It doesn't matter, Isa. That's not what matters or why I saved you."

"And why is that?" I ask, tilting my head and flicking the bacon between my fingers. "Why did you save me?"

"You were my patient for months. I spent, at times, days beside you. Trying to figure out what it was that was happening upstairs in that head of yours." He turns around completely, his legs now spread to my side. "I became obsessed with wanting to know your story. Why you were there."

"Because of my dad?" I ask, searching his eyes.

He waves me off, his head cocking back. "Fuck your dad."

I burst out laughing, and god it feels good. My shoulders vibrate, tears spill from my eyes, and for once, they aren't tears that are a product of pain. They're tears of happiness.

I swipe at my cheeks. "I'm sorry. That was just very funny to me." His face is serious, his lips in a flat line. I instantly still. "Sorry. I didn't mean to—"

"—no, that's not it." He shakes his head.

"Well what is it?" I ask softly, though I'm not sure I want the answer. I can't help but notice the invisible draw that I feel toward Max. But I can ignore it.

"I've thought about what your laugh would sound like for what feels like years. I've wondered what your smile is like, too. Now I got them both and I gotta say..."

"Say?" I urge, though I don't know why I'm hanging off every word.

"That your husband was a dumb motherfucker."

I laugh again, turning back to my bacon and cutting off the moment we shared. "You sure you don't know Bryant? Because motherfucker was one of his favorite words." We fall into easy conversation and Max tells me that Fate was the only place he could bring me to and it be safe enough for us to relax and concoct a plan—which he also admitted to not actually having one. I feel at ease with Max, a peculiar comfort that unsettles me to some degree, because of my past experiences, I shouldn't be so quick to warm up to people.

"So where are we if you think my father won't find you? He's the President of the United States. I'm sure he could if he wanted to."

"That's the thing," Max says as we wash up our dishes. "I know he is. I have no doubt that he has the whole of America looking for you. It makes him look good." I fold the dish towel and place it onto the counter, leaning back.

"My father has let me down many times as I have grown up," I confess. "I used to be so envious of all the little girls who had a dad who loved them. I wanted a father who didn't care about money, appearances, or fame. I just wanted a dad. Not a fucking president." I didn't realize what I had said until Max shifts directly in front of me, leaning against the counter.

"I'm sorry those two assholes let you down, Isa. What do you want to do?"

I ponder over his words. "I want revenge."

Max nods his head, as if that's a given.

"I want to destroy them both."

Another nod.

"I want you with me."

Max stills, his eyes searching mine.

I continue. "And I know that that is very selfish of me to ask, considering all that you have already done for me. I don't know if you have a family, or a wife, or children. But I want you with me."

Max kicks off the counter and takes a step closer to me, which is very close considering Fate is small. "You want me?" He holds my stare. My heart picks up its pace at those words leaving his lips, and my hands sweat. Why am I feeling a certain way about him? He licks his lip. "Then I'm yours."

I exhale loudly and fling my arms around his thick neck. At the connection, my muscles relax. The tension liberated from my tight limbs. I bury my nose into the crook of his neck, my eyes closing. I can feel his skin against my lips, his smell now having the same effects on me as a shot of heroin. "Thank you," I whisper against his flesh. Only when I mouthed the word 'you' it felt more like a kiss.

He tenses. "Anytime."

Pushing back from him, I head into the bathroom to quickly scrub up. Squeezing soap into the palm of my hand, I take special care into rubbing the perfumed suds all over my body. I want to trust him, and I think a part of myself has slightly opened for him without even realizing it, but there's a bigger part that has a strong grasp around my insecurity. That very same insecurity that is completely occupied by Bryant and my father.

I looked forward to my thirteenth birthday since the day I hit puberty. It was the day me and my girlfriends planned for weeks on end leading up to it. We were having a sleepover, we were going to watch movies, and then, when my parents were gone, we were going to raid my father and Lydia's alcohol cupboard. We had it planned out to a T.

My friends from school were all downstairs in the home theater with sleeping bags and pillows, all giggling and talking about some new hot guy at our school, when I started jogging up the stairs. Dad kept his best alcohol in his bedroom, and I just so happened to be dumb enough to break into it.

I slipped through their door, flinching when the creaking broke through a little too loudly, and made my way to the small bar they had set up in the corner. Leaning down, I flipped open the glass door and took out a half-bottle of vodka. One that maybe he wouldn't notice. When I stood back up, a photo caught my eye on the mantle. It wasn't in a frame. It looked out of place, as if it had been thrown there in haste.

I picked it up. It was a woman standing in snow. She had long brown hair, a pixie face, and eyes that seemed to have seen too much evil to hold any life.

I didn't recognize her.

Placing the photo back onto the mantle, I slip the alcohol under my oversized hoodie before making my way back downstairs.

Rubbing the water from my eyes, I shake out of my flashback, allowing it to linger around me like a fresh memory. To this day, I don't know why that photo was there. The rest of the night went exactly how any thirteenth birthday party would go. But it was also the last birthday party I ever had. Everything from that point onward was full steam ahead with my father and politics. I didn't know at the time what my father was planning. I didn't think about it much at the time, either. Ever the selfish teenager. I was always the disappointment, but from that point onward it only got worse.

Turning off the shower, I step out in a plush wool towel and dry myself quickly before dressing in skinny jeans and a loose V-neck. I don't know whose clothes these are, but she had taste. Once I'm back in the bedroom, I toss my dirty laundry in the basket when a box catches my eye from beneath the dresser. I bend down and reach for it, pulling out the old shoebox. Flipping it open, I find that it's filled with photographs on top of photographs. There's a wedding band and a Polaroid camera too. I flip through the photos, seeing selfies and candid shots of Max and a woman. I don't know what the woman looks like, because her face is always hidden behind her hands, or her long dark hair, or an oversized hoodie. I gather she has a beauty that complements Max.

"She was my wife." Max's voice shocks me from the doorway and I jump, dropping the photo back into the box.

"I'm sorry. I didn't mean to snoop."

Max shrugs, kicking off the doorframe and bending down to sit opposite me. He flicks through the photos and hands me one. I take it, studying the photo of Max standing outside Fate. "Wife was everything I really wanted. She hated Fate. Said it gave her the creeps. It reminded her of all the ghosts that were too bad for Heaven and too good for Hell." He shakes his head, flicking the photo back into the pile. "Fucking loved her anyway."

I gulped through the emotion. Why couldn't I have married someone like that?

"Loved?" I ask softly, pointing out the past tense. "You don't have to talk about it." Even though I had only seen their connection through photographs, it was discernible. Especially in the way he looked at her. I wanted to ask why she never showed her face, but it didn't seem like something that was any of my business.

"Yeah." He shut the lid, pushing it back under the dresser. "Turns out, I didn't know her as well as I thought I did."

I inch closer, wanting to know more. Maybe take some of my dark clouds away and replace them with his. They seemed easier to deal with.

He snorts when he notices my obvious attention. "You're not the only one with trust issues. We'll keep it at that for now."

I flinch. "I'm sorry, Max."

He shrugs, standing back to all his six-foot-whatever-inches. "It is what it is, Isa. There's not much I can do about it."

He takes a seat on the bed. "Do you know what you want to do yet?"

I tuck my hair behind my ear. "Where are we?"

"We're in the Pacific Northwest. Far enough out in the mountains."

I bite my bottom lip, finally ready to admit the one thing I wasn't ready to admit to earlier. Max is... well, he's very good looking. He's not beautiful, but he's not handsome, he's—well, he's damn *hot*. He has a roughness about him that I didn't know I liked in a man. Or maybe it's that he's the opposite to my fucker of a husband. "Let's go to New York."

THREE

How many times can you fall in love?
Infinity with the right man. - Isa

We left for New York the next day, after giving myself a mini makeover. It was snowing right now, which meant we were around December or late November. My memories are coming back slowly, but my confusion with the date is one thing I struggle with daily.

Max leans into me as we collect our bags from the carousel. "You really think that hair is going to be enough to hide you?"

My hand touches my freshly bleached strands. It took a few box dyes to get it to this color, but it will have to be enough. It has an ugly yellow tinge stuck to it though, so I've told Max that I will need to do a purple shampoo run before I even think about showing my face in front of Bryant. If a man breaks your heart, you better make sure your next appearance breaks his balls.

"Yes?" I sigh. "I don't know. I hope it's enough." Reaching

for the handle of my suitcase that's filled with his wife's clothes, I shrug. I didn't have much to pack, because I owned almost nothing. How sad is that? At twenty-five years old, I had nothing to my name. My father starved me of love and gave America everything.

Max takes my hand with his as I shove my cap lower, covering my eyes with Ray-Bans. He wore aviators to hide his own with a baseball cap. "Come on. We have to move fast." As we pass the lobby, the TV that's hanging in the corner catches my eye and my father's face comes into view.

"We are a happy family. There is nothing I wouldn't do for them. We are confident that we will find my daughter. If you see her, please contact authorities immediately without approaching her."

Fucking liar. Lying bastard!

I squeeze Max's hand without even realizing I was doing it as he shoves me under his arm.

His lips press to my head. "Come on."

I relax beneath his guidance. Once we're outside, Max calls a taxi down and blurts off directions to our hotel. An hour later and we're hauling ass up an elevator and onto the second floor. I didn't know where or what he had booked. I didn't care, to be honest. I just want this to be over, Bryant to be dealt with, so I can go back to not having a life to live.

"You okay?" Max asks, pushing open the door and allowing me in.

I offer him a polite smile. "Yes, I just want this over."

He nods, kicking the door closed behind him and dropping his small suitcase to the ground. "You and me both."

I remove my jacket, noticing the one bed that was in our room. It was a queen, but there was only one.

One bed.

Shit.

Max seems to look at the same time as me, his eyes shifting to where I was standing. "I can sleep on the couch."

I shake my head, blowing out a breath of air. "No. Don't be crazy."

He chuckles. "What's crazy is your hair. Damn."

I touch the ends again. "I didn't think it would turn a mix between brown and blonde. Basically *bronde*."

Max makes his way into the kitchen laughing.

I didn't tell Max what I was planning to do, mainly because I was afraid what he would say, but I need to talk with Bryant alone. I want him to see me, the real me. I want my fucking revenge. He left me at the hands of my father to be eaten alive, only he didn't know that my father's appetite was bottomless.

We both lost Harper, but he didn't lose me. I lost him.

"Want a drink?" Max asks, peeking around the corner while holding a small bottle of wine. I should say no. I don't need any alcohol in my body to influence me, especially when I'm around Bryant. But I need something to take off the edge.

"Sure." Only a little. I watch as rich pinot slowly fills the glass. Sighing after taking the first sip.

"Isa, listen..."

I shake my head. I don't want to hear what he has to say, because I'm partly scared that it will be a confession. I'm not stupid. I know. I pick up the vibes that he sends out. Or maybe he really is a good person who wants to help me, and I've been around the wrong kind of men my entire life.

Which judging by the current situation that I'm in, is looking like the more realistic reason.

"Max, if I clear your name with my father, will you be happy?" I try for a distraction that would work on both of us, because I'm needing it too. I'm thinking irrationally. The old Isa would have jumped straight into bed with this man the second she found out that her husband had left her out to rot, but this time I want to do things differently. *I have to.*

"Define happy?" He leans back, kicking his feet out in front of himself. His carefree persona is only more hypnotic.

I place the red wine onto the table in front of me. Obviously, I don't need any bad encouragers when it comes to Max, and red wine to me is what a molly is to a teenager. "If I get your job back..."

He shakes his head. "I don't want it, Isa. I don't want that anymore. I can't work for someone who doesn't share the same vision that I do."

I relax into my chair, bringing my glass back to my lips. I'm at a loss for words, and that doesn't happen often. What does he want? Why did he help me? As my eyes connect with his, I can't help but think of every single question that I thought of when I woke to find him in the cabin.

"You're thinking too much..." Max interferes as if hearing my thoughts out loud. "Stop thinking. You're too smart."

I snort. "Too smart? I'm certain that's not it. Have you met my husband?"

He leans forward and licks his lip. "I know you want to see Bryant. I know you think he's still your husband." He fishes out a folder from his backpack and slides it across the table. It's yellow. Actually, no, it's mustard. *Ew*. It's as though yellow took a shit on brown and smeared it all over this folder.

My eyes shoot to his. "What is this?"

Max brought his glass to his mouth. "Take a look."

Bryant Saint Royal.
   Occupation: CEO of Royal Enterprise Holdings. Entrepreneur.
   Reason for filing: Mental incapacity at time of marriage.

I gasp, slapping the cover closed. "He filed for divorce?" And then I read over the words again. "And that fucker filed under mental incapacity? Is he saying that I was fucking insane at the time of the wedding?" I breathe in and out, my eyes closing. I'm trying to be a better person, but right now I want to take to Bryant's balls with a scalpel and tear off his dick.

Max nods, the edges of his eyes crinkling in worry. "I didn't want to tell you. He did."

I try hard to ignore the pain that shoots through my chest. *The day I got locked up?* "Asshole." Why would he do that to me after everything we fought for to get to where we were. Why did he fight so hard for us when all he was going to do was tap out?

"Indeed." Max leans farther forward, his hand coming to mine. "You're no longer married, Isa." I search his features, his hand still on mine. I won't think too much into the PDA, or even the unmistakable eye contact, or the fact that my body seems to like it when he's around me.

"What do you want from me, Max?" I ask through a whisper, though I'm almost certain I know the answer.

He cranks his head. "I think you know."

I lick my lips. "True." My palms twitch, slicked with sweat. I swipe them over my legs to get them dry. "I just—"

Max shakes his head. "I realize this is very one-sided, Isa. I've known you for months, whereas you have only just met me."

I wince. I didn't want to feel this way about Max, but I'd be lying if I said that I didn't. He is beautiful, caring, and had just enough edge to bring out my dark side, but there was something wrong.

He still wasn't Bryant.

And until I saw him, I couldn't promise anything to Max. Period. Bryant may have walked away from me, but I was crazy enough to chase him anyway. At least for answers.

"Give me a few?" I ask, hoping he would understand. I'm

not sure how we managed to go from one point to this one, and the more I thought into it, the more I found it strange. So I stopped thinking. I didn't need any more confusion inside my head.

His shoulders fell slightly. "Always."

I tip my glass back and swipe the residue from my lips. "You know, a long time ago, I would have climbed onto your lap willingly. I was a reckless woman and a borderline nympho." I snort, tucking my hair behind my ear. "Actually, not borderline. I was—or—" My eyes meet his. "Am a nympho."

Max laughs, his head tilting back before his eyes come back to mine. They're hungry. Starved. As if he's been fasting for thirty days and I'm the first meal he's seen. "Are you? Or have you just not been fucked right?"

I almost choke on my drink. Not because of the crassness, but of how wrong he is. Not only has Bryant violently fucked me into a coma—amongst other things—but Devon wasn't half bad either.

I leave it. Not wanting to damage his ego.

I went to bed not long after that, tired and overwhelmed from the travel and daily revelations. I have to admit, I feel lighter. But I also know that the storm hasn't even started. This was the calm before it. It was the universe warning me that nothing worth living ever comes easy.

My heart aches when I think of Bryant, because in my head, it was still fresh. I fell in love with him. We had our happily ever after and our story was supposed to continue between the two of us, without the words 'The End' written in cursive.

Only that wasn't the case.

The next morning, I'm in the kitchen pouring a mug of hot

coffee when Max strolls in, wearing dark sweats. His hair is messy and his beard scruffy. He's wearing no shirt and his abs are on full display. They're not as defined or shredded as Bryant's—not even close—but he was still solid. *Why the fuck am I comparing the two?*

"Uh," I mumble through my stupor. "Coffee?" I need to pull myself together.

"Sure." He runs his hand through his hair, reaching for something in the fridge as his muscles contract. My mouth dries. Why was I becoming more attracted to him?

I need to see Bryant. For whatever reason, I feel like I owe it to him to beat his ass before I even think about beating it up on someone else's dick.

I begin stirring creamer through my coffee. Enough for my coffee to look more like toffee. Sweet but a touch bitter, just like me. "I'm going to Royal Enterprise today. I need to see him."

Max freezes before turning around to face me. His features are hard, as if he doesn't understand why I would do that. "Why?"

I take a sip of my hot coffee, hoping it will gain some time for me to think of a valid excuse. "I need to, Max." Should have taken longer.

He seems to think over my words while shuffling to the table, dropping down onto one of the white leather chairs. His big, burly shoulders lift slightly. "Then you do what you got to do, Isa."

"Wait for me?" I ask the same question I did last night, searching his eyes while selfishly pleading that he does.

I need him to wait for me.

For my ego or for my heart, I wasn't sure yet. It was too early to tell.

"Always." He gently smiles before hiding it behind his coffee.

I step around him, heading to the bedroom and pulling out some clothes that I packed. I settle on a relaxed white blouse and skinny jeans. They are washed denim and the blouse hangs loosely off my figure, while displaying the color of my bra underneath. Red lace, obviously, and I made sure to pop open the two top buttons, knowing I was about to see my asshole ex-husband. Squeezing on leather knee boots and a leather jacket lined with fur, I made my way back into the kitchen, but Max isn't there. Just as I reach for the door handle, his voice stops me in my tracks.

"Take this." He tosses a phone at me. I catch it midair, my eyes landing back on his. "It was an extra one I had. My number is in there and if you need me, Isa," his pained eyes come to mine and for a second, I feel guilty. "Call me."

A small smile tugs on the corner of my mouth, one that couldn't promise anything but wanted to say so much. "I will, Max." Then I turn the handle and leave.

FOUR

The difference between a dream and reality? You can have me there but not here. - Isa

I hail the first taxi that I see and slip into the backseat on the worn leather seat.

"Sixty-two Wall Street, please." I scroll through the iPhone that Max gave me. It's blank. There are no contacts but his and no messages at all. Twenty minutes later, the taxi pulls up to the curb of a stone building held together by four pillars at the front. I tilt my head while swinging the door open.

Royal Enterprise Holdings

...was engraved delicately into the steel above the entry. Before I can flip the sign off, I quickly shuffle through my pockets to hand the taxi driver some cash. Slipping out of the back seat I'm instantly slapped in the face with the loud streets of New York, I shut the taxi door and squeeze the phone that's in my hand. Why does he have to own this city? I mean literally too. He owns every single piece of realty that was worth owning, and then rented it out, and he did that because he was bored, not because he needed the money. Bryant makes, roughly, around two-hundred-thousand dollars an hour. Nothing he ever does is for money, it's for power.

Dashing past the reception, I hurry toward the elevators and push the arrow up. I was lucky to move past them undetected. I don't really like to fight while wearing white. Blood stains can be a bitch to get out, and I don't have many clothes as options.

As the numbers climb, my belly flips erratically. As the numbers grow higher, so does my anticipation, until tingles are electrifying my fingertips. What am I going to say to the man that promised to never leave me, only to dismiss me as if I was a maid in his life? I didn't think this through thoroughly.

The doors ping open and before I can change my mind, I put one foot in front of the other and make my way down the stark white lobby. Everything is clean, a complete contrast to the filthy bastard who owns it. Right to the diamond chandelier that drops down over the middle of the reception desk.

"Excuse me, miss!" A young blonde who looks fresh out of college pounces out from behind a marble desk, her heels clinking against the glass tiles. Her eyes came to mine. "Can I help you?"

"You?" I ask, cocking a brow. "No." I shove past her as she clambers dramatically back behind her desk, picking up her phone. Maybe she knows who I am and was told to call security on me if I walked in here, or maybe she was as dumb as she looked and didn't think at all. There is only one problem with that theory, and that is Bryant never employs someone whose IQ is below one-twenty.

Shoving through the glass doors, I ignore the bright sun that shines through the floor to ceiling windows, displaying all of the people who are seated around the rectangle board-room table, obviously mid-meeting.

My eyes found him instantly.

Bryant Saint Royal.

Ex-husband and second most disappointing male in my life. Second to my deadbeat father.

Everyone in their seats turns to face me. Most of them seem confused, some shocked. I wasn't a stranger around here; he was my damn husband. We had a child together. There used to be photos of us in his fucking office.

He shot up from his chair, his eyes on mine. For a second, all of the oxygen is filtered out from the room and all I can hear is my heavy breathing. *In and out. He left you. He would always leave you.*

He looks sinfully good.

Bryant wore a suit like a soldier would armor, and every day he went to war, only this was a battle that he wouldn't win.

"Husband." I smirk, folding my arms over my chest.

"Wife," he seethes. I take this moment to breathe in his appearance. His shoulders larger, his jaw more prominent. He was always beautifully fit and articulate, but he looks differ-ent. His skin is still glowing, yet it isn't as flawless as it used to be. He doesn't look older, he just looks—different. For a thirty-one-year-old man, he was every bit the monster that I dreamed of in my head. The monster I softened enough to marry, although I'm not so sure I softened him at all.

"Everyone get the fuck out," he barks, but his eyes never leave mine. Everyone split around me as they exit the board-room and I watch as he leans forward, his hand coming to the back of the chair. He squeezes. "How'd you get out?"

"Well," I murmur, making my way farther into the room and taking a seat at the head of the table. "Not with the help of you, that's for sure."

He bares his straight teeth. It'd look beautiful if he wasn't so feral. "You're not my problem anymore, Isa. Because of you, I lost everything." The door bursts open behind me, but I don't pay it any attention, my eyes staying on Bryant. Sure enough, he waves his hand toward the security guards until they're scurrying out the door.

"Did you know that my father has been drugging me for god knows how long, using my brain as his own personal science project for some new pharmaceutical drug? I'm not fucking crazy, Bryant. My father—"

"—Stop!" Bryant glares at me from across the table. "I don't want to fucking hear it. I've heard enough fucking lies from you."

I push up from the doorway and stumble my way toward him. His size is still every bit as intimidating as I remember. He towers over people like his buildings tower over New York. Dark, moody, and controlling. He's built so large that he not only physically takes up the atmosphere in any room, but it is also mentally draining to be in a room with him. He exudes pure alpha energy. It's intense on the best of days. His aura is rougher than his beautiful exterior. My ex-husband is a beast, but I'm no beauty. I know exactly how to draw energy from him. I just had to get close enough.

"Isa..." he warns, his eyes coming to mine. He's wearing an incredibly perfect Armani suit, tailored to every single curve of his body. That was Bryant, though. A brute in a suit.

"Bryant..." I whisper, bringing my hand up to his cheek. His jaw flexes beneath my palm, but just like an unexpected power cut, the door behind us flies open, interrupting our moment.

"What the fuck do you want!" I yell, spinning around to face the security guards again.

Only it wasn't the security guards.

It was a tall, skinny blonde woman with enough makeup on her face I could scratch my name into her forehead.

Her eyes are on Bryant first, before they slowly draw to me. Blue sapphire with a hint of gray.

"Who the fuck are you?" I tilt my head.

The woman steps forward, her eyes cutting back to Bryant as she slowly lifts her left hand. "I'm his fiancée." My heart splits open in my chest, the ache almost unbearable. "But I know who you are." I want to lash out. Be angry. Take hold of the anger and pain that has so viciously risen to the surface and throw it right back in his face, but I have too much pride to show weakness. To show this woman, or Bryant, that they got to me.

He just fucking replaced me.

I blink back the tears that threaten to expose my pain and straighten my shoulders. "Funny how you know who I am, yet I don't know who you are..."

"Isa!" Bryant growls, but I ignore him. He has long since punched his ticket to board the *tell Isa what to do* train.

I take one step toward the leggy blonde. "You seem familiar."

She shakes her head. "No, I don't." There's an air of diffident that clings to her. She's Bryant's old type, before he met me.

My eyes narrow as I take another step as Bryant's fingers flexed around my arm. Spinning around, I cut him with a glare. "She was my daughter, Bryant. I lost her too, not just you."

He searched my eyes. "What do you want, Isa?"

So cold. It was like taking a step back in the past, where I don't mean anything to him again.

Only I know him now. I know his soul and his heart.

I look down to where his fingers are still around my arm, before pulling myself out of his grip. "I don't want a fucking thing from you."

He sighs, stepping back and loosening his tie in the way that I know he did only when he was frustrated. "Come to dinner tonight. I may as well write your check."

"My what?" He better have not said what I think he did.

Barbie behind me clears her throat. "Bryant, did you want to see me?" Her eyelashes flutter, her shoulders hunched in a submissive stance. It was as though she was too afraid to look the man in his eyes.

I throw my head back and laugh. "If you think you're going to last ten seconds with Bryant, you are so very wrong. To marry a wolf, one must become a wolf, and you seem more like the prey."

She dismisses me without a single word, turning and walking out of the conference room.

"She won't bite, Isa." Bryant's voice cuts through my anger, and I close my eyes.

Inhale.

Exhale.

Motherfucker.

I slowly turn to face him. The sun is setting behind the large floor to ceiling windows, leaving a burnt orange hue across the sky and offering the perfect lighting to shadow every defined feature on his face. "You replaced me." I said the words aloud, but I was really repeating them to myself again. Needing to hear it once more. Maybe it will solidify the fact that I have to let go.

He doesn't want me.

He allowed my father to take me.

He didn't save me.

I hate him. I should hate him. I should want to hurt him.

I will hurt him.

He takes one step toward me. "She won't bite because she's trained not to do so."

I don't answer. My brain is still trying to wrap itself around my own words.

You replaced me.

His hand comes to my chin, tilting my face up to his. He peers down at me and I don't know if it's the proximity, or my mind playing tricks on me, but I see a flash of the old Bryant in there. My Bryant. Only deep down, I know that every part of this man is mine. Will always be mine. "You look good, Isa."

I swallow past the hurt. "Don't say things you don't mean."

The cushion of his thumb glides over my bottom lip. "Am I the type of man to use my breath on lies?"

My eyes collide with his. "Why did you replace me?"

"I didn't," he answers, dropping his hand. I instantly miss his touch. The hunger of not having him in my life all-consuming. I may not survive this. "You're irreplaceable."

"And you talk a lot of shit." My anger once again ascends to the surface. His eyes snap to mine and his shoulders tighten. "Remember who the fuck you're talking to, baby, or I'll have you bent over this fucking desk with bite marks on your ass."

He steps back. "The house in Connecticut. Be there. On time at six." I take one more look at him. The pain that flashes over his eyes before his fingers dig through his hair distracts me briefly from the pain he has caused. "Leave."

I head for the door, flipping off the pert little bitch at the reception desk. As I stepped through the open doors of the elevator, I duck my head out and catch her glaring at me.

"For your information, Bryant is my husband, so next time I walk through this fucking building, don't call security unless you want to be jobless."

Then I step back inside and let out a long breath as the doors close in front of me.

I hate this.

The elevator lowers, taking me to the lobby as I step out and rush through the doors and onto the busy street. I love New York, it is my favorite place in the whole United States, but right now, the towering buildings only remind me of the monster who owns them.

Arriving back at the hotel room, I toss my jacket onto the small table that's right behind the door and find Max on the bed, his knees drawn up.

"Everything okay?" His eyes are slightly frantic as he nibbles on his bottom lip softly.

It's a side I haven't seen from Max, since he's all *Me Tarzan, you Jane.* Usually.

"Fine," I say, running my hands through my dark blonde hair nervously. I hope Max agrees to come tonight. Since Bryant has clearly moved on with someone else, I want to make it as if I have too. "We have to go to his house for dinner tonight."

"We?" Max quirks an eyebrow, standing from the bed and making his way toward me. I want to step back. Not give him any more of myself than I already have, but then images of the blonde bitch flash through my brain and I step forward instead of back.

"Yes, we, because if he's taking his fiancée, I will need you there." I pull open the fridge and take out a bottle of water, flicking open the lid and bringing it to my mouth.

Max takes a few steps toward me, his head tilted. Seeing

Bryant again was like swallowing acid, now his presence is stuck to my throat and refusing to let go. I'll drink his poison and die for all my sins. I'm that stupid.

"Then I'll be there," Max says.

I want to thank him, and I should feel relieved, but all I feel is this heavy throbbing in my chest and instead of it becoming lighter, it's gaining weight and speed and soon enough, there's going to be a gaping hole where it was and I'll be left with nothing but a shattered soul, and a broken heart with a big ass hole in it. Again, I'm that stupid.

For the rest of the day, I spend most of my time laying out on the bed and obsessing about all the things that could go wrong tonight. The butterflies are no longer fluttering in my belly, they've just straight up eaten it. It's now five p.m. and I've moved on to obsessing about what I'm going to wear. It doesn't help that his fiancée is all prim, pretty, and pert. My options for attire are also slim, (again, not in my favor), but I can and will make whatever I have in this bag work. Because I may be a mess, but I'm a stubborn mess. Red was Bryant's favorite color on me, so I know I need to shop for that.

"I need to go to BOA." I scoop up my jacket.

Max watches me in passing before grabbing me by the hand. "You think you can withdraw undetected?" It's not that I think I can withdraw money undetected, it's that I no longer care. I won't let my father get away with whatever he has been doing to me for almost all of my life.

My palms drip with sweat as I swipe them down my thighs. I went for tight red skinny jeans, boots that close around my ankles, and a black blouse. It's sexy without noise. Which has always been my style.

After a drive that seemed to go on forever, the taxi comes to a halt outside the mansion I'm a little too familiar with.

The floor to ceiling glass windows gives the home an executive style setting, but the stark white pillars on the wraparound porch offer the home a warm traditional welcome. It's a complete contradiction to the two styles but is what Bryant intended it to be.

"You okay?" Max asks worriedly, grasping my thigh. His touch instantly shocks me out of the hole I was successfully dragging myself into. The memories of this home are burned into my brain, although I don't have many. Our collection of memories are built into the walls of the apartment in the city.

"Yeah." I clear my throat, stepping out of the car as Max pays the driver.

Once the taxi has disappeared down the driveway, he brings his hand to mine. I relax slightly, somewhat appreciative of his presence. I can't imagine having to face Bryant and his fiancée on my own. Max is the strength I didn't think I would need. It's funny how a stranger, someone who I never knew, has become someone that I rely on to a degree.

At least for now.

We make our way up the milky marble steps and it's like stepping back into time. This was Bryant's home *home*. The one away from the city. We had plans to move here eventually, what with it being in suburbia, but obviously, fate had other plans.

Max reaches up to knock, but I'm already twisting the gold plated handle and flinging the door open.

"Ah..." Max looks from me to the inside of the house. "Isa..."

"This was my husband, Max. I'm not knocking on his door."

His face contorts, displaying his apprehension, but he enters anyway, obviously trusting my judgment.

I slam the door closed just as blonde Barbie walks down the foyer, wearing a short mini dress that clings to what curves she has and bright red lipstick smudged over her lips. A little loud, but good on her. I only take her obvious display of formal attire as a hint that I have her insecure. You don't need a short skirt to please Bryant, you just need to drop to your knees and call him daddy after he rearranges your insides.

"Oh, you let yourself in," she says curtly, but it was more to herself than to me.

"I did," I answer, hanging my fur coat on the hanger and hooking my arm into Max's. "Max, this is…" I tilt my head, signaling for her to tell me her name.

"Stacey," she says, and I watch as they exchange politely. "Hi, Max, nice to meet you. I didn't realize Isa was bringing a guest. I'll have Trevor set a place for you."

"That'd be great. Thanks."

"Don't let that sweet smile fool you. This girl is trouble." I freeze at the new voice, side-stepping away from Stacey and Max.

"Jerry!" I scream, bolting toward the tall glass of muscle. My legs wrap around his waist, my arms hooked to his neck. "Oh my god!" My muscles loosen at his familiarity. Jer is everything I would have wanted for a father, and I think over time I found myself looking at him in that way.

His chest shakes from his chuckle, his thick trunk for arms squeezing around my waist. "Hey, trouble. You been well?"

My smile falls, as I slowly lower myself back to the ground. Tucking my hair behind my ear, I smile softly. "Sure." I find it strange that he doesn't know about me being locked in the asylum. Just how much does Bryant know? There were never any secrets between Jer and Bryant.

"It's been quiet without you." His hand caresses my cheek, but when his eyes fly over my shoulder, landing on Max, he drops his arm. "Does bossman know about this?"

The clench of his jaw and instant shift in demeanor illustrates Jer's disapproval.

I shrug. "He doesn't get much say."

"Hmmm." Jerry sizes up Max, his thick brows pulling in. Jer looked good. But then, he always did. Now his thick beard had a scattering of gray through it and a few lines had risen around his eyes. God, I missed him.

"Interesting." Stacey comes up beside me, her eyes on Jerry. "I've never seen you speak more than two words, Jer."

"It's Jerry, and that's because I don't want to talk to you." I notice the way he shifts away from Stacey.

I wasn't mad at it.

My laughing dies out when I feel the energy in the room shift. Suddenly the atmosphere is as cold as the marble tiles and expensive glass double stairway that leads to the second level of the mansion.

When a shadow shifts behind Jerry, I suck in a deep breath, tucking my hair behind my ear and slowly—very fucking slowly—bringing my eyes to where Bryant stands. My heart thunders in my chest, and damn near flatlines when I see what he's wearing.

No suit today. Loose faded jeans—*Phillip Plein* probably—and a casual white Dolce & Gabbana shirt with the words *Million Dollar Psycho* printed over his chest. His hair is damp, the ends of his dark hair dripping wet. He's clean-shaven and has a cigarette tucked behind his ear, a zippo flicking between his fingers. His skin is smooth, tanned, and flawless, and his jaw is every bit as sharp and angular as I remember. It's as if the gods cut his features from stone. His eyes are deep blue, his lashes fanning out over his cheekbones.

I flush, flustered with how much his presence distracts me.

Only he's not looking at me.

His eyes are on Max. He's scowling, but not in a noticeable way, more in a way that is calculated. Bryant will never display his cards unless he intended to.

"Oh, hey, baby." Stacey waltzes toward him, her hips sashaying with every step. "Have you met Max? Isa's boyfriend?"

My jaw slams closed. *Little. Bitch*. I didn't introduce him as my boyfriend.

Bryant ignores me. Not once does his gaze shift to me. It's as if I'm invisible, or just not important.

Finally he breaks eye contact with Max and I can breathe again. For now.

Max strolls beside me as we follow Stacey and Bryant farther into the foyer. "Nice house."

"It's alright." My tone is barely audible, more like a grumble. I don't want to pay attention to anything in this house, too afraid I'd notice something. We turn the corner of the foyer and head into the dining room, where a rectangular table that could easily seat twelve people sat. There was a gold and black chandelier hanging from the ceiling with the table setting delicately set out.

Bryant sits at the end of the table and I take the seat beside Jerry, with Max on the other side of me and Stacey opposite Jerry but beside Bryant.

I don't even know if Bryant has seen me yet. It's silent, but not awkward. I could never feel uncomfortable around Bryant. Ever.

"Bryant..." I mutter. "Are you going to be polite and say hello to my friend?" Finally, his eyes slide across the room and land on me.

Now that I have his undivided attention, I don't fucking want it. My god, he looks feral. The corner of his mouth curls up. "No?"

Oh, here we go. It's fucking showtime. All of that anxiety

I had earlier was really my gut telling me to run while I still had the chance.

Just as my mouth opens and I'm ready to reply with something sassy, a small blonde girl walks in carrying a tray of food.

I freeze.

"Ashley?" A smile so wide my face could crack replaces my scowl that was pointed at Bryant, and I stand abruptly from the table.

Ash has been with Bryant for longer than I knew him, but she and I clicked instantly the first time that I met her. She was like the little sister I never knew I needed. Her and another girl who works for Bryant, Amanda, are like two peas in a pod. I'm closer to Ash, though, always have been.

She smiles brightly, placing the tray onto the table. "Mrs. Royal? Oh my god!" She rushes forward while still holding a bottle of Champagne with her other hand, her arms flinging around my neck. "Are you back?" I want to bask in the glorification of being called Mrs. Royal, just for a little longer.

"Great," Stacey muttered from across the table. "Another one who knows her."

I take the bottle of *Dom Pérignon* from Ashley and pop off the cork while sitting back down. "Well, no. And as far as I've just learned," I start pouring the champagne into my flute, my eyes back on Bryant, who is now leaning back lazily in his throne. I can't help but know he's loving this little cat and mouse game. "I'm no longer Isa Royal."

Bryant's jaw tenses, his focus never straying from me. It's as though it's just he and I and our chemistry that's in this room. My blood loudly gushes through my ears to a rhythm I don't know the choreography to.

"Well," Stacey jokes. "There can't be two of us..."

"There can't?" Bryant answers her, but his eyes remain on mine. The corner of his mouth is cocked up in a grin, flashing part of his straight teeth. Teeth I want to knock out after that comment.

I narrow my eyes. "Oh, it's like you don't know me at all, husband, or have you forgotten..." I tip back my drink and when his eyes fall on my damp lips, I drag my tongue out and lick the tangy champagne off the bottom. "I don't share."

Max's hand comes to my thigh and I jolt slightly, my eyes flying down to the connection and then up to Max's soft brown eyes.

"You okay?" he whispers.

"Yes." I clear my throat, taking another long sip from my flute. "He makes me crazy."

Ashley excuses herself from the room to go back to work, but only after telling me she wants to talk later. I didn't miss the dirty stare she gave Stacey either. At first glance, I thought Stacey was nice enough. Demure. Soft. Too gentle for my wolf. But the more I spend time around her, the more I don't like her, and I didn't like her to begin with, so I'm balancing on hate right now.

I sigh, resting back in my chair once the alcohol is pulsing heavily through my bloodstream. "So. What's up, husband. Why am I here?"

Bryant's eyes go to Max. "Do I know you?"

Max tenses slightly beside me. *Deflect, deflect, deflect.* Bryant is good at that. "I was Isa's doctor."

Max takes a swig of red wine. So different from Bryant. Where Bryant only ever really touches hard liquor, Max is happy with wine.

"And you broke her out?" Bryant further asks, his finger working the top of his mouth.

His tattoos sneak out over his fingers and I notice new ones all over his neck and throat, even one near his ear, on the side of his face. I can't make out what it is from here, but I have to fight the urge to jump over the table and—

"—Isa!" Bryant snaps, drawing all of the attention in the room to me.

I freeze, my eyes zoning back on him. His jawline is tense. "Care to remain focused? Or have you lost your will, and do I need to remind you where it is?"

I can't stop the half smile that sneaks onto my face. It's the alcohol, it's bringing out the worst in me. The trunk of my flute glass dangles between my fingers. "No, no need to remind me." I lean forward, cocking my head. "Up to the third level and first door on the right, right? Tell me, did you end up opting for the spa bath or did you listen to me and go the more classical route by choosing the clawfoot?" I watch as fury flashes over his eyes while I bat my lashes innocently at him. I can't even revel in my triumph for two seconds before a sadistic smirk creeps onto his mouth.

Bryant shakes his head at me, leaning toward Max. "You broke her out—why?" I take this time to watch Stacey. To see how she's reacting to mine and Bryant's back and forth, only she's not looking at either of us, her attention is on Max. She seems on edge, probably trying to distract herself from the shitshow that's playing out in front of her.

Max nods, running his hand through his hair. "Yeah, I did. I had been watching her for months since her father checked her in. Her characteristics were like nothing that I'd seen before. A lot of the nurses had already put her into the schizophrenic category, before I had completed a full diagnostic."

My eyes remain trained on Stacey, who still hasn't taken hers off Max. I've noticed he's not paid her any attention. None at all.

Max continues. "I stayed after-hours to run all the tests I needed to do. MRI scans, blood work, studying her sleep patterns, and how she reacted to certain environments of sleep and sounds. She seemed normal until they'd give her her daily drugs, then she'd be out again, sometimes for days at a time. She would either wake up as Isa or as Brooke."

"That." Bryant snaps his fingers, leaning back in his chair. He snatches the pack of smokes off the table and puts one into his mouth. Flicking open his Zippo, he breathed in the sweet nicotine. "That's what her father said. She was a schizophrenic and her other personality was called Brooke. As if she was possessed by her."

Max grunts, seeming uncomfortable with the current conversation. "Yes and no. Brooke was a real person—"

"—I fucking know that," Bryant snaps, flicking the ash off the tip of his cigarette.

Max clears his throat when he notices Bryant's hostility toward the woman who *killed our daughter*. "What I mean, is that Isa somehow placed all of her bad characteristics into a personality and called it Brooke. In her head, the same story would play, only different from the true events of what happened. With Isa, she was the one who killed Brooke. Brooke exposes herself, rapes her, and then Isa kills her, or Brooke kills Isa. How the ending finished in her head would depend on who Isa would wake up as."

Bryant leans forward, snatching up his glass of whiskey before taking a sip.

"Where were you, Bryant?" I finally ask, my eyes fluttering closed. Grief has decided to take anger's hand and now I'm left with a cocktail of feelings stirring inside of my soul with no outlet. *This isn't going to end well.* "You didn't come for me?" When I finally open my eyes, I find him focusing solely on me.

"I couldn't," he simply answers, as if it's just another question that I had asked. As if it didn't pain me to even ask him to begin with. To display raw emotion to the person who has shown me none. *Agh*. He could be so impossible. I didn't fight my rage anymore, but I also didn't want to have this argument around other people.

Stacey stands from her chair, picking up her glass of champagne. "Am I the only fucking one who thinks this is weird?"

"Excuse me." Pushing off my chair, I exited through the kitchen and made my way out to the main lobby where I knew the guest bathroom was. I pause in my tracks when a piece of artwork catches my eye down the hallway. The splash of color against a concrete canvas with gray stencil is a dead giveaway on who the artist is. *This is why you weren't looking for things. Because of this. Now you've found something.*

I feel his presence behind me before I see or hear him, but I remain focused on the art. "I thought you said that you'd never hang Banksy on your wall..."

Silence for a beat. "That was before I lost you."

I freeze, turning slightly to face him. My eyes clash with his, a tornado of torment and pain aching to be understood. "You didn't lose me, Bryant. You left me. There's a huge difference in that."

He steps forward, his glass hanging from between his fingers. He chuckles, swiping his mouth with the back of his other hand as he gets closer.

I back up until I'm colliding with the wall. There's no way out. I didn't become a wolf when I married one, I'll always be his prey. The single meal he always wants, the only feast to satiate his wild hunger.

One hand slowly comes to the wall beside my head as he takes another long pull of his whiskey. His eyes remain on mine. He finishes his sip leisurely before his tongue sneaks out and absorbs the liquid from his swollen bottom lip. "One, I didn't leave you, and two." He grins. "You're not going anywhere now."

I shove his chest. "Leave me alone, B."

His eyes drop down to where I just pushed him before slowly coming back to mine. He deliberately places the glass on the table beside us before pressing the palm of his hand to the other side of my head. Now I was caged in, and with Bryant, there's no escaping the cage that he confines you into.

"I didn't leave you," he repeats, his tone bored but forceful. This is my first warning that I'm treading painfully close to him losing his patience with me.

I tilt my head in challenge. "Sure you did. That's why you didn't save me."

His hand is at my chin so fast I almost missed it. He squeezes while tilting my head up to face him. "I. Didn't. Leave. You."

Third warning.

My eyes narrow. "Then why the fuck was I still there until Max broke me out?"

He shakes his head. "You were a different person, Isa. I thought I was doing you good."

I grab his arm when he pushes away from me. "What?"

He stumbles back slightly until he was against the wall. "You didn't see you during your episodes. You don't get to tell me how I should have handled you when I didn't even fucking know you during that time."

I blink. "So you didn't try."

He tenses. "I fucking did."

"What stopped you!" I yell, frustrated.

Bryant brought his eyes to mine, baring his teeth. "When you never came back to Isa and stayed as Brooke. I don't know what that fucker has told you, but you haven't been Isa for a long fucking time. You were—essentially dead."

Tears threaten to spill. "He told me it was bad, just not that bad." Probably for good reason, Max didn't want to lay it on thick right away. "You thought I was gone?"

Bryant glares at me. "Why the fuck else would I move on?"

I'm frozen in the spot. Momentarily paralyzed by his confession. "I don't…" I stumble backward, struggling to suck in any oxygen.

"You need to pay very close attention to the next words that are about to come out of my mouth, Isa…" Bryant mutters, grabbing onto my arm before I collapse onto the ground.

I yank away from him. "Why the fuck would I do that?" I hiss, before spinning around and making my way further down the hallway, passing all of the familiar artwork. All of my favorite pieces by Banksy.

"Isa," he growls, annoyed at my rebellion. Ever Bryant. He caresses my rage before using it as his toy. I continue down until I take a random right turn, not wanting to head straight through the red doors at the end of the hallway. My footsteps pick up in pace until I'm eventually jogging through a library and flying out a door that opens onto the patio at the back of the house. Untouched and cool air slaps me across my face, pulling my attention back to the here and now and out of my near panic attack.

Inhale.

Exhale.

I know that he's behind me, and I don't know if that's what's making something so simple like breathing difficult, but I can't seem to get it under control.

"Baby." His voice is soft from behind me and my eyes drift closed as the syllables wrap around my flesh and sink into my pores. "I need you to listen to me." I slowly release the breath I was holding, finally turning to face him.

He's a foot in front of me now, close enough for me to lean forward and reach him.

"When I say these next words, I need you to not react. Can you do that for me?"

I nod, running my tongue over my lips. Despite it all, and whatever else Bryant is telling me, I want to go back to trusting him.

"We need to go back in there and pretend like nothing has happened."

"Why," I whisper, my shoulders sagging from the defeat and withdrawal of energy.

He watches me closely, and I know deep down that I don't know if I'll trust his next words. "Because Stacey and Max are not who they say they are."

I still. My senses now on full alert. "What do you mean?"

"Stacey and Max know each other. I don't know what they're playing at right now, but we need to go along with it." I believe him to an extent, but something doesn't make sense. I know he's not going to let me all the way in right now, so I do what I know I have to do.

My eyebrows slant in. "Why the fuck would I do that?"

Bryant exhaled. "Because this is more than you and I. This is you, me, your father, Jess, and—" His eyes came to mine. "Devon."

FIVE

Bryant

Best friends can hurt you just as much as a lover can.
Love is the weapon. People are just collateral.
-Bryant

Seeing her squirm beneath my revelation raise old feelings that I thought I had squashed when I thought she was gone forever. I should have known better than to trust a word that her father said, even if he was telling the truth, which to be honest, I'm not sure. Ever the fucking liar and manipulator— I knew better. I don't know if I chose to ignore the signs, or if I simply believed him because I was tired.

Tired of feeling pain.

Tired of the anguish.

Tired of the mourning.

I wanted it to disappear. I turned my wrath into goddamn poison and forgot how to protect those I loved from being touched by it.

"What do you mean Devon!" she snaps, the fire in her

eyes only igniting the very same inferno that I put out while she was gone.

"Exactly what the fuck it sounds like!"

She flinches at my tone.

I feel like shit for snapping at her. For about two seconds before I remember exactly how we are. How Bryant and Isa are. We fight dirty but it only serves as foreplay. We turn our dirt into a storm and kill everyone in our path. It is how we are, and fuck me if it didn't feel good having her standing in front of me right now. She looks good with lighter hair. Maybe even better than her brunette.

I step forward when my cock strains against the zipper in my pants.

I want her. Fuck talking about Devon right now, she'll soon learn what's up with him.

She counters my step and walks backward until she hits the wall.

I cage her in with my hands on either side of her and tilt my head. "Miss me?"

"Never." She keeps her eyes on mine, the defiance only making my palms itchy to have her feisty ass bent over my knee while screaming, bleeding, and coming all over my skin.

I dip down to nibble on her ear. "Still a fucking liar, my sweet little pet."

"If that's how you treat your pets, Bryant, then I hope you never own a dog."

I chuckle, reaching one hand up to curve around her slim throat. "Kiss me." I feel her inhale sharply, her swollen lips opening slightly to tease mine.

"Where is Bryant!" I groan when I hear Stace's voice echoing through the house. She's a pain in my ass.

"Oh!" Stacey says, and I don't miss the smart-ass tone behind her hostility. She pokes her head out the door. "There you are. Wondered where you both disappeared off to."

"I got lost," Isa mutters, ignoring her. "On my search for the bathroom."

"Huh." Stacey seems to think over Isa's lie. "How long did you live in this house?"

Isa was quick, and I couldn't take my eyes off her. "I didn't. I lived in his penthouse. We came here a couple of times but not enough for me to remember where a bathroom is in a twenty-bedroom, intricately architectonic building."

Stacey dismisses her, and I have to stop myself from physically putting my hands around her skinny little throat and choking her to death for the sheer disrespect.

Just for looking at Isa the wrong way.

Jesus Christ. I need a drink.

Stacey hooks her arm in mine, tugging on me gently. "Come on. Food is ready."

I flash a look to Isa, her pale cheeks now displaying a pool of red. Either from me rubbing up against her or from the anger of seeing another woman wrapped around my arm.

I wink at her just to work her up before setting off back inside. Back to play the usual game that I set out to play. Back to why it is that I chose Isa.

Back to Stacey and Max.

I take a seat back in my chair, my eyes drifting to Max. He underestimates me if he thinks I don't know who the fuck he is. Which is good. I need him to underestimate me in order for my plan to work.

Before I can rile him up even more, Isa enters the room and takes her place back on her seat. When Isa is around, the whole world fucking stops. I don't mean that in a cheesy way, I mean people around her literally stop and stare. The impact her beauty has on people that she doesn't even know is cataclysmic.

"Sorry." She flutters her eyelashes at Max. "I got lost."

My fists clench from beneath the table.

Max shrugs and digs into his food.

I skip it, reaching for the paperwork from beneath the table and tossing it across to Isa.

Her eyes fly up to mine as she grabs it. "What's this?"

"Exactly why you're here tonight." I pick up my whiskey and swirl it around in my glass. I watch as her face morphs into anger as she flicks through each page.

Attempting to hide my smirk behind my glass, I chuckle as she tosses the papers down onto the table. "You're legally binding me to this house under the grounds of my unstable mental health!"

"I am," I answer smoothly, taking another pull of the soft whiskey. Her hate only makes my dick hard, so I will always win.

"As in I can't leave this fucking house."

I drag my tongue over my lips, smirking.

"As in I have to stay here like a prisoner."

I chuckle, placing my glass on the table. "You're being dramatic."

"Wait!" Max interferes, and my jaw clenches to stop my fist from flying across the table and punching out all his fucking teeth. "You're not married anymore. You can't serve her with shit unless a lawyer is present."

"Actually." I lean back in my chair and spread my knees wide. "I can."

"How?" Max argues, his face turning an embarrassing shade of *I'm a little bitch.*

I can't help it. I want to inhale this moment. Fucking roll it up in some blunt papers and smoke it. "Well, I guess I never divorced her."

Isa

My ex-husband isn't an asshole, he's just straight-up evil. The kind you can't tame, let alone pour holy water on.

"You can't force me to stay here." I don't know why that's all I can reply with after he so ruthlessly dropped that bomb.

Movement out of the corner of my eye distracts me as Stacey launches off her chair. "Why would you do this?" Oh good. She's pissed too.

Bryant ignores Stacey, his focus solely on me. "Actually, I can, and I will, or have you forgotten how persuasive I can be?"

I hadn't. I don't think I ever will.

Stacey tosses her hands in the air. "Why, Bryant?"

He continues to ignore her.

I like playing with fire, especially when the starter is Bryant. "And if I don't?" I ask, rounding the table to take a seat on Max's lap. If Bryant wants to play, I can play. I watch as his eyes harden, the veins beneath his ink on his arms pulsing as he clenches his fist.

It bothers him that I'm on Max.

Good.

Max's hand flexes around my thigh.

Bryant leans forward, his eyes on mine. "I think you know very well what I'm capable of, *Mrs. Royal*."

I flinch at the use of his last name, sliding off Max's lap. As much as I want to poke the bear, I'm painfully aware of what he said before coming back in here. I need to know what he needs me to play along with.

"Fine, I'll stay."

"What?" Max shoots up from his chair, just as I slide into the one beside him. "You don't have to do this, Isa. We can figure out another way."

Oh sweet Max. He underestimates Bryant immensely and knowing Bryant, that would appease him.

I shake my head. "No." Pinning Bryant with a cold stare, I add, "I will stay. But what about your fiancée?"

"Thank you!" Stacey exhales, huffing theatrically. "What about me?"

As if in slow motion, Bryant's head slowly turns toward Stacey, his cold, dead eyes up to hers. "You'll stay too."

Max shuffles on his feet. "*Both* of them?"

Bryant's evil chuckle doesn't sit right with me. It's like curdled milk after being left on the counter for too long. "Both for different reasons, Max. Pay attention."

He's planning something. There's no way Bryant would be this calm if he wasn't.

SIX

Romance died the day you stopped loving me.
-Bryant

Jerry directs me to my bedroom, leaving Bryant and Stacey arguing in the kitchen. I feel sick that I'm doing this. Living in his house with his fiancée, but I know Bryant, and he doesn't do anything without a plan. A reason.

"You'll be alright in here. trouble?" Jer asks, gesturing to a bedroom at the opposite side of where I know Bryant's room is.

It's beautiful. There's a small porch that drags out and welcomes the morning sun with mesh curtains that drift in with the breeze, but it's not where I want to be. I don't want to be this close to Bryant.

"Actually," I murmur, reaching out to Jer's arm. "Could I take one of the rooms on the ground level? I would prefer to be able to come and go without the devil lurking around every corner."

Jer laughs, nodding his head. "I don't see why that would be a problem. Come on."

This room is not as big or beautiful as the bedrooms on the third level, it's actually more of a granny flat, but it's what I need. Something that doesn't remind me of Bryant. That I'm living in his house. Away from the riches and crystal chandeliers. It's tucked behind the kitchen, so away from the other wing of the lower level. I haven't seen that area yet. Whatever is behind the red door.

"I'll get Amanda and the girls to bring all of your clothing and personal items that you left with Bryant down here. Ash is busy right now." Jer leaves, closing the door behind himself.

I venture into the room. The queen bed is against a clean white wall and there's an open sliding door that leads out to the wrap-around porch. The curtains are the same color as the walls, and the sheets and bedding a soft beige.

I like it.

It feels sterile.

Quiet.

There are two other doors inside the room. One leads to a bathroom with a medium-sized tub, and the other to a small walk-in closet. Even the lesser of the bedrooms in this house is licked in opulence.

A gentle knock on the door pulls me out of my snooping. Amanda and another girl, a little older than us, are holding bags and suitcases.

Amanda drops everything onto the floor and flings her arms around my neck. She pulls me in deeper. "I missed you."

I exhale. "Same."

Pushing me back, she searches my eyes. Amanda is in her early twenties, way too smart, but had a rough start to life. She takes care of everything that Bryant needs, whether it be cleaning, cooking, housekeeping, gardening. She also manages the rest of the cleaning and housekeepers that Bryant has on staff. She grew on both Bryant and I instantly after meeting her. We went through applicant after applicant to try to find the right person to help us out with Harper, but all of them were either too old, too tired, not enthusiastic enough, or too enthusiastic. Amanda walked into Bryant's office and told us she didn't want to be here.

The rest was sort of history.

"What is going on?" she whispers, picking up the rolling suitcase and dragging it into my room, with the other woman following closely behind her.

I sigh, shutting the door. "I don't know."

"Bryant is up to something..." She begins pulling all of my clothes out and slipping them onto hangers. The other woman is already folding and tucking things away into my closet.

"Oh, I know." I fall onto the bed when a small shoebox catches my eye. I take it, flipping it open.

"That's all of your personal items."

"Bryant kept all of this?" I can't see Bryant keeping anything of mine actually. It's not like him to be sentimental.

"Well." Amanda cringes, quickly dashing into the closet to put away more of my clothes.

"Amanda..." I warn. "Spit it out."

She pops her head out from behind the door. Her shoulders sag in defeat. "Okay fine. When he found out about you *going away*, he ordered me to get rid of everything, but I didn't. I put all of your things into the storage room. I had a feeling that you were coming back. As stupid as that sounds."

My heart is pounding in my chest. How many times can you feel disappointment before the pounding goes numb? "Right," I whisper, attempting to hide my washed-out sadness. "Yeah, that sounds just like him."

She comes closer to me, the palm of her hand on my cheek. "It's only because that's his way of mourning, Isa. He lost two of the most important people in his life. Just because someone doesn't know how to cope with their mourning, it doesn't make it wrong. There is no right or wrong way to deal with heartbreak, there's just survival, and you do what you need to do to get through it."

I chuckle past my swollen throat. "Ever the theorist." Next out of the box is my cellphone, wallet—thank god for bank cards—and other small items I had. My favorite earrings, my—"wedding rings."

Amanda is in front of me again. "I figured you might still want those."

I toss them back into the box and slam the cover over it. "He's marrying someone else."

Amanda places some folded chiffon sleepwear on the bed and pats it. "I don't know what he's doing, but Isa?"

I look up at her, choking back my tears.

"Give them both hell." She winks before finally losing herself in the organization of my crap. Picking up my sleepwear, I pad into the bathroom, sighing when I shut the door. Amanda must have already placed some items in here because there's a couple of bath bombs, soaps, and shampoos placed on the counter, as well as a toothbrush and paste.

I hit the faucet on the bathtub and watch as water fills to the brink. Amanda knows me, to an extent. She knows what I'm capable of and how much havoc I can create.

So if he wants me to stay here.

Then stay here, I will.

SEVEN
Bryant

When someone dies, the memories you have of them slowly die too.
—Bryant

She's fucking ruthless. I knew that she wouldn't want to be in the bedroom down from me. Actually, I fucking expected it. What I forgot was how people gravitated toward her. She's the rebel without a cause. The recluse. Yet, people couldn't help but be drawn to her. She attracts all kinds of people. Jerry, my heartless ex-SEAL who killed people on a regular, and did it without blinking, couldn't stop his concrete wall from tumbling at her very hand. She does this. Isa fucking Royal will change everything you thought you knew about a bad woman.

She's someone I can trust.

I can go to war beside.

But now, I'm not going to war beside her, I'm going to war against her.

"Cat got your tongue?" she purrs, and I watch as her lips

wrap around her strawberry as she sucks the cream off the tip.

My eyes narrow. "Never." It took all of my power not to kick down her door last night and fuck her until she bled.

Her white teeth sink into the fruit as juice drips down the corner of her mouth. She leans forward. "What is this, Bryant? I don't want to play games anymore. I just want answers."

I used to trust her more than I do now. More than I trusted anyone. But can I trust her with this? *Not yet.*

"Morning." Stacey bounces into the kitchen, fresh from a run and leans down to press a kiss on my lips.

Isa flinches, only slightly, and if you weren't me, you wouldn't have caught it, before leaning back in her chair and averting her eyes out in front of her. Her phone vibrates on the table and she swipes it up, scrolling through the text.

A soft smile graces her mouth as her fingers fly over the screen. With a sudden change of attitude, she stands from the kitchen chair, revealing her sleepwear. The one I'm all too familiar with. Pretty sure the fucking thing is still torn from my teeth.

"Where'd you find your sleepwear?" I pause, looking down to her phone. "And your phone."

Isa shrugs, dipping her finger into the cream pot before sucking it all off. "Guess someone gave enough of a shit to hold on to some of my things." She raises her hand up at me, flashing her fingers and her damn *Lorraine Schwartz* emerald cut solitaire diamond ring. That twenty-four-carat bastard is about as heavy as my regret for not breaking her out. "Including this." Only the multi-million-dollar ring isn't on her marriage finger, it's on her middle finger.

She giggles like the psychopath that she is, flipping me off. "Thought you'd like that, husband."

I wave Stacey off, my eyes locked on Isa. "What is it you want, Isa."

Her eyes narrow. "What do you mean?" There's a long pause, long enough to hear the old grandfather clock that sits in the foyer.

I lick my lips, ignoring Stacey crashing cutlery around in the kitchen. "I mean, what do you *want*?" It's a double-edged question.

I take in her features. Even having just woken up, she's flawless. Her milky soft skin and pinched red cheeks, even her long dark blonde—*or what even color is that*—hair twisted into a messy top knot is perfect, and don't get me started on the soft curves that she's somehow gained, just begging to be grabbed onto. Isa being on the curvier side lately gets my heart racing way more than it did when she was slim. More to bite on.

"You want to know what I want?" Isa slowly walks her round ass around the kitchen table. I watch as fire flashes over her green eyes, the defiance she tries so desperately to bury fighting its way to the surface. I want it. I want all of her. When you marry someone, you don't just marry the parts that you like about them. You marry every single inch of that person. The good, the bad, the evil, and in Isa's case, the recklessness.

"I want you to tell me that you knew I wasn't gone. I want you to tell me that my daughter is still alive and that I really did see you outside my room door when I was locked up in purgatory." My fingers flex as she draws closer. With her hands now on my thighs, my muscles tense. "And I want you to get rid of that walking excuse of a plan, because have you forgotten?" Her index finger glides down the side of my cheek. She leans down to my ear and nips my lobe. *Jesus Christ.* "I. Don't. Share." She attempts to push up from me, but I snatch her wrist, pulling her straight back down onto my lap. Her legs spread wide over mine as she sinks into me. I'm done fucking around with this. I need my cock in her ass just to remind her who fucking owns it.

I open my mouth. "Fin—"

"Isa?" Max's voice is like a bucket of cold water. Water I will happily drown him in.

Isa grins, gauging my reaction. Her eyes stay on mine. "Max!" She swings her legs off me and makes her way to him. "I'll just get changed and then we will go."

"Go where?" I snap, glaring at her and not paying Max any attention. I readjust my stiff cock in my pants.

Isa turns to face me. "To see Devon."

I freeze, my hands clenching. "Why?" She doesn't know the depth of Devon. Not even fucking close. *Fuck.* And I was supposed to have that conversation with her last night.

"Because he was my friend before all of this happened."

"Was he?" I push from the table and stand to my feet. "Or was he simply on a job?"

She pauses, turning back to face me. "What?"

"As much as I'd love to watch you both verbally abuse each other, can I have a word?" Max interrupts, his hand around her arm.

She smiles up at him. "Sure. Follow me."

As they both disappear down the hallway, I pace around the table until I'm in the kitchen where Stacey is sitting on one of the bar stools.

Her eyes come up to mine, and it's the first time I've seen her sad. Wish I could say I cared, but I don't. Stacey is a complicated piece of ass. She always has been.

She pulls off the ring that's on her finger and places it on the table. "You're still in love with her..." It wasn't a question; it was a fact.

"She's my wife. I didn't marry her because I didn't love her."

"And what about me?" she snaps, her eyes colliding with mine as she pushes up from the stool. "How was this all supposed to go down?"

I lean back onto the counter, crossing my legs at the ankles. "I can't answer that question."

"You've been colder than normal toward me, Bryant. To be honest." She rubs her damp cheeks. "I wasn't sure how I was supposed to do this without gaining deep feelings for you." There's so much I should say to her. She deserves that. I may be cold and ruthless, but I make exceptions at times, and Stacey is one of them. Not as important as Isa—no one fucking is—but important, nonetheless.

She stammers toward me, her hand pressing against my cheek. I want to slap it away, but I fight the urge. "Give me a few days to get my head back in check."

I watch as she disappears into the foyer. I'll give her those days, after all...

Pulling my phone out from my pocket, I hit dial on *The Reaper*.

"To what do I owe the pleasure?" he asks, but the sass in his tone is obvious.

"Isa is back and she's out for blood."

"Oh, I know." Devon chuckles. "But it's not my blood she wants."

I roll my eyes. "When do you get back?"

He pauses, and I hear chatting in the background as he answers. "I'm already back."

EIGHT

If it doesn't make sense, then don't pay it a cent.
-Isa

The longer I sit and think about everything that I've been through over the past year, the more clarity I tend to get. Devon and Brooke. How their roles played out with my internal battle. My mind has been so manipulated that it doesn't feel like I own it. My plan is to take back that power from my father.

"Are you sure about this?" Max asks, looking at me from over his arm.

I nod. "Devon won't hurt me."

"But when you were out, he was an enemy. You had put him on the bad side—" My blood pressure drops to dangerous levels at the near mention of her name. Saying her name inside my head was easy, but hearing it out in the open makes me uncomfortable.

"Brooke was an enemy. But Devon, I'm not sure where he came in to play when it came to my mental characteristics."

Max reaches over and squeezes my knee. "I'm here. Always."

I give him a polite smile as we pull up right outside the coffee shop Devon and I would go to while we were in New York. The dark maroon paint that's glassed over the entry brings back memories of all the good times Devon and I had together.

All of them.

Before I was married to Bryant, we would travel to New York a lot. It was our playground before my world spun out of control.

I climb out of the passenger seat, slamming the door closed behind me while turning to face Max, my hand flying up to his chest. "You can wait here. Devon and I need to have this conversation with just the two of us. Is that okay?"

Max looks over my shoulder briefly before meeting my eyes. "Yeah, alright. I'll be here."

"Good." I pat his shoulder before making my way to the entry, the bell dinging above my head as I walk over the threshold.

I find him right away. His styled blond hair sticks out as his lean body rests against a table, chatting with one of the waitresses. He sees me come in and smirks at her, tapping her shoulder and planting a kiss on her cheek.

"Don't stop on my account," I sass him, pulling out a chair that's tucked beneath a graffiti-ridden tabletop.

Devon's face falls as the girl disappears behind me. "What? I don't get a hug?"

I glare at him. "No. Maybe if you had tried to rescue me, you would, but the answer is no."

Devon drags a chair around the table and plants it directly in front of me. He sits down, his hands coming to my cheeks. "Isa, I thought you were gone."

I whack his hand away from my cheek. "So what? The

Devon I knew would have taken me even if I was crazy Brooke."

Devon kicks out his legs and squeezes his hands into a fist. "A lot changed since you married my cousin."

I sigh, massaging my temples. Devon looks good. His blond hair combed back and his bright blue eyes twinkling in mischief.

"Who was that that you came with?"

"Hmm?" I try to play dumb, as if that would ever work on him. He comes from a long line of over-intuitive family members.

"The tall, hulk dude. Who is he?" Devon leans forward, resting his elbows on his knees with a devious half-smile on his mouth. "Does my cousin know about him?"

I wish I could remember the clear details of finding out that my best friend and my husband were related, but the niceties are hazy. All I know is that I *know*. I'm hoping someone can clarify the parts that don't come to me straight away.

"He knows, but I don't care. Since he has a fiancée living in his house now and won't let me move out."

Devon chuckles, shaking his head while leaning back in his chair. "Moving you in? Damn. He's always so dramatic."

"Dramatic?" I raise my eyebrow, signaling to the waiter that we were ready to order. "I don't know if that's the word I'd use, considering the man is Bryant Royal."

Devon seems to ponder over my words, his index finger working the top of his lip. "Who's the man, baby?"

"What man?" I ask, just as the young waiter appears at our table.

"She'll have a venti latte and I'll have a long black," Devon whisks off effortlessly, his eyes remaining on mine. Once the waiter has gone, he repeats. "Who's the guy with you?"

I fidget beneath the table, my fingers wrapping around

each other like tiny little vises. "He was one of the doctors at the ward I was being held in."

The corners of Devon's eyes crinkle around the edges before he exhales, leaning back in his chair. "You know it was for your own good."

I freeze at those words. I hate being told something is for my own good. No one knows what is good for anyone unless they're that person and know what good feels like to them. What the fuck does he mean it was for my own good? "What?" I lean forward until my elbows were pressing into the table. "You mean to tell me that me being locked in a psych ward while my father played Dr. Jekyll and Mr. Hyde on me was for my own good? Devon, you're a fucking idiot." I go to push off the table and stand to my feet when his hand covers mine on the table, pausing what was going to be my dramatic exit.

His skin is pale against mine and the leather bangles that clench around his slim wrist match the black ring that's over his thumb. My eyes fly to his in fury. "Get your fucking hands off me, Devon."

He doesn't.

His hand remains on mine. "No. And Isa, I'm not letting you go this time because you're going to hear me out."

I don't want to hear him out. I feel myself slowly slipping into self-consciousness with whether or not I should be trusting my friend. My only friend. My mind is saying don't be stupid, but my heart is saying we know this particular brand of stupid.

"Jesus Christ, Isa," he exhales, and I faintly hear the legs of his chair scrape against the tiled floor. "Come on. We need to go somewhere more private." He takes my hand in his and leads me out of the coffee shop, pushing through the entry doorway. I don't know why I allow him to do this so quickly after pissing me off. Maybe it's as simple as me wanting to, or maybe it's because deep down I still trusted Devon. It's not hard to trust someone when the seed was already planted there from the beginning. All you have to do is water it.

Max is waiting outside of the car when he catches us walking out. Instantly he's strolling directly to us, probably sensing danger. "What's going on?"

Devon glares at him up and down, the corner of his mouth tipped up in a snarl. "You think Bryant is scared of you? He's merely heating up his meal before he eats you for a snack."

"Devon." I slap him with the back of my hand.

Devon turns around to face me. "He can't come."

"Why?" I ask, my hands waving in the air.

Devon shrugs. "Simply because I don't trust him."

I run my tongue over my bottom lip, thinking over Devon's words. Devon may always be the life of the party and the obvious extrovert in the group, but make no mistake, he's every bit instinctual when it comes to reading people, so his simple declaration of not trusting Max has wriggled inside of my head.

Exhaling a pent-up breath, I turn to Max. "I'll call you if I need anything." Devon beeps unlocked a Porsche that's parked behind Max's hired car.

Max shakes his head, the obvious unease possessing his features in ways that he probably doesn't even realize he's exposing. "I don't like this, Isa. Your father could be working with them, trying to get you back in. I can't help you if this is his doing."

"Yo! I'm not a fucking Republican!" Devon yells loudly from the driver's side of the Porsche.

I roll my eyes. Devon doesn't even politic. I squeeze Max's hand. "Please. You've done so much for me. I will call you."

"You trust him?" Max asks, the wariness rolling off of him in waves.

Without a pause, I nod. "Yes. I do. Unfortunately."

Max releases a breath that I didn't realize he was holding. "Okay. I will go back to the hotel and wait for your call." Waving him off, I slide into the passenger seat of Devon's new ride.

"What the fuck are you playing at, Isa? You really wanna strip dance with another man right in front of the beast?"

I lick my lips. "Why don't you like him?"

Devon floors us out of the parking lot. "Because he's wearing fucking loafers with jeans."

"God, Devon!" I yell, turning to face him. "What the fuck happened while I was away?"

Devon shakes his head. "After you left, things turned to shit."

"Are you really the damn reaper, or did I imagine that?"

Devon smirks, picking up speed as we make our way onto the highway. "Oh no, that you didn't imagine. I very much am, but as far as Brooke is concerned, she and I were never working together."

"I don't know what's real and what isn't."

"That's what your dad wanted, Isa! He wanted to fuck you up like that! Have you seen Brianna?"

I flinch at the mention of my sister's name. "No."

"Well, she's a fucking Stepford wife. Like you didn't already expect that to happen anyway. Divorced and re-marrying."

"And the baby? She was pregnant with me, with Harper."

"Yeah, a boy. He's cute as shit." Devon glares at me from over his shoulder.

"Damn," I sigh, shaking my head and resting it against the cool window. "I really lost the plot there."

Devon laughs so loud I find a smile on my own mouth. "Yeah, you did."

"Also, in my dream state, or whatever it was that I was

going through, you wanted to get me pregnant for some reason. I later found out that you weren't there. We don't know why I put you on the bad side of the fence."

"Well, I mean, I'd still like to fuck you until you get pregnant. Does that count?" He's joking, and it feels familiar, like home, but there's still a sadness that seems to linger within me. One I haven't been able to shake. "In all seriousness, it probably has to do with the way I make you feel. I don't make you feel good things. We, you and I, we were toxic. We fucked, did drugs, and repeated. We weren't good together. It makes sense why you would unconsciously place me in the dark, I've been there through all the dark moments." I want to engage with him in this conversation because it seems a legitimate reason, but there's one thing I have to ask.

"Why didn't anyone save me?" My throat tightens around the words, as if my body is too stubborn to let the words go. To expose my vulnerability.

His hand rests on my thigh. "Baby. It's not Bryant's fault. Seeing you as Brooke was something none of us could handle. You never wanted any of us around. Straight up refused to see us whenever we would ask for you. Your husband may have connections on that side of the law, but your father had everyone on both sides. Even if we wanted, he wouldn't let us through."

I sigh, squeezing my eyes closed. I was so fixated on Devon's words that when we slow down, I only just notice that we've pulled into Bryant's long driveway. "Oh Devon!" I yell, turning in my seat to face him. "Why are you bringing me back here!"

Devon pulls up the emergency brake and shifts in his seat. "Because you and he need to fucking talk. Away from the fiancée and away from your new toy."

I smirk, pouting. "Are you jealous that I have a new toy?"

Devon rolls his eyes, leaning over to my door handle and

pushing it open. "Get out of the car. Pain in my ass. Once you and he have talked, then we will talk about what to do from there, but as of right now, Isa, you need to be back on his lap."

"I'm not a dog, Devon..."

He bites his bottom lip and winks. "Oh, but don't you like it?"

"Fuck," I grumble, stumbling out of the car while staring up at the mansion. This time with new eyes. Stacey's car isn't here. Actually, no cars are parked out front. The sun is setting behind thick trees, with an overlay of green from the leaves. I suck in a deep breath, just as the front door opens and my husband is standing there with a glass of whiskey hanging between his fingers and his tie loosened around his neck.

"Inside, baby. Time to talk."

NINE

Bryant

I didn't want to ruin her. I just wanted to love her.
-Bryant

If I had the option to walk through Hell or go through everything that I have been through this past year, I'd run toward the gates of Hell.

Isa straightens her shoulders, and I can't help but take in her body. I need to get her on my dick as quickly as possible. I need to fuck her, and I need to do it now. The thought of her soft curves bruising under my hand has me fighting the urge to throw her over my shoulder and dragging her upstairs.

"Husband." She grins, taking the steps one at a time while keeping her eyes on mine. "Really, this is how you wanted to get me back here." She pauses right in front of me, but just as she's about to step past, she brings her hand to my tie and yanks it off. She bats her eyelashes. "Could have just called me." She's walking past me while tossing my tie around her neck when my hand catches hers in passing and I yank her backward, slamming her against the wall in the foyer. I can feel her heart beating against my chest, her breath on my lips. I press one leg between hers while keeping my hands planted on the wall on either side of her head. "Watch it, wife. You know how I get when I'm angry."

"Oh..." She runs her finger over my jaw. "I was counting on it."

Fuck. My lips collide with hers without even thinking, my hands at the back of her thighs as she wraps her legs around my waist.

She didn't fight me.

She wouldn't. *She should have*.

I grind myself against her, needing to be closer. "Bryant," she whispers over my lips.

I pull back, searching her eyes. "What?"

She hits me in the chest with the back of her hand, her expression morphing into obvious disgust. "You moved on."

I groan, annoyed that she wanted to bring Stacey up right now. She starts wriggling in my grip, attempting to get out of my hands.

"Let me go!" she cries, and I see them, the tears that prick the corner of her eyes.

"Hey!" I try for the gentle route, circling my thumb over her cheek.

She doesn't listen, and if anything, her fighting becomes more forceful.

"Isa!" I yell, my hand now at her throat. Squeezing, I flex my fingers around her frail neck as her fighting is instantly subdued. I bare my teeth at my victory as her eyes crash into mine like angry clouds of warfare, threatening to bring a storm.

So close. She was *so close*.

I lean in closer, running the tip of my nose over hers while staring her down. "I didn't fucking move on. It was always going to be you, but what the fuck was I supposed to do, baby? Stay alone forever? Fuck the endless options of women just to keep my dick wet?"

She holds her stare; her shoulders square and her jaw set, but her stubbornness loses when tears begin to trickle down her cheeks. "Yes, Bryant. One hundred times fucking yes!"

"Isa..." I watch as her focus begins to shift. I'm losing her and I know it. "Baby, look at me."

She wouldn't, so I flex my fingers around her chin and forced her eyes to mine. "I fucking love you. There was never going to be anyone else. I had to do this for a goddamn reason, now are you ready to talk, or do you want me to fuck some sense into you first? Maybe throw you around a bit until you bleed?"

I feel her defeat roll off her body as her head falls to my shoulder.

"I missed you."

She looks back up at me with her perfect doe eyes.

I run my thumb over her bottom lip. "Is that a yes to wanting to be thrown around?"

"We need to talk. You're right." I step forward and let her fall down to the ground, taking her hand in mine before leading her to my office. I don't know how this is going to go, and to be honest, I haven't thought much about the execution.

Once we're inside, I shut the door, squeezing my fist against the wood before I brave myself to turn around and face her. *Just how much...*

I turn around to find her on my chair with her high-heeled shoes on my desk and a cigar clenched between her teeth. "Well, let's talk."

Jesus fucking Christ. I married Tony Montana.

TEN

He may be a monster, but that monster is my pet.

-Isa

Bryant's eyes slanted in challenge when he notices where I'm seated. I did it on purpose. This is Bryant and Isa. Completely challenging. I think we will both be this way until the day we die and the way we die will probably be at each other's hands.

Bryant slides in behind the back of the desk, picks me up from under my arms and slips into the chair while planting me back on his lap. "Your father told me you were schizophrenic. That I couldn't have a future with you because you were the worst case that they had seen. I believed him when I came to visit you because you were Brooke. A completely different person. The doctors in the psych ward confirmed it all, and fuck, Isa. I didn't know what to think. You didn't recognize me when I came in to see you and then you eventually stopped wanting to see me. You hated me. It became unbearable to watch. Eventually, your father cut off all visitations to you and put you into isolation. He said that you were self-harming and that he needed to keep you monitored. I believed him. When I have a crazy wife screaming at me like a demon on crack and a president as a father-in-law whose word I trusted, it was easy to pick who to believe."

I want to interrupt him and question things, but I don't. He needs to talk and I need to listen.

"I need you to not worry about Stacey right now but trust that I know what I'm doing." He turns me around to face him so I'm straddling his waist. "Know that you come first. Everything is for you."

He licked his lip and I had to force myself not to lean in and bite down on it. "Max is also planning something, and I'm almost certain that I know every single fucking move."

"What do you mean?" I ask when the rest of the information becomes too much. I don't even want to bring up Stacey until I've gotten to the bottom of my father and now Max.

"He means that you didn't escape that asylum, babe," Devon whispers from the doorway.

I jump, turning my head over my shoulder briefly before resting my eyes back on Bryant.

Bryant nods as if reading my thoughts. "They let you out, and your man Max? He's part of it."

My brows furrow. "Stacey..." I think over my time in Fate. "The photo..." I whisper out the thoughts that were rushing through my head. "She's—she—"

Bryant nods. "Max's wife."

I exhale through a hiss, resting my head on his shoulder. He begins massaging my lower back, the cool touch of his Rolex against the warmth of my skin. "Max is with your father, but we can't let them know that we know."

I still. "You mean Stacey too?"

Bryant shuffles in his seat. I notice the tense of his muscles instantly. "Sure."

Before I can question what *sure* is supposed to mean, Devon leans against the side of the heavy mahogany table, crossing his feet at the ankles. "It's true. We can't."

"So, what does that mean?" I swing my legs off from Bryant and make my way to the alcohol table. Pouring a glass of vodka, I drop two ice cubes into the liquid and swirl the glass around between two fingers.

"It means you have to play nice," Devon mutters, pressing himself against my ass while his fingers sprawl out over my tummy.

My eyes closed as I tipped the liquid down my throat. "I don't play nice."

Devon chuckles, his lips skimming against the nape of my neck. "We know, baby."

"We have a plan." Bryant takes my glass off me and brings it to his lips. "And you're about three seconds away from losing your cock, Devon."

The vibrating in my pocket distracts me and I reach down to fish it out, seeing Max's name flashing over the home screen. I hit ignore and slip out of Devon's grip, turning to face him head-on.

"Some things are coming back to me," I say. "Like the parts that I created in my head from the drugs have almost faded to nothing and the things that actually happened feel as though they've only just happened. You and Brooke?"

"We fucked. Before the wedding day. That's it."

I search Devon's blue eyes. Eyes I had trusted for years. Eyes I could still trust, even though I shouldn't. "You and your cock, Devon."

Devon flashes me one of his trademark grins. "Hey, I mean you never complained about it before."

I ignore him. "And what you do for Bryant?"

Bryant interferes. "Not just me, he has many clients."

I shake my head, making my way to the large window that

overlooks the driveway. Thick trees line the manicured lawn, a fountain built from stone in the middle. "You're an assassin?" The words fall from my lips before I can swallow them.

"I prefer the term reaper, but in essence, yes, I am."

I exhale, snatching the glass off Bryant when he comes close enough for me to reach. Kicking off my red bottom heels until they're scattered on the ground, I bring my legs up to my chest, leaning on the back of the glass. I love this office. This seat that's built against the window. "You knew about me when you moved in with me?"

They both remain silent.

I open my eyes onto Bryant, who is now watching me closely. His shadow over his jaw is growing thicker, borderline beard. It suits him. Bryant is a feral beast, tamed and conditioned to aim his anger at the right people. He's respectfully poised, and has no problem sitting and waiting his turn to bite, which is exactly what made him dangerous. He never acts irrationally. He does everything with intention, with purpose, so you knew that when and if he was about to end your life, there was no way you were walking away from his wrath.

"Baby." Those simple words said from complicated lips erupted emotions that were dead inside of me and raised them to the surface. Bryant runs his hand over his jaw, bringing a cigar to his lips. "Yes, Devon knew who you were when you became friends. He knew who you were when he moved in with you. He knew who you were the whole fucking time." Bryant lights the tip of his cigar and I watch as smoke filters through the air, the soft sweet hint of marijuana burning with the strong scent of nicotine.

"Because I killed your brother." I'm not so much asking, more thinking out loud. "Because you wanted revenge?" Deep down, even as I say those words, I know that nothing with our life is ever easy.

Bryant sits beside me, resting his elbows on his knees as his eyes come to mine from over his shoulder. "No."

My head snaps toward him like the damn exorcist.

Bryant takes another puff of his cigar. "That day that you and Brooke came to the tent, we knew who your dad was, yeah. The truth, Isa, is your dad owed me a great debt."

Tension builds between my eyebrows as they pinch together. "What do you mean?"

Bryant licks his lips. "He owed me for something I did. Something I helped him with. As a backup, if he didn't pull through with what he promised me, I needed to get close to you. Easier to kidnap someone when they're willing to get in your car..." he whispers off the words with a smug smirk on his face.

I want to slap it off.

I rise from the seat, shaking my head. "Wait. So—" Reality slams into me like a sledgehammer right to the head. "Wait!" *Breathe, Isa. Breathe. You can't go to prison.* "So you proposing, wanting to marry me, the reasons why you told me you loved me, were actually lies?"

Bryant looks up at me from hooded eyes, the veins on his arms popping out. I hate when he rolls his dress shirt up to his elbows. He has perfect arm porn.

"Baby..." Devon reaches for my hand. "What happened to *get you down that aisle* and *everything up to this point doesn't mean anything on what we both are now.*"

I'm on my feet in a flash and before I can stop myself, I slap Devon across the cheek with a loud clap. He takes the hit, shrugging me off. "I knew that they had played me, Devon. I knew that my father and even Bryant had cooked something up." Tears stung the side of my eyes. "But I thought you were different! I trusted you, Devon! Even when I was unconscious and fighting the battle of Brooke in my head, even when I saw you with Brooke in my head, deep down I still trusted you!"

Devon came closer to me, and before I can run, his arm is hooked around my back as he pulls me into his chest. "Fuck you, Isa. You know I love you. You know how I feel about you and what I would do for you and only you, Isa." He squeezes me, and my emotions are fighting silently with his right now, because the crack in his voice shatters my core. "Because I didn't want any other girl on my dick. Just you. Always just you. So I went to men, because every single time I was cock-deep in another fucking pussy, all I thought of was yours. So fuck you if you assume less of me. I'm not responsible for the shady shit your brain created."

My heart sinks at his words, the pain almost unbearable. I need to be alone. Devon releases me, stepping backward to allow me my space. I knew Devon was in love with me. I truly and beneath it all knew all along, but I slept with him anyway. All along, I was messing with his feelings and didn't even realize.

Bryant was in the same position, watching me. When I bring my eyes to his cold, dead ones, his jaw tenses.

"You got anything to say for yourself?"

"Yeah," Bryant says. "I'm not done. So if you could sit your fucking ass down so I can finish, maybe I won't need to beat your ass to make you compliant. And Devon can watch."

My arms cross.

"Stop acting like a brat, Isa. You know damn well how both he and I feel about you and you fucking know that no one walking this earth would ever be able to get near you."

"Really?" I snap, glaring at the both of them. These two infuriating men who mean more to me than I could ever attempt to explain. "Because last I checked, you both fucking left me in an asylum." As soon as the words leave, I already know I'm beating a dead horse. We know this. I've been through it. I'm starting to feel like the words are losing their substance every time I say them.

Bryant stands from where he was sitting. The air shifts as he eats up each step. Closer and closer. Any other woman would crawl back into her shell. He's intimidating and he knows it.

"One, I believed him when I saw the state you were in. We both did. The asylum was legit. We thought you were in the best care. Why would your father go to this extreme at keeping you hidden, hmmm?" Another step. I take one back. "Two, if you doubt my feelings for you one more time, Isa, it will hurt."

I bang into the desk, my hands squeezing around the edges of the wood.

My phone starts vibrating again. "So, to be clear..." I say. "My father offered me to you to pay his debt?"

Bryant nods.

"Not the worst thing he has done, obviously," I grumble. "And I see how it would benefit you both in some way. This is what happens when men have too much damn power." I shake off my thoughts before I veer off track. "One more question before I ask my next one."

"That doesn't make sense, by the way." Devon snickers from behind Bryant's massive body. "You should just say two more questions."

I flip him off while keeping my eyes on Bryant. "Why did my father owe you?"

Just when I think my question will be left on deaf ears, Bryant says, "You're not ready for that answer yet. Trust me."

I tense. "Tell me, Bryant. I'm not going to go along with any plan unless I know everything. I will not be blindsided again."

Bryant pushes away from me. "Fine."

I slide up on top of his desk. "Your father owed me because—"

Devon coughs from behind me. "You don't want to know this..."

"Yeah," I mutter. "I do."

Bryant's head shakes, but I can sense his underlying agitation. "We helped with something that happened years ago."

"What? Helped him with what?" Why do I get the feeling that I'm not about to like what is said next?

I can't hear anything when Bryant's mouth starts moving. It's as though my brain knew that the next words that were about to come out of his mouth were going to be something that I wouldn't like.

"Do you?" Bryant urges, and I didn't even realize that his arm was hooked back around my waist or that my face was almost pressed against his chest.

"Do I what?" I ask, resting my palms against him to give me some space. His cologne is toxic but mixed with the cigar smoke it's lethal.

"Do you remember the boating accident?" he repeats, only this time his tone is careful. He's searching my face as if looking for clues. Any clue to see if I'm lying.

"No?"

Devon shuffles from behind me, dropping down into my favorite seat.

"You were young. Really fucking young. Like, sixteen..."

"Wait!" I stop him with a simple flick of my wrist. "You've known me since I was sixteen?"

Bryant flexes his jaw. "Yes. Your father, he reached out to Devon and me for our... services."

"Services?" I ask, an eyebrow cocked. "What do you mean services? What would he want with a CEO and a—" I pause, as a pool of saliva fills my mouth. The reality of his words finally pulsing through the membranes of my brain. *Did he mean what I think he meant?*

I step away from Bryant as his hands fly out to my arm to stop me. "And an assassin." My vision is blurred on Devon. "What the fuck!"

Bryant seems to lose focus on me as he stumbles backward, reaching for the bottle of whiskey while running his hand through his hair. He leans against his desk and takes a swig from the glass bottle, his focus back on me. He swipes his mouth with the back of his hand. "Before I started Royal Enterprise, I was just like Devon."

I want to scream. Hit him. Ask him what this meant and why. Why was he telling me this right now and what did it have to do with my father and me?

Bryant continues. "Your father dialed in a job for me."

"A job?" I ask, blinking. "What was the job?"

Bryant stares. "You."

ELEVEN

Not all men are fit to be a father. Some are only equipped to be dads.
-Isa

Past

"I got a text." *I flicked through the message that was open on my phone, as Devon stumbled out from his back room with a bottle of vodka hanging from his fingers. Devon was eighteen and I twenty. I never planned to have this gig as a long-time thing. In fact, a business deal was about to go through next week that was sure to set me up for fucking life.*

I couldn't tell Devon right now though, he loved that we did this together too much. Like Batman and Robin, only we weren't fighting bad guys. We were the bad guys.

"What'd it say?" *Devon asked, nudging his head at my phone.*

I glared up at him with a smirk, kicking my legs out in front of me. "To meet him at Clay Harbor. Two hundred fifty thousand dollars." *I watched as Devon froze as I said that number out loud. Same for both of us, both our parents were rich. But a trust fund couldn't buy me the most expensive thing of all.*

Control.

"How do we know it's not a setup?"

I shrugged. "We don't." The phone that we used was basically a burner phone. We changed every week and put out feelers so that people had our new number. Everyone knew who Devon and I were. The Reaper and The Beast. That's all we were ever known by.

Devon smirked, tipping the bottle of vodka to his lips. "Then let's fucking party."

The drive was quick because we knew exactly where to go. I was slightly distracted about the business meeting that I knew I had next week, but when we pulled the car up to the parking lot, with the loud crashing of waves creating the perfect scent of sandy air to whisk through our cranked open windows, I knew this would be my last gig. I needed to get into business clean. My hands were dripping in blood, but today was going to be my last job.

I climbed out of the car, slamming the passenger door. I noticed the man standing nervously in the corner from a mile away, and it wasn't because his anxiety stuck out, it was because I had seen his face splashed on television for the past few months. A fucking senator.

I approached him carefully, with calculated steps. "You call this in?"

The number that clients would use was exclusive. No one could get their hand on it unless they gained it from a reputable source, and we made sure to keep our sources small. Seven men on every continent. Who also happened to be my closest friends and one being my shithead brother.

Senator ran his hand through his hair nervously and met me half-way. "I did." His eyes were flying all over the place, as if he was waiting for someone to jump out from the bushes.

"You a rat?" I asked. I didn't care. We had a backup plan if we ever did get set up. We were untouchable.

"No." He shook his head. "My daughter. She's who I need you to take care of." He turned over his shoulder, and I followed his sight to a boat bobbing over the waves. "She's asleep on there. Make it look like an accident or never have her body found again."

*My fists clenched at my sides. Piece of shit. "We don't do kids."
And congratulations, now I'm going to kill you instead.*

*He shook his head, glaring at me as if in disgust. "No, she's older.
Much older. An adult."*

*I knew the rules. No asking questions, and that's why we get paid.
No judgments. I'd lost count of how many I had taken, but never once
had I felt like I needed to ask questions. Not until now.*

*The white and blue super yacht rocked back and forth against the
small waves, as I brought my eyes back to Johnston. "Got the cash?
You know how this goes."*

*He took out a phone from his suit pocket and punched in numbers,
transferring the funds to our offshore account. My phone dinged with
a notification to say it had been instantly transferred.*

Just as he was about to pass us, I turned around. "Why?"

*He paused, rubbing the stray tears that were falling down his
cheeks. I continued. "You're not necessarily what we're used to either.
You have too much remorse. Usually, we don't allow people to back
out. But I'd make the exception this once. I will refund the money
right back if you want to stop this shit now."*

*Devon cleared his throat from behind me. I knew why. I never
gave anyone this option. Ever.*

He stared back at me through regretful eyes. "Just do it."

I shrugged as we both made our way to the boat.

"Wait!" He came up to us. "I'll come with you. I'll hide."

*Bile rose in my throat. "So not only are you putting a hit out on
your kid, but you want to be in the vicinity while it happens?"*

"You don't understand," he muttered, walking ahead of us.

Devon and I shared a puzzled look.

*"You're fucking right, I don't." I shook my head. What a fucking
idiot. Not my kid, not my drama.*

*Once we were on the boat, I drove us out until we were far
enough out to have no one around us. Devon ducked underneath the
hood where she was tied up in one of the rooms.*

He came back up, shaking his head. His skin was pale. "She's real fucking pretty."

I rolled my eyes. "Everyone is fucking pretty to you."

"Not everyone." Devon smirked at me. "You're not."

I flipped him off before making my way down to the anchor. Tearing off my shirt, I tossed it onto the chair that was on the side and made my way to the room.

"She blinded?" I called out.

"Yep!" Devon answered as I shoved the door open.

I paused.

She looked real fucking small.

Too fucking small.

"Where—" she slurred as if drugged. Her movements were slow but hostile.

I clenched my jaw and stormed back out, making my way to the other room at the front of the boat. I kicked the door down. "How fucking old is she?"

Johnson sighed, running his fingers through his hair. "She's sixteen. You don't understand. She's trouble. Reckless. If I run for president, which I am, I can't have her running around making a mockery of my name."

I scoffed. "And you get America's vote of sympathy if she disappears."

Pig.

I shook my head. "I don't fucking do kids, and sixteen to me is still a fuckin' kid!"

Finally, he brought his eyes up to mine. "I know. I thought this was what I wanted. It would answer all of my prayers if she just disappeared, but now that I'm here..."

Maybe she's older and deserves it. I don't need my reputation going to shit because I can't end a girl who probably deserves it. Why else would he be here? He's not my usual client. "You want to or not, because the more we fuck around, the more time that has to get inside your head."

He nodded. "Do it."

I shut the door and set off to do what I was supposed to do.

I made my way back to her room, grabbed her by the ties that were around her wrist and dragged her tiny body to the back of the boat.

Devin stood silent, watching me carefully. He knew I didn't want to do this. Not really. I hate doing women. In fact, I'd only ever done one before—and it was justified. As much of an asshole that I am, my relationship with my mother and my sister was flawless. It's why I struggled with it. Women make the fucking world spin. We all came from one. They deserve fucking respect for that alone. Period.

Devon glared at me harder, sensing my anxiety. He also knew how I felt about this. He used to call me the silent feminist, until he saw how I fucked.

He rolled his eyes and grabbed the girl from the back of her neck, slamming her down onto the chair and tying the anchor around her ankles.

I squeezed my eyes closed. Fuck. We can't do this shit. This is fucked up. Turning around, I made my way back to the room to try to talk her dad out of it. That way, Devon won't get itchy for murder if he backs out.

I opened the door. "You can't do this."

His eyes came to mine, rimmed red from tears. "You're right. I can't. I will just have to find another way to get rid of her."

I shook my head. "You're a sick motherfucker. I could ruin you."

I took my phone out from the back of my pocket and snapped a shot of him before grabbing him by the collar and shoving him up with one hand, coming nose to nose with him. "I'm going to keep an eye on that girl for the rest of her fucking life, and if she so much as falls off the radar for a second, I'll drown you, motherfucker. Understood?"

He swallowed sharply. "Understood. Keep the money."

"I fucking will, fucker."

Turning back around, my steps faltered when I caught Devon

standing, a cigarette in his mouth and his cock out, pointing toward the ocean as he took a piss.

"Where is she?" I called out, even though we don't speak during jobs.

Devon swung around. "Oh, down there. Don't worry, I took care of it for both of us since I knew you couldn't."

"No!" her shitty father wailed in the background, but before anyone could say anything else, I dove right into the water and swam until I saw the dark shadow of her body sinking to the bottom of the ocean.

Silence.

Isa crawls into a ball, tears streaming down her face, her eyes closed. I can't imagine what she must be going through inside. I feel like every bit the piece of shit for not telling her about this sooner. But how? How do you tell a woman that her daddy wanted to have her killed at sixteen?

"I'm sorry, baby. I saved you, cut you from the anchor and brought you back to the boat. I kept an eye on you for fucking-ever. Part of that was putting Devon in your life. I've always felt protective over you."

Her eyes snap open as she springs up from her position, storming toward Devon. Her elbow rears back, and her fist flies into his face. Blood splatters everywhere. "How could you!" she screams so loud I'm almost certain a few of her vocal cords snap in her throat.

Devon swipes the blood from his nose, tears pooling in his eyes. Only one person walking who could make death cry, and I was dumb enough to marry her. "Isa, I didn't know you then. You were just a job. I—I—it all changed when I came to know you."

"Yeah?" Isa snaps. "What about all those people you

killed, Devon, someone would have felt that way about them too and you still killed them!" She was angry. Feral.

She spins around, swiping the stray tears from her eyes and points her finger at me. "I will do this with you, Bryant. To bring my father down once and for all after everything he has put me through, but after that? We are done. I will file for divorce." I wince at the impact of her words. "And you will fucking let me go. You will never break my heart again because you will never have the privilege to hold it again. You can't break what you can't hold." She spins around and leaves, slamming my office door behind her.

"Well, that went about as well as I thought it would, which by the way, why the fuck did you tell her?" Devon is already at the alcohol stand.

"Because he is going to tell her anyway, and because I knew she'd break your fucking nose."

"Damn," Devon says, swiping the blood while flinching. "I think it is actually broken."

"Call the doc." I pull my phone out of my pocket, typing out a text.

"B?" Devon calls softly as my hand rests on the door handle. "You just lost her, you know that, right?"

Pain. "We both did, motherfucker."

TWELVE

A love lost wasn't yours to keep.

-Isa

I pace around my room for hours, thinking back to everything that just came to life. I let it stew in my brain.

My father hates me. Why else would he do all that he has done? I knew I was a rebel child. I was always doing things I shouldn't do just to piss him off, but beneath it all, I wanted his attention. A child should never have to fight for their parent's attention.

How could he not see that?

Part of my heart has broken beyond repair. Not all wounds can be fixed.

I want to hold my daughter. I need my daughter. I need to feel real love. The kind that isn't conditional or filthy.

I tap out the numbers on my phone and bring it to my ear.

She picks up on the fourth ring. "I'm coming."

"Is it safe?" she asks. It's good that she asked. It's why I can trust her.

"Yes. I'll be there in one week. I have some things I need to sort out and then I'm done." I breathe in and out. "How is she?"

Later that night, I call Max and invite him over. I have to keep up face with him, so he doesn't know that I know who he is and what he's done, but it's hard. Every person I thought I could trust has let me down one way or another. Max is just another name to add to the list.

"You okay?" Max asks, running his finger down the side of my cheek. I search his face. His beard, his gentle eyes. His thick muscles. He's hot. It's a shame that he's not who he says he is.

I wonder if he and his wife had a rule, like say, no sleeping with the psycho patient. I wonder just what their game is. You don't need to learn the rules to break them, you just have to want to win bad enough.

I lean up on my tippy toes and bring my lips to his. Soft cushions melt into me as he pauses for a second, before slowly his lips part. He hooks his arm around the back of my waist, pulling me in closer until I'm crushed against his chest.

I shrug off my top and then reach for his. He hooks his arm around my back and pulls me farther into him. "You sure about this? I feel like your husband is watching."

My eyes fly up to the little red light that's flashing in the corner of my room. Bryant having cameras isn't exactly shocking. He's a control freak by nature, so the cameras are a given. It's when he put that particular one in this bedroom that worries me.

I lean over until the tip of my tongue touches the warm

skin of Max's neck, my eyes remaining on the camera. "I'm counting on it."

A resounding growl pulsates from his chest, as he picks me up from the floor and throws me onto my bed. His fingers flex around the buckle of his belt as he unbuttons his jeans, all while moving closer to the bed.

I lick my lips.

Bryant wants to play games?

Okay. Let's play.

If he wants to see just how far done I am of his shit, then he can watch. Shrugging out of my jeans so I'm in nothing but my panties and bra, I grin up at Max as he lowers himself on top of me, his mouth back on mine.

I'm lost in the feelings that are buzzing inside of me. I've always used sex as a weapon against my demons. For those minutes, I feel good. Fulfilled. All of the empty and broken parts inside of me are mended back together for those minutes while it's happening. The part that sucks is the after-math. When your body declines and your mind spirals, and then all of a sudden, the wounds are back open again, only this time with more scar tissue. It's a toxic cycle. The lead-up, the foreplay, the sex, and then the comedown. There was only one person who satiated me more than the others, and he and I hate each other right now. It's also why Devon and I always worked. We were the same, only I'm not a coldhearted murderer.

Max's hand dips beneath my bra, but before the tips of his fingers even reach my nipple, the door flies open. We both don't look. I can't help the smirk that's covering my face.

Thank god. I don't really want to fuck Max, but if I had to prove my point, I would. Bryant knows that.

"Isa, baby, why are you playing without me?" Devon purrs from the doorway.

My body stills.

You can't act like this or Max will know.

I internally shake off my hate. Or simmer it at the very least. Peeking around Max's body, I flash Devon a grin. "Jealous because you want to join?"

Devon matches my smirk. "Maybe later. When everyone is asleep. For now, Stacey is here, and dinner is ready."

I tap at Max's shoulder, thankful for the distraction. When Devon disappears, I flutter my lashes up at Max. "Later?" This might be harder than I initially thought. Dancing around someone who is flat out lying to me is a distraction.

He swipes the corner of his mouth with the cushion of his thumb. "Yeah."

While he's standing there semi-distracted, I dip into the closet and start pulling down some clothes. "Hey, I want to say thank you. You know, for being cool with this. I know it's not an ideal situation to be in, in fact, it's pretty fucked up. So I appreciate you not running for the hills, or back to your cabin." I'm glad I have the confines of my closet to hide my expression, because my facial expression would dead ass be giving me away right now.

I wriggle into something revealing. I opt for short linen shorts that barely cover the rim of my ass and a loose black t-shirt with no bra underneath.

I'm feeling reckless.

Entering back into my room, I gesture to the door. "Ready for family dinner?"

Max's eyes drop down my body before coming back to me. "Ah, yeah."

We make our way out and when I reach the bottom of the stairs, Jer and I give each other a low five quickly. I love being around Jerry. He will always feel like home to me.

Turning the corner to the dining room, I see everyone already seated. Now that I know about Stacey and Max, it's obvious how much they tense whenever one another is in the room. I don't know how I didn't pick it up earlier.

I don't know why Bryant is playing this game. Why doesn't he just kill them both and get it over with, since that was his specialty.

"Wife." Bryant smirks from the opposite side of the table.

I slide into my chair, clearing my throat. I need this to end in one week, because then I'm done. I'm gone. And where I'm going, they will never find me.

"Husband." I reach for the glass of water and take a sip, wishing it was vodka. Dinner is served almost instantly, which I'm appreciative of because I can feel my mood slowly balancing on the off-side. I ignore everyone and cut into my steak, dipping each piece into the creamy mushroom sauce.

I can't believe he was the one who saved me in the water or that my father had tried to have me killed.

All these years, my dad had told me that someone tried to kidnap me and kill me by throwing me off the boat and that he saved me.

All these years, I believed him.

All these years, I was married to this prick who knew the truth all along. In his defense, we never spoke about that day, but he knew about it, and that makes all the difference.

"Isa," Bryant says, but I'm too busy slicing into my meat. Fire burns beneath my flesh. Hot, molten fucking lava is bubbling below the surface of my cool demeanor and soon enough, something's going to need to be cut open to let it all out. "Isa..."

I throw my cutlery down onto the table with a crash and everyone silences instantly. "You know what? I'm not hungry." I push up from my chair just as Bryant reaches for me. I didn't even catch him getting up from his chair, he was that quick.

"What's wrong?" he asks, and for the first time in a long time, I see the worry in his eyes. Undiluted fear.

You know what's wrong. His touch. I pull my arm out of his grasp. "A word. Please."

"You two need to stop fighting so much, I'm always walking around with a hard dick."

"Ew, that's your cousin..." Stacey snaps judgingly. You can't judge someone who doesn't give a fuck, and Devon is the epitome of zero fucks given.

He glares at her, bored. "Not for him, you sick bitch."

I roll my eyes before leading Bryant out of the room. I'm heading for his office initially when I find my feet taking me to the back door in the lounge room. I know he's following me from behind, and it should bother me. He should bother me. I know that no matter what, my decision won't change. I'll still be leaving, and I won't be taking him back.

I shove the door open, the cool air of the night instantly slapping me across the face. There's so much I want to say, but anytime I think of the words, they never reach my lips.

The click of him shutting the door is the only sound that I hear. I can't think. I don't know what to say or do or where to even start. My emotions are boiling over the top, and they're not all good ones either.

"Isa, what—"

I spin around before he can say another word and my lips crash against his.

He pauses for a second, his lips frozen and unmoving.

I fist his shirt in the palm of my hand. "I need it."

It was all I needed to say before he's lifting me off the ground.

"I know, baby," he murmurs into my mouth, because he does. *He does know*. Above everyone, he and Devon know every single dirty part about me. Bryant has seen my washed up, unloved soul, but instead of adding to my daddy issues, he placed it gently into the palm of his hand and loved me twice as hard. He is very well acquainted with how I abuse sex.

"Hard and fast, Bryant. Please."

"Shut up," he growls against my mouth. "You don't make the rules."

Did I say gentle? I only meant with my soul, because the filthy way he fucks is enough to make even the darkest of sinners seem like angels.

My insides melt, my chest heavy. I want to scream; the feeling is way too overwhelming. I want it to just be him and I and infinite time. I feel my addiction being fed through an IV.

He tugs his jeans down with one hand while keeping his other arm hooked around my waist. Slamming me against the wall on the patio, in the dark where no one can see, he tears off my shorts and his finger slowly dips inside of me.

"You wet for me or for him?" he asks, his finger hitting every nerve inside of me.

"You, only you."

"Only you, *what?*"

I lick my lips.

He retracts his finger and presses his thumb roughly against my throbbing clit. "What, Isa?"

A scream erupts out of me as my hips buck, needing a release. Fucking Bryant is like chasing a pretty fairy unicorn, only when you finally catch it, you realize he's really one of Satan's hounds.

A soft whimper oozes from my lips, as I drop my forehead onto his shoulder. "Only you, *daddy.*" He knows I hate when I say it, and I know he loves when I do, but right now I'd give him anything just to have his cock deep inside of me, filling those broken parts.

He slips his tip over my entrance and enters me slowly. I

whimper, cry, yelp as I open and stretch for his girth. *"Oh my god."*

When he pulls out, the rim of his cock rubs over my G-spot and I lose it. My muscles spasm, my heart flatlines, and all too quickly my release fucking drowns me.

He slams his hand over my mouth to silence my screams as he fucks me raw up against the wall. With every thrust, I nibble on his palm, twisting and turning as my orgasms spill out of me.

"Fucking missed this pussy."

He continues to thrash inside of me as if his cock is a weapon and he needs to destroy every inch of my insides. I clench around him like a vise, needing to soak up everything that he's giving me, bullets and all.

Bet you did miss it.

His hand comes to the front of my throat and he squeezes until I can't breathe. My fingernails dig into the flesh of his shoulders as his lips come back to mine. He grunts inside of my mouth until I taste his pleasure on the tip of my tongue. Bringing my fingers up to his face, he catches the red blood seeped into the tips and leans forward, wrapping his lips around my fingers and sucking the blood off. His lips crash onto mine as his pelvic bone thrusts over my clit. Sweat pours out of me with every second that passes, his arm hooking around my back to bring himself in closer. I need him closer. With his rock-hard chest against my nipples, his head sinks into the crook of my neck.

"Mine."

The animalistic sounds he growls out every few seconds is enough to send me over the edge. Every time he drives inside of me, my body is thrust against the wall. I feel the warmth from that IV drip fill me like a fucking junkie does with heroin. He's my drug and I'm his addict. Finally, he sucks my flesh into his mouth and all at once he bites down roughly, enough to draw blood. I feel my walls contract around him as cum drips down my thigh. My—I've lost count—orgasm slams into me at speeds I can't calculate, just as Bryant hisses through clenched teeth, eyes rolled back. I feel his cock throb inside my swollen pussy as he empties himself inside of me. We take a few seconds to come down, our breathing ragged.

Silence.

Tears prick the side of my eyes from the betrayal. Betrayal from Bryant, from Devon, from my father. Men are disappointing, I need to change to women. His thick body holds me up as our silence turns from seconds to minutes. His heavy breathing dances with mine as we both attempt to catch our breath. *Oops.*

"Isa," Bryant whispers, pressing a kiss against the curve of my neck where he just bit. "I love you."

I can't get past the irony of his words and the placement of his kiss. Enough bittersweet love to kill you, but the right dose of pain to remind you that you're alive.

"You don't." I push away from him, my fingers flexing against his suit shirt. "If you did, I wouldn't feel the way I do right now."

He slowly lowers me to the ground. "You don't think I've protected you?" He zips up his slacks.

I square my shoulders while pulling up my shorts and running my fingers through my now messy, matted, and damp hair. "I know you haven't, Bryant. Everything is a lie."

He steps into me, forcing me back against the wall. One hand comes to one side of my head, the other resting against my hip. "Do you love me?"

I take a few seconds to recollect my thoughts. I know that I do, but a big part of me doesn't want to give in to his ego and say yes, so I say, "I did." Then I duck under his arm and straighten my clothes while quickly making my way back inside the house. I shouldn't feel bad for telling him that, I should feel powerful. I want him to hurt, to feel betrayed the way I do, but the ball that's swelling in my throat and the wild emotions running rampant inside of me right now are telling, like something else.

Something like regret.

I take a seat back at the table, picking up my glass of champagne and swallowing in one go.

"Everything okay, baby?" Devon asks from his chair right beside Bryant. It's funny, because when I didn't know their connection, I would think that they could never be friends. Actually, I get the impression that they aren't exactly friends either, but the more I see them together the more I see their bond. Friendships don't need to be loud or proud. It's not about what your friendship looks like to other people, it's about how that person makes you feel.

"Fine." I begin cutting into my meat again, the blood seeping out from my steak triggering the memory flash of Bryant sucking off his own blood from my fingernails. Blood that's still smeared over a couple of my fingers. I flush bright red as my cheeks heat. Damn. But that was hot.

I push my meal out of my way as Bryant moves back into the room, sitting back on his chair, or should I say throne. Reaching for the bottle of champagne, I tip the rest of the dry bubbles into my glass and take another few gulps.

"Hey," Max says, his hand coming to my knee. He gives it a soft squeeze. I want to squeeze his balls in the palm of my hand just for touching me. "You want me to stay tonight?"

My eyes meet his. "No, it's okay. I think I need some alone time."

And now that Bryant has fucked the stupid out of me, I don't want to be near you for as long as I have to.

Dinner and dessert go through much quieter than when we first started. It was as though the electricity that crackled in the room before Bryant and I fucked some of our tension out simmered down. We could see straight.

Ashley walks into the foyer once I've let Max out. I'm sitting on the cold marble floor, my head against the front door and my knees drawn up to my chest. "Mrs. Royal, is everything okay?"

"Ash." I smile at her. "Just call me Isa, please."

"Sorry," she apologizes, kneeling down and taking a seat beside me. I need silence, but the atmosphere is loud. Everything from the gold and diamond chandelier that hangs above me to the marble floors that are laid out all over the house—including the twin staircase. Seriously. Who the fuck puts marble on the stairs? Rich bastard.

"You know, I don't trust many people. I know a lot of people say that, but I really don't." I clear my throat, keeping my eyes fixed on the Banksy piece that's right in front of me, hanging on the wall. It's an intense reminder of the love Bryant tries to show without using his words. Ash doesn't interrupt. "There were two people I trusted with my life. With my daughter's life." My throat swells. "And they failed. Now I have no one."

A soft hand comes to my arm, and I turn toward it out of instinct. "You have me." Bringing my attention up to Ashley, I take in her soft blonde hair and baby skin. She's so young, yet so wise. I don't trust her, unfortunately, but I do like her. You don't have to trust someone to like them.

"Thanks, Ash."

"What are you doing?" Bryant comes into the foyer, a glass of whiskey hanging from his fingertips and his suit shirt now fully unbuttoned. I can see the tattoos beneath now, the tight abs and angry muscles. I know I've put on a bit of weight since he last saw me, though it seems to be dropping the longer I'm here, but he doesn't make it obvious that he has noticed. It may only be a few pounds, but If I was any other girl, having a husband who looks like Bryant would be intimidating. If there's one thing Bryant has never failed at, it's making me feel secure. He doesn't just make me feel wanted, he makes me feel hunted.

"Sorry, I'll go back to work." Ash stands from the floor.

Bryant glares at her in passing, baring his teeth while slowly coming closer to me. He's such an untamed beast, I almost want to lock him in a cage.

"What's the plan? I need to know what we're doing and why I have to keep face with Max," I say robotically. My energy is drained, my focus waning. I'm not even sure I want any revenge at all anymore. Revenge on who? I believe Bryant and everything he's saying, and I to an extent believe Max. Especially about the drugs.

"You won't for long." Bryant bends down to my level. I can smell sweet elements of the expensive whiskey teasing the tip of his tongue.

I bring my eyes to his, knowing the risk of losing my soul at his mercy. "Bryant..."

"Yo, so we need to tell her the plan—"

Bryant's jaw tenses at the invasion of Devon.

"Yes." I roll my eyes, standing to my feet. "Please tell me the plan."

We make our way into the sitting room, where a fire is lit and crackling in the silence. I drop down on the sofa and cross my legs under my ass. "The sooner this is done, the better."

"Why?" Bryant snaps from the other side of the room, where he's pouring more whiskey into his glass.

"Jeez, husband, have I pushed you to drink?" I smirk to myself, resting my head back against the rim of the sofa.

"Only after you've fucked me."

"I fucking knew it!" Devon gasps, and I lean up to glare at both of them.

"Knew what?"

"That's your sex hair and it hasn't changed much at all." Devon takes a glass from Bryant and brings one to me.

I shake my head.

"Never one to turn down a drink." Devon quirks his eyebrow at me. "Are you pregnant?"

I snarl at him. "I've had too much champagne already and I do want to sleep tonight. Besides, you know how I get on whiskey."

"I do." Devon smirks, winking at me. He grips onto the back of the couch and thrusts his hips into it. "Will. Never. Forget."

Bryant drops down on his chair, blatantly ignoring Devon and his antics. "You gonna sit on my lap or continue to play hard to get?"

I roll my eyes. "Your fiancée is in this house, and by the way, I'm not playing hard to get. I just don't want to be got. It's not a game."

His eyes continue to penetrate me from afar, as if they hold enough hunger to eat up the distance between us.

"Here's the plan," Devon mutters before Bryant can snap at me. He drops beside me. "And you might not like it."

———

The next night, I'm slipping into a silk gown when there's a knock on my door. Running my hands down my wide hips, I smirk in the mirror, seemingly satisfied with my appearance. "Come in!"

The door swings open, and I have to quickly recollect my composure when I see it's not Bryant, but Max. I'm not entirely sure how I feel about Bryant and his decisions regarding me, but I'd still like to crush his nuts about it. Make him hurt a bit.

"You ready?" Max asks, stepping inside my room.

My jaw snaps closed. I have to fight with myself every single time he's around. I want to hit him. I want to lock him in Bryant's basement and force him to tell me what exactly he's playing at and why he's doing this to me.

"I am." My eyes meet his in the mirror as he wraps an arm around my torso and leads me out the door. Something inside of me pulls and twists anytime he touches me. It's identical to the way I felt when I woke in the cabin. It's an eerie silence that sneaks down my spine, but enough comfort to warm me. It's confusing.

His grip tightens around my hip as he hands me a black lace mask. I take it from him, the strings falling over my hand.

"Didn't think you'd have brought your own, so figured..."

"Thanks." I look up at him, searching for anything. Any hints as to why he would do this to me or what his plans are. I trusted him when I woke in the cabin. *I trusted Bryant too.* I freeze, quickly diverting my gaze away from him. I think it's safe to say that my judgment when it comes to the people that I should trust is lopsided.

We pause once we're outside the mansion, my red bottom shoes clicking against the marble patio. Ignoring the figures I see from the corner of my eye, I turn toward Max. "You look good. Really nice." My eyes drift up and down his body. *Someone call the fucking Oscars.*

Tapping my foot, I divert my eyes to the front of myself as we wait for our car. Why does this fountain look old as fuck? The house itself isn't old, yet this massive statue quite clearly carved from ancient stone looks like it has been shoved into a time machine and fast-forwarded to this century. I can feel Bryant's eyes on me before I've even seen him, burning through the side of my head. When the waiting becomes too unbearable, I turn to Bryant.

"This fountain is ugly. Who chose it? I sure as fuck know I didn't."

"I'm hurt, baby. Tell me what you really think..." He ignores me, tapping on his phone.

"What the fuck is taking them so long..." I mumble under my breath, inching closer to Max.

Stacey, who's tucked underneath Bryant's arm, (and doing everything in her power not to look directly at me), answers, "There's only one Jerry."

"Yeah." My eyes snap to Bryant. "And he's mine, so Bryant will have to drive you both." As if on cue, a black Bentley slides up in front of us and Max opens the door for me, gesturing for me to slide in.

"Hey, Jer," I mutter, gathering the silk from my train up and placing it in a pool at my feet once I'm secured in my seat.

"Hey, trouble."

Max slips into the seat beside me. I've been going back and forth with Max and my judgments when it comes to this situation. I've trusted the wrong people all of my life and it has damaged a part of myself that I will never repair. *Can I trust Max?* Trust. That word is supposed to be one of promise, a display of loyalty and love. It's nothing but another lie to me.

"Max?" I watch the trees pass by as we drive down the long driveway. "Can I trust you?" I turn farther to face him, searching his eyes. *Give me anything.*

He smiles, but it doesn't reach his eyes. I finally notice it. Or maybe I'm thinking too much into everything because Bryant has told me that he's working for my father.

"You can." The words are clipped enough to come off as honest.

"Can I?" I snap, narrowing my eyes on him. The passing streetlights illuminate his sharp features and scruffy beard.

Max tilts his head, seeming to study me closely. He's obviously picking up on my sudden hostility. I don't know why Bryant put me onto this, he of all people should know that I can't be fake to save my life.

Literally.

Anyone else remember the pig farm incident?

I cross my ankles together. "Never mind."

His hand comes to mine, but instead of relaxing beneath his touch, I tense. "Hey, talk to me, Isa. What's he been whispering in your ear?"

I don't say anything. I shouldn't say anything.

"What?" he jokes, a small smile tugging on his mouth. "You don't think that now that you have your two broody bodyguards standing by your side that I haven't noticed your sudden displeasure with being around me?"

Damn. He's a good liar.

I hate it.

The only thing worse than a liar is someone who believes their own tales. There's no redemption for them. They spin their web of lies, but instead of untangling them and becoming remorseful, they move in and make it their home.

"It's not about them..." I whisper, and it's the truth. We pull up to the curb of the hotel, where a red carpet spews out from our car to the front entrance doors. "It's about what's right." Max's and my conversation is no longer my first priority, as the face of my enemy hangs over the front of the hotel.

My father's exclusive ball. He holds the same one every year. I've always thought it was just one big pissing contest for my dad and his friends to flash around their money, and the older I got, the more I realized how right I was.

Max shuffles out of the car and turns back to face me, holding out his hand.

I pause, clutching the silk of my gown in one hand while the other squeezes the back headrest of the driver's seat.

"Come on, Isa. We can talk later."

I don't particularly want to take the hand of an enemy, an enemy that I still, underneath all of the confused feelings, feel something for. What? I don't know.

Cameras are flashing from behind him and my heart panics.

"Get her out of here!" Bryant roared from the other side of the alter, his teeth bared. I hadn't ever seen Bryant flash such pain as he did that day. He bled out his humanity and let it spill over the floor.

"Come on." Jessica took my hand, but I squeezed Harper in my arms, her blanket draped over her little body.

"This..." I shook my head, unable to form coherent words inside of my head. "Has my father all over it."

My eyes flew around the venue as people laid spilled out over the ground, frantic and panicked. They all witnessed a murder. Multiple even. I couldn't find Brianna amongst the chaos, and when I tried to seek her out, Jessica was in front of me.

She grabbed me by my elbow and helped me to my feet. "We have to go. Come on." She brushed the tears from her face as we began running down the aisle with Harper in my arms. I'd leave the rest to Bryant. Right then, I had to be here. I needed no one to touch Harper. To go near her.

We reached a waiting car at the curb, and my steps slowed as my eyes came to Jess.

"Jess? What's going on?"

Her mouth opens, her eyes falling to Harper. "Do you trust me? Take my hand."

Snapping myself out of my deep memory, I take Max's hand and step out of the car. If it's true, and Max is working for my dad and my father did intentionally release me, I need to know why. I won't learn that if I fight Max, so for tonight, I'll play the game.

We make our way down the carpet, my mask securely placed around my eyes. No one knows who I am. Bonus. Screaming and yelling erupt from behind the cameras, just as we're safely inside the hotel and I turn over my shoulder to see reporters all rushing to snap Bryant and Stacey. Bryant is in a black and white suit, with a blood-red tie.

He looks to die for, but it won't be me. For once.

Max takes my hand and I follow him toward the two security personnel at the door.

"Names?" they ask, searching the list that's connected to a clipboard.

Max hands him two tickets and the guard flashes a look between the both of us, shocked. "Go right ahead."

I should ask what that was about. I'm not supposed to know about Max and my father, but I don't. Because I can't be bothered, and I need a damn drink. I'm so tired and drained.

"You go find our table and I'll grab some drinks." Max disappears behind me and I twist the piece of paper in my hand.

Table 001.

That can't be good. That sounds like a table where the president would sit. *What the fuck*.

Max comes back to me, holding two champagne flutes. "What table are we at?"

I grind my teeth. "Double oh one."

Max freezes, his fingers flexing over his glass. I watch as some of the condensation slides over his middle finger. "You sure?" He leans over my shoulder to look at the tickets. I bring my glass up to my mouth and tip my head back, sinking the whole lot in one go. I am not here to pussyfoot around anything or anyone tonight. Isa Royal is tired as fuck, so if anyone wants to test me, now would be the time. Fuck what I allowed in the past.

We begin walking toward the front table—that is thankfully empty right now—when Max's finger connects with mine.

He tugs me into his chest gently, brushing my hair away from my face.

Why do I feel a connection to him?

When you're fed empty promises all of your life, your soul is always starving.

I take my seat, just as Bryant and Stacey sit opposite us, his eyes remaining on mine. Always on mine. I roll mine to the back of my head and fight the urge to flip him off and drink more instead. The games were always fun when we first met, but games take a lot of stamina, and eventually you get tired.

That's what I am.

Tired.

"Is this your doing?" I say to Bryant, who seems to be sitting beside Stacey rather comfortably. It should bother me, and it does. There's an eternal fire burning beneath my skin that was ignited with a match that had Bryant's initials carved into it. I just have to contain it and not pour gasoline over it.

For now.

He tilts his head. "Why would it be my doing? I hate your father as much as you do."

I lean forward, placing my flute onto the table. "True, but I broke free from his mental ward, Bryant. Now you're telling me that he placed me at this table?"

Bryant's eyes slit. "I don't give a fuck what you want to believe, Isa."

Stacey snorts loudly, making my eyes instantly snap to her. "How the hell did you two get married when you fight so much?"

I raise my brows in challenge. "We fucked more, that's how."

She chokes on her drink. "Sounds toxic."

I smirk. "Pure poison, but the thing with poison" —I glare at Bryant— "is it tastes so damn *good*."

He remains flat and emotionless, but I see the curve on the side of his mouth, just wanting to come out and play.

As if a magnetic force is being pulled from behind me, the hair on the back of my neck stands up abruptly and my muscles stiffen. Out of instinct, I find myself searching for Bryant, as if I need an anchor for my security. A safety net. His presence offers me the solidarity that his words do not.

The reason why my body has shut down had nothing to do with the fact that the room is erupting in loud bursts of cheers and clapping, and had everything to do with the way tension settled into my bones like walking through a haunted childhood memory. As if an invisible grip is squeezing around my throat, causing my heartbeat to slow. My breath becomes more desperate because I don't know if this will be the final day that he decides to take it from me.

Bryant's eyes stay on mine, and I can't hide the panic that I'm feeling. I'm sure he's sensing it. As if on cue, he stands from his side of the table and makes his way to my side.

"Bry—" I hear Stacey yap off opposite me, but she doesn't matter. No one matters. The only thing that exists when I *need* Bryant, is me. I never should have second-guessed his feelings for me. The only woman who owned whatever was left of his heart, was me.

I need him beside me to get through this and he knows it. We may fight, we may hate each other at times, but he loves me when it counts.

Right now, it counts.

His hand comes to my thigh as movement out of the corner of my eye screams for my attention when two people take a seat on the other side of Max. I'm thankful he's seated beside my father and not me.

Finally, I turn my face toward the man I thought I could trust. The man who was given me to protect, but did everything in his power to destroy.

"Father."

He looks different. Older? His skin is worn, his smile rough and his eyes have lost the softness that they once held. Or maybe I'm now looking at him through the eyes of a woman, and not those of an innocent child who put all her trust in someone she shouldn't have. There's that filthy word again.

"Isa." Father's mouth curves in what I know is a fake, gentle smile. "I'm glad you could make it." He takes a seat with my stepmom, Lydia, carefully falling to the one beside him.

I seek Bryant again, turning to face him. Our eyes connect like a loud clap of thunder on a still night. He leans in, bringing his thumb to my mouth and slips it between my lips while leaning into my ear.

"Just go with it, baby. You know these arms are big enough to catch you."

I want to say that they didn't catch me. They did absolutely nothing to help me when I was locked in a mental ward, but I'm guessing now isn't the time and I'm almost certain he's sick of me complaining about it. Aside from that, I don't think I can form coherent words because my heart is still on cloud nine from those simple words that flew out of his mouth fluently.

I gulp, picking up my glass and pull away from Bryant. I don't mean to pull away from him in an obvious way, and what he said was sweet enough to challenge Willy Wonka, but it also reminded me about the arms that I needed during the darkest time of my life, and how they weren't there.

He growls softly at my resistance. "Still stubborn."

"Isa," Lydia murmurs from across the table. "It's so, so

good to have you home. We can't express how happy it makes us feel."

That's when it hits me.

Placing my glass back to the table, I straighten my back. Bryant must sense my unease because he squeezes my knee in warning.

I whack his hand away from me while turning to see the cameras that are all flashing.

At me.

At everyone at this table.

Turning to face Max, I narrow my eyes. "What was your role in all this?"

Max licks his bottom lip before smiling. He covers his next words behind his glass but leans in close enough so I don't miss a word. "Hmmmm, I'm not sure right now is the time." That's bullshit code for; 'I'm hiding shit but I need enough time to form another lie to hide the other lie.'

Everything seems to make sense now. Why I'm here. At this table. With the cameras. This is yet another setup to make my father look like the golden man that America needs.

I clench my jaw while looking at Stacey. "I know she was your wife."

"I know," Max says, swiping the excess wine from his lips with the back of his finger. Guess he's finally ready to spill some truths. "But we're not together anymore."

"And what was her role?" I ask, genuinely wanting to know for God knows what reason. There is no shock in learning that people have betrayed me. I've been hit in the same spot too many times and now I don't feel pain.

Max shakes his head, bringing his hand to the back of my neck. I still at our connection. "Oh now, that is a story that will take *years* to explain. Isn't that right, Bryant?" When Bryant glares at Max, his nostrils flaring, Max continues. "In her defense, she was a mere pawn in a game that you were the main component in."

Bryant's hand comes back to my inner thigh and I instantly reach for it beneath the table. Grabbing onto one of his fingers, I twist it backward as hard as I can. He coughs into his drink and pulls away from me. I'm not done with him, and I don't trust him right now or his intentions with this setup. For too long, I've been an object in my father's games to win voters, money, power, fucking *pharmaceuticals*.

I've reached my breaking point.

Inhale. Exhale.

I count to ten.

Stretching a wide smile that spreads over my straight teeth, I flash my eyes at Lydia. "I'm glad I'm back too, Lydia. It's good to see you're perfectly happy."

Lydia seems to falter before sipping from her glass. I don't know exactly how much she knows, nor do I care right now.

"Baby..." Bryant warns from beside me, his whisper still hot on my ear. "Don't go jumping to conclusions."

I sidle into Max, pulling away from Bryant. Not sure why, the man has just admitted to being a damn fraud. Turning over my shoulder to look at Bryant, he's glaring at me with raised eyebrows. "Really?" *Oh yeah, that's why.* Because I want to be petty. For a few more minutes.

Before I can hound my father for answers that I'm sure I will never get, the lights drop low and the MC walks across the stage. I sink into my chair, reaching for the bottle of champagne in the middle of the table and pouring. His balls are the same every year. A few bands play, some famous Hollywood singer will come on, people spend money on shit they don't need with money they have too much of, and then everyone gets drunk.

"This has nothing to do with me." Bryant's arm is hooked

around my chair and he pulls me closer beside him and farther away from Max.

I bring my glass to my lips, not listening to a word that's being spoken. "I don't trust you."

"I know." Bryant's hand comes to my inner thigh and I freeze. He moves higher and higher up until my dress is lifted from the ground and the palm of his hand is coating my skin. "I need you to go with it tonight."

As everyone starts clapping, the MC turns to face the screen that's playing in the background. "We have compiled a video of all that the Johnson and Taylor families have done over the years to help poverty-stricken families throughout the state of New York. The crime rates in those areas have dropped immensely. Ladies and gentlemen." She gestures up to the screen.

The first thing I hear is my voice.

THIRTEEN

Memories aren't reliable. Unless they've been recorded.
- Isa

Bryant collects his glass from the table, but all I can focus on is the screen and what's playing.

"No! No. Someone has to help me, please. He's trying to kill me. Daddy!"

My hand flies to my mouth to stop my gasp from spilling out.

I push back from my chair, but Bryant's fingers sprawl out over my thigh. "Baby, I'm going to need you to watch this."

My eyes fly back to the screen, like a delusional moth to a flame, I need to get closer to what I know could very well destroy me.

I'm strapped in a straitjacket, my hair matted to my face from sweat. That's when it comes back to me...

"Dad, please. I don't want to be here."

My father turned his back on me, as if I meant nothing, which was exactly what I meant to him—nothing. He cleared his throat and began talking to one of the doctors beside him. "Max, I need you to up her sedative. If we continue to push through the trials, this will change everything. It would be enough to cure the fallen medical economy and will have my name all over it."

Max turned his head over his shoulder. "She seems young, are you sure you want to do that?"

"She's not. She's old enough and has caused enough chaos in my life to send me to an early grave. As your president, I order you to do this."

"Why her?" Max asks, and I bring my eyes to his. Desperate.

My father finally turns to face me. "Because I made a decision to keep her alive a long time ago. That day, I found out that a deal that I needed had gone through for a clinical trial ." He brought his eyes up to Max, and I gulped past the boulder that felt lodged in my throat.

"What kind?" Max asked.

"I'm going to cure schizophrenia and insanity."

What? I yank on my arms, my breathing ragged. I don't have schizophrenia.

"How?" Max asked, crossing his large arms across his chest. His coat stretched over his thick muscles. "That's not possible. Forgive me, but schizophrenia is a mental illness and there are therapy exercises to help the clinically insane. There doesn't need to be a cure."

My father's eyes bored into Max. "None of that works. So are you going to help me or not?"

Max turned his head over his shoulder, his eyes coming to mine. Tears stung the edges of my sockets and my brows pulled together. I shook my head. "No! No!"

I shake out of my memory as the video playing cuts into something else. This time Max isn't in it, and my father is talking with Taylor. They seem to be in a stretch limo, the camera filming them from somewhere in the corner of the vehicle.

"How do you know that Max will do this?" Taylor, my father's VP, asks.

"Because he feels a connection to her. He will want to fix her, help her."

"An awful lot riding on your feelings." Taylor stilled, and I watch as a flash of pain bares itself over his eyes. Only briefly. "I knew her as a kid too, Johnson. Watched her grow."

My father smirked at Taylor. "Oh, Max will do as he's told, and shut up, Taylor. You know this is what I need."

Taylor seems to be over his brief flash of sense. "How will Max obey?"

My father seems to pause slightly, thinking over his next words. His hand comes up to his mouth, his finger teasing his mustache. "Well," he begins, reaching for the bottle of whiskey that's in the minibar. "I guess because he will feel inclined to. They'll both feel bonded to each other but won't know why."

"And what am I supposed to do with that, Johnson? This is too far. Even for me," Taylor jokes, shaking his head. I always thought Taylor was the smarter one of the two, the one with more humanity. At family barbeques, he would always be the loudest in the room and bring my sister and I toys and candy. We liked him, a lot. That changed drastically when my father became president—well, at least for me anyway. You give some people power and they not only abuse it, but they weaponize it. That's Taylor. Taylor's eyes turn serious. "What do you mean?"

My father chuckles. "I had an affair earlier in our marriage. They're fucking half brother and sister, Taylor. Jesus Christ, have you always been this fucking slow or is it becoming worse with age—"

I fly out of my chair and to my feet before I can recollect

my erratic heartbeat. Guards surround my father already, preparing him to leave. Because even a shitty human being can be guarded if he has enough money and status. There's more commotion I can hear popping off behind me, but I can't focus.

"Did you know!" I scream at Max, disgust contorting my face.

He rears back. "No! Fuck no!" His arms fly out to the side of him, his eyes frantically shifting to my father. "What the *fuck!*"

I glare straight at my father. "You're disgusting."

He stands from his chair, his eyes going straight past me and landing on Bryant. "You think you've won? You may have this one, and you may have the last laugh, but remember who you're messing with, Royal."

Bryant grabs me by the hand and glares at Max. "What will it be, motherfucker. You wanna get fucked or be the one doing the fucking?"

I can't comprehend the meaning of what Bryant is spewing right now, because my mind is spiraling out of control.

I kissed my damn brother.

Max looks between us and my father as I attempt to fight the tears. Slowly, Max hooks his arm in mine. "We need to get her out of here."

I pull out of both of their grasps, spinning around to look directly at my dad, who's being escorted by security. I ignore the flashing of cameras in the background and the heavy guards surrounding our table. "Was it worth it?" I don't know why, but it was the first thing that I could think to say.

My father's eyes harden as he grips onto his suit jacket and buttons it up. "You think this is all me to blame, then you're even more blinded as I thought."

The cruelness of his tone is like a bullet right in the heart.

It's not that I expected anything more from him, but I guess a girl can never get used to being on the receiving end of her father's disgust.

"It was always you. But why?"

"What's happening?" Lydia starts squealing off beside him as another man dressed in all black takes my father by his arm.

"What's happening, is that he had me locked in an asylum and drip-fed me drugs for the past six months, that's what's happening, Lydia. He!" I point at my dad when I notice one of the guards shift in front of him protectively.

"Isa, baby, stop..." Bryant growls softly in my hair. "Don't show all of your cards right now."

I swipe at the tears that were pouring down my cheeks, straightening my shoulders from the words Bryant just whispered into my ear. "You know what? Not right now."

I spin around as Bryant takes my arm and Max shifts around the other side of me. The room begins to tilt, a buzzing sound screaming in my head. Colors and circles warp my vision, right before everything turns black.

FOURTEEN
Bryant

The sex bruises I leave on her skin are nothing compared to what her hate has left on my heart.
- Bryant

Forgiveness isn't an emotion that Isa feels. Whether by what the world has given her by its withered hand, or by her choice, she doesn't forgive often. If ever. I already know what she's going to ask when she comes back to us.

Did you know Max was my brother? Then I'm going to have to say *yes*.

She's going to ask *why* I didn't tell her, and then I'm going to have to tell her everything.

Telling her everything means I'll lose her, but I can't have lies between us anymore.

"She's going to kill all three of us. You know that, right?" Devon murmurs, gesturing to both me and Max.

I lean back in my chair, flicking a cigar between my fingers. "You love her."

"Of course I fucking do!" Devon yells, throwing an empty bullet casing at me. "What the fu—"

"—not you!" I snap, sneering at Devon. I look up to Max, who's watching the flames lick around the fireplace. "You."

Max doesn't turn toward me, he leans against the mantle of my stone fireplace, arms tense. "Yes. Slightly repulsed that I kissed her, and almost other things."

"It's hardly incest. You're her half-brother."

I shake my head at Devon. "Shut the hell up for a second."

He raises his hands in the air in submission. Devon is a pain in the ass, but I've known him all of my life. He didn't get his name Reaper for being soft and I didn't get The Beast for being a fucking puppy. Don't let his pretty Ken-like features fool you. Fucking Barbie doll.

"It's still classed as incest." Max rolls his eyes, pushing off the fireplace and takes a seat on one of the many chairs I have scattered in my office. He runs his hands over his face. "I should have been smarter with this. I knew I felt something for her, and I thought well, she's beautiful, so it must be attraction. It clearly wasn't."

There's a hint of authenticity in the way he articulates his words, but fuck if I trust this idiot. Keep your friends in your pocket, right beside your enemies, and never tell them who is who.

"Or was it?" Devon adds, wriggling his eyebrows.

I cut him with a glare to shut him the hell up.

He runs his middle finger over his lips in the zipping motion.

"Continue. You need to start talking. Whether you live to see tomorrow or not, depends, I have to be able to trust you around Isa. So." I lean back in my chair and light my cigar. "Tell me fucking everything."

Max exhales. "I was fresh out of college when Peter

offered me a job at Banks Psychiatric Hospital. I thought I hit the jackpot. Offering six figures already with no experience? Damn, that never happens."

"Should have been your first flag, just saying," Devon again. I have to count in my head to calm down before I hit him.

Max rests his head back. "I started working and over the five years I was there, built a relationship with Peter. I respected him a hell of a lot too." He pauses, and I lean forward to flick the ash off the end of my cigar. "When he brought her in after your wedding"—my fists squeeze at the mention of my darkest day ever—"she fit the profile. She was erratic, multi-changing, and hostile." He pauses. "Do you know what happened? With what she was seeing in her head?"

"What do you think?" I grin around the thick trunk of my cigar, before slowly sobering and shaking my head. "I know that she replayed everything in her head, from the moment she ever met me to the day of our wedding."

Max nods. "And the drugs in essence stopped her brain from using the prefrontal cortex, which is the front part of the brain that helps us think logically to categorize our thoughts. It was as though all of her irrationality was tipped into insanity. On top of that, she began to compartmentalize all the good of her personality and keep her Isa, but sometimes she would wake up feeling evil, and call herself Brooke. Just to be clear," Max's face falls serious. The lines around his eyes crinkling. "Brooke was real?"

My jaw tightens. My fingers squeeze my cigar as I nod. "Yes. She killed my daughter on accident on our wedding day. The bullet was for Isa, or me, but she hit Harper."

"I'm sorry," Max whispers, and I want to feel the sincerity of his words, but there's something. I don't fucking know what, because he's telling me all the right things. I get the feeling that he really does care for Isa, but there's something else. "I didn't know he was feeding her drugs and using her as a test dummy until the night before I broke her out."

"But you didn't break her out. He allowed you out," I add, my jaw clenched. "I'm not a man you can lie to, Max. I'm very resourceful and know exactly how to utilize those resources to also make you disappear without so much as a whisper of a fucking trace. Don't fuck with me when it comes to Isa, because bodies drop when her safety is at risk. That, son, is something I can fucking promise you."

"Jesus Christ," Devon adds behind a chuckle. "Daddy's home."

Max nods his head without a second thought. "I wasn't finished, but yes. I knew that there was no way I could make my way past his guards, and if I did, there's no way he would never find me. He is literally the most powerful man in the world."

"—was," I correct, but don't want to dabble into why I chose the past tense. He's a fucking dead man walking. I've already made my mind up.

Max narrows his eyes at me, licking his lips. I can already see the hunger in his eyes for revenge. Revenge for what I don't fucking know, he doesn't know Isa well enough to be slapping on armor for her.

"Or was. So, I propositioned him with an idea. I convinced him that she wasn't responding to the drugs correctly, which wasn't exactly a lie. He wanted to kill her right then when I told him, but I countered that by telling him I could break her out, reconcile her with her family at his famous yearly ball where there're media outlets and paps, and he could earn the sympathy of America all while lining up a new subject."

I chuckle, my top lip curling as he continues.

"He bought it, and we had the plan. My ex going after

you? I don't know what that's about. Maybe she thought that I had feelings toward Isa because I would talk about her when I'd come home from work. Mainly fascination from before finding out she was drugged on trials. When I left her, she decided to go after you. Your and Isa's marriage is all over the magazines and televisions. It didn't take her long to add it all up, probably."

"I knew who she was all along," I murmur, only telling half of the truth while running my finger over the top of my lip. *Oh sweet fucking secrets and stupid fucking fools.* "What and why was her father suddenly interested in turning people crazy with the drop of a pill?"

Max clears his throat, shuffling on his feet. The question made him uncomfortable. Fucking good. It's what I want. "Well, he wasn't creating it to turn people clinically insane." He pauses, and I see the flash of honesty rear its ugly head over his eyes. "It was to cure it. For what or who, I couldn't tell you. I never asked."

I ignore that for now and put the information into the little box of secrets inside my head. "You love Isa."

He loosens his tie. "I do."

I stand to my feet, making my way to the bar and taking down a bottle of whiskey. "Good, because she's going to need you tomorrow."

Devon shakes his head. "We are all so. So. Dead."

FIFTEEN

Not everyone dies with the taste of love on their lips.
-Isa

I can feel submission leak its weakness into my brain. I've felt battered, trampled on and played with so many times now that it's basically a new emotion.

I blink, keeping my eyes trained on the roof above me. I hate this room.

I hate this house.

I yank the covers off my body and make my way downstairs. I woke last night and found myself looking for Bryant, only when I found him, I caught all three of them in the middle of a conversation about me. Shocking. They don't know that I heard what Max said about his involvement, but I did, and right now, I don't know left from right. Any direction I choose is ultimately going to be the wrong one.

Pulling out a bar stool, I sink into it as Devon turns around to face me, his gray sweats hanging dangerously low and his chest glistening with sweat.

"Let me guess." I can't help but scan him up and down. "You haven't fucked in two days so now you've gone back to running." Devon only ever does cardio if he doesn't get fucked enough. I just eat.

Devon slides over a mixed berry protein shake and I take it, wrapping my fingers around the cool glass. "Something like that."

"Devon." I reach for his attention with my words. "Why did Bryant set up that video?"

He ignores me.

I swing off the bar stool, making my way toward him. I'm well aware the kind of effect I have on Devon, and yes, I may be a bitch right now for using it to my advantage, but the way I see it, that's all these men ever do. Manipulate their position in my life.

I lick my lips and run my fingers through my hair, swiping it all up to the top of my head before tying it up. I'm wearing a loose silk nightie and fluffy slippers.

Bringing my finger to Devon's rock-hard chest, I run them down, over his pierced nipple and curves of his abs, swiping the glossy slickness of his sweat until I get to the band of his briefs.

"Fuck," he groans, falling against the counter while letting me have at it. His blue eyes come to mine. "What do you want to know?"

I step between his stretched legs, my hand at his crotch. I know Devon's body like the back of my hand. I know exactly how he likes to be fucked, and he knows exactly how I like to be fucked. We were each other's enablers for years, some-times we would fuck for days until we would eventually fall into a sex slumber.

I run the cushion of my thumb over his swollen tip. "Everything."

"Really?" Bryant grunts from the other side of the

kitchen, and I smirk, slowly bringing my eyes up to him. His eyebrows are raised. "You're weaker than I thought, Devon. Like a fucking lost little puppy dog."

Devon snaps out of it and groans while painfully pushing me away. "Can you blame me?"

Bryant ignores us both and heads straight for the coffee. "Yes?"

My heart stammers in my chest and Devon no longer exists. Bryant is wearing slacks, but no shirt, so all of his tattoos are on display, and his tattoos are not to be taken lightly. They're demonic and entrancing. Every single flick of pattern tells a story of his past. Of what he lives with on a daily basis. He's not a "get a tattoo just because" kind of guy. Every single thing is calculated and thoroughly thought through, just like the art that hangs on his walls.

"Bryant..." I try his name on my lips like I would the first sip of an enticing new drink.

He turns to face me, and I'm momentarily paralyzed by the way his eyes peer into mine.

I can't breathe.

I need distance, but I'm backed against the kitchen counter and he's directly in front of me. "Back to Bryant? Not *husband?*"

I cross my arms. "Not anymore."

His eyes fall to my chest. "Nice tits." He closes the gap between us, his arm hooking around my back to pull me into his chest. He runs the tip of his nose over mine. "Can almost remember how they felt suffocating my cock."

I suck in a deep breath, my fingers sprawling out over his smooth chest. "Stop."

"Keep going?" Bryant growls softly, leaning forward and sucking my bottom lip into his mouth. He bites down on it roughly. "Devon?" The tone is gentle, but I knew that the next words he was about to say wouldn't be. "Get the fuck out."

"I want to watch..." Devon whines from somewhere behind us.

Bryant ignores him, his eyes still on mine. "The fuck out, Devon."

My breathing becomes erratic with every breath my heart feels as though it's being weighed down by boulders. I recognize the shift in him, and I'm well acquainted with it. I've sat down and bled with this side of Bryant, rolled with it in the dirt and come back out fucking destroyed. *I need him.* I need to feel his raw animalistic presence kill me from the inside out.

"Max could come down and catch us."

"Bet he won't look for long, motherfucker knows not to play with me. On your knees." He cocks his head, seeing the slight defiance flash over my eyes. "Now, Isa."

I fight my legs to stay upright, unmoving. My defiance wants to challenge his need for control, but every time I try, I know I fail. My knees weaken as I collapse onto them, my eyes staying on his.

Running his fingers through my hair, he dampens his bottom lip with his tongue, sipping his coffee. "Stay there." Placing his mug onto the bench, he moves to the cutlery drawer.

Shit.

Squeezing my eyes closed, I silently plead with the Good Lord, or whoever will listen, that he isn't going to do what I think he's doing. Metal clinks together as if he's trying to find something, and then the drawer is slammed closed.

This doesn't mean I forgive him, nor does it mean that I'm not going to ask questions about what his play on this was. This means I need sex, something to tip me over. Having Bryant walk around me shirtless, knowing I can ride on him at any time that I want, is like a needle being flashed in front of a junkie all day.

Eventually they'll crack.

His fingers sprawl around my chin, just as I hear music spill out from somewhere in one of the other rooms. I know it's Devon and part of me wants to know what he's doing playing Marilyn Manson midday, but I can almost guarantee that it will include alcohol. Right now, he's reaching for something, anything that will get him off. I feel for the poor person who dares walk up in there while Devon is in a mood.

"We're going to play a game." Bryant flashes me a crooked grin, flicking a knife in front of his face.

I shake my head. "Pass."

"It's cute that you think you have a choice. Up."

I stand to my feet, just as his hands slide beneath my armpits and he lifts me onto the counter. Placing the knife down beside me, his hands are at my thighs in a flash as they slowly slide up. I want to squeeze them closed to feel some kind of pressure down below as my skin burns to life beneath his palms. I watch as the tattoos on his tanned hands disappear beneath my pale silk gown.

My lips browse over his teasingly as his finger presses against my clit. At the connection, my head swings back. Pleasure ripples through me at his simple touch.

"Still so fucking needy."

He lifts my gown and I push up, allowing him to untuck it from under my ass.

"Don't act like you're not hungry." I flash him a smirk. "Have at it."

He dips his finger inside of me while his other comes up to my hair, releasing my long locks from the top knot it was in. Tilting my head back, I'm grinding against his finger when I feel the warmth of his mouth cover my pussy.

"Bryant," I moan, biting down on my bottom lip.

"Mmmm, not loud enough..." he growls, each syllable being spelled out over my clit. His tongue flicks against it roughly, igniting a deadly fire that for sure will burn us both down if not tamed.

My insides solidify, my hips bucking in their search for more as the stubble on his jaw scratches the inside of my thighs. I can feel sweat drip down my face as my body yearns to spill over the top of the mountain Bryant so expertly carried me to, only his hands clamp down on either side of my hips, holding me captive. Marilyn Manson screams about "Say 10", and I bury my hands in Bryant's hair, twisting the ends as he flicks, sucks, and assaults my pussy the exact same way that he does my heart. My body jerks around my release as my orgasm screams like a desperate bitch, after scratching and clawing her way up my throat. The animalistic sounds of Bryant sucking all of the evidence up like a starved beast distracts me briefly before he stands to his full height.

When my eyes meet his, I'm thrown by how devilish he looks. Dilated pupils, hair disheveled, and the glossy moisture that coats his lips. They're all part of the elements that create Bryant's wild energy when it comes to fucking. He snatches my soul every single time he takes me and then shoves what's left of it back inside of me when he's done.

Slowly, he pulls his belt off, and I watch as he raises it to my mouth. "Bite and drop to your knees."

Sweat drips down my sternum, but I do as I'm told. Opening my mouth and biting down on the strap. The rich scent of leather slaps me across the face as the sweet smell from his cologne clings to the back of my throat. He continues to wrap it around my head before pulling it tight, creating a DIY gag with his belt. Stepping back, he lifts my silk gown up above my head and throws it onto the floor. Now I'm sitting naked on the kitchen floor, gagged with my husband's belt in my mouth. Classy.

If this doesn't sum up our marriage, then I don't know what will. All that's missing is a murder or two.

Hooking his arm around my back, he lifts me from the ground and walks me toward the dining room table, obviously changing his mind about the kitchen floor fantasy. His hand is at my throat, my ass pressed into his crotch as he kicks my legs wide. I groan as his finger dips inside of me, my fingernails scratching the tabletop. He circles inside of me, pulling out while tugging on my hair, yanking my head back.

"Want Devon to fuck your ass while I eat your pussy?"

I wriggle against him.

"No?" He must lean closer because his hot breath is on the nape of my neck. "Then stop fucking teasing him." He bites me before pulling back. I hear the zipper of his jeans glide down. "Isa..." he whispers, and it's then that I feel his mouth back on my pussy, this time from behind. I feel exposed, on display for him to take what he wants, how he wants. "Who owns this pretty little pussy?"

Oh Jesus.

I wriggle, but don't answer.

"Do I need to force you to answer me, baby?" My defiance doesn't want to say a word, so when his palm lands on my ass and a loud slap sounds out around the room, I'm not even half surprised. "Wanna answer me? Or you gonna wait until I beat this ass up?"

My tongue drags over the leather. I want to push him. I know I shouldn't, but I want to. I know he's pissed at me for seeing what he did when he walked into the kitchen, so may as well let him get all this anger out.

I bite down on my bottom lip after he slaps me again, the sting this time penetrating my butt muscles. *Damn. That was hard.* It will get worse, I know this.

"Tell me you're not going to touch another fucking man, Isa, and I'll stop..." I don't. I'm lost in the way the sting turns into pleasure as it moves over my pussy, adapting to the sensation he's slaughtering me with. His finger slips inside my entrance. "You fucking love it."

I nod, just as he pulls his finger out and presses it against the entrance of my ass. I tense and then relax.

Slowly, he moves his fingertip inside of my ass, and he's curling it forward, hitting nerves inside of me that I didn't know were there. I love anal, always have. Double P is even better, but with anal, I've always been fucked hard and ruthlessly. Never once has a simple flick of a finger been enough to have me sweating, panting, and crying for more. The sensations that are dancing around in every single corner of my body are almost unbearable. Tears prick the corners of my eyes as his other hand is covering my pussy. The pressure his finger is creating in my ass and the thrusting of his hand over my clit is enough to send me over the edge. Biting down on the leather band, the veins in my neck stretch as a brutal scream fights against the object in my mouth. My legs liquify as I fall to the ground, only Bryant catches me.

"Nah, uh, give up, baby. Tell me you won't touch anyone else or I'll make you come until you stop fucking breathing."

Away from this situation, I'd joke that he's threatening me with a good time, which is what I want, until I feel my body damn near shutdown from the accumulation of every orgasm. Pulling out of me, his hands are on my hips as he lifts and spins me around until my ass is seated on the table and he's standing between my legs. His fingers flex around my lower back when he yanks me into his crotch, his thick cock stressing against the zipper of his pants. *Oh god.*

"Mmmmm," he growls, running the back of his hand against my cheek.

My eyebrows are pulled in together, tears streaming down my face, and I'm breathing heavy. I'm almost certain spit is hanging off the belt too from my mouth being stretched over it for so long.

"Such a stubborn little bitch." His eyes fall to the belt as his hand comes to the back of my head and he loosens the buckle.

I sigh when it falls onto my lap, the pressure of it being clipped around me finally released. It's probably going to bruise or mark.

I lick my lips, swiping my mouth with the back of my hand. "That's how you like me."

"True." He circles into me, leaning forward and biting my neck. I yelp at the sting as he stands back to his feet. "Answer me, Isa..." His forehead rests on mine as his arm comes around my back, locking me flush against his body. It would feel intimate if I wasn't bruised, aching, and fighting the sting that's still itching my ass cheek.

When I don't answer him, I expect him to do something else to humiliate or hurt me, but he does the opposite, his lips glide over mine softly. "Are you mine?"

My insides melt at the simplicity of his words and the intensity of his action.

I bring my hand to the front of his pants, gripping the thickness of his cock. "Depends," I murmur over his swollen lips. I can taste the sweetness of my release all over him— exactly as I like it. "Are you mine?"

He pauses slightly before the corner of his mouth tips up in a smirk. "Always have been, baby, damn, all you had to do was ask..."

I bite my lip and squeeze his cock. "Then fuck me."

His hand is at my throat instantly and I'm being shoved down until my back is slammed against the tabletop with a crash.

"Ouch!" My eyes roll to the back of my head as the pain continues to vibrate through my brain.

Before I can climb back up and cuss him out for manhandling me rough enough to knock my ass out, he's filling me to the brink. I flex for him until he's inside completely and his balls are pressed against my ass.

His fingers flex around my throat but right under my jaw. He uses it as a damn handlebar as he pulls out and drives back in with a slap. The table scrapes against the marble floor as he continues to slowly drive in and out. When he picks up speed and slams into me relentlessly, I scream out, my arms spread wide and my fingers searching for anything to grab onto so I don't slide off the table. Only his grip tightens while his other hand comes to my hair to hold me in place.

He yanks on it so tightly that I can almost feel the ends being ripped out of their sockets. His body is hovering over mine, his hips riding into me. He tilts his head and I watch as sweat slips down the edges of his hard jaw. I want to lick it off, lick all of the sweat that's dripping all over his beautiful body.

He speeds up until our bodies slapping together is the only sound in the room. The grunting, panting, yelping, and moaning all mixed with the smell of sex and forgotten anger. Right now, I don't care about anything. My core squeezes and I tighten around him.

"Close?" He pants, leaning down to my face and licking inside my mouth. "Hmm?" His hips continue at the same speed, yet he seems so fucking controlled. *How?* I'm about to come all over him like a desperate kitten drowning in the lake.

"Yes," I whisper.

He slides over my body and I'm truly impressed that this table hasn't broken now that he's on top of me. He releases the grip on my hair but keeps his hand on my throat. It's his reach for control, because he knows that he can't control me when we're not having sex. His mouth comes to mine and he kisses me, all while his hips continue to ride against me. I moan, reaching behind his neck, twisting my fingers in his damp hair. He never breaks the kiss, not once. He slows his lips but slams into me harder, rougher.

"Bryant," I whisper between kisses.

"Let go, baby, have at it..." My body releases itself and I feel the wetness drip down my thighs. He groans into my mouth, pressing into me harder as his cock pulses.

"Fuck." He bites on my bottom lip, enough for the metallic taste of blood to cling to the back of my throat. Pressing another kiss to my lips, he slides off my body and slaps my pussy. "It's mine whether you fucking admit it or not. She knows who her daddy is."

Slipping off the table, I wince from the pain on my ass cheeks, the tightness of my actual asshole, and the swollen bruise around my mouth. "You gave me smile lines."

Bryant pulls up his jeans but leaves them unbuttoned. "Good. Don't fucking touch anyone else or you won't have them again."

I don't know why, but I want to sulk. I'm obviously being sensitive, too sensitive. I know how Bryant gets during sex and I usually love it, but something about this time felt as though there was too much anger, distrust. I know that it's only a symbol of our current situation and I'm thinking too much into it, but that doesn't stop me from taking a step away from him, ready to hide in my room for a bit until I lick my wounds better. Literally, almost.

I'm only two steps away from him when his hand is at the back of my neck, turning me back around and yanking me into his chest. He tilts his head, squeezing the back of my neck to keep my eyes on his. "I love you."

I smile weakly, pleading for the scary bastard with my eyes to let me the fuck go. "I know."

He releases me, collecting his belt from the floor and

disappearing out of the kitchen, and probably up to his room. I'm low-key worried about the sanitizing of the table, so I quickly pull open the cupboards beneath the sink and take out disinfectant, quickly wiping down surface, focusing on the areas both our bodily fluids are probably on.

I know I should've followed his lead upstairs, or at the very least have a shower, but by the time I finish cleaning up, I'm slightly distracted by the music choice that's spilling out from the lounge. The lounge is connected to the kitchen through a small atrium-style room. The ceiling is clear, perfect for stargazing at night and always catches the perfect daylight. I enter the living room, finding Devon dancing around the room, swiping white powder off his nose.

"Why are you playing in the snow?" I raise my eyebrows. "What happened to just weed?"

"Heaven Upside Down" by Marilyn Manson vibrates through the room as he dances toward me, moving his hips with the beat. When he's close enough, he leans into my ear and sniffs. "You smell like sex, that's why."

My stomach falls to the ground. I know Devon has always felt a certain way about me. The connection between us sexually was nothing short of toxic, but now I'm beginning to think that he's headed down a path that not even I could bring him back from.

I push off from the doorframe, ready to head for a shower when he calls out to me.

"Party tonight."

"Celebrating what?" I ask, turning my head over my shoulder.

He grins at me while rolling a hundred-dollar bill between his fingers. "You'll see."

Later that night, I'm brushing all the tangles out of my hair when my door swings open and Max stands on the other side. My mouth is now healed, thank god, but my ass cheeks are still tender and I've just lost a whole bunch of hair thanks to Bryant's savagery.

I sigh. "I'm getting really pissed off at all the testosterone that lingers around this house."

Max chuckles, entering my space while seemingly interested in taking in what little things I have scattered around the place. "I thought Bryant had a sister?"

I freeze mid eyeliner, my hand hovering over my eye. It takes me a beat to recollect myself. "She's not around." I continue with lining my eyes. *Leave it alone.*

"Your room is plain."

"I'm a minimalist." Spinning around, I tilt my head. "What do you want? I'm still slightly repulsed by what happened between us."

He grunts, dropping down onto the bed, his hands on his face. "I'm sorry I lied to you. Had I known you were my sister—"

"—half."

"Half-sister," he corrects, leaning his chin on the palm of his hand. "I would have gone about things a lot differently."

I tighten the silk robe around my waist.

"Are you going down to the party Devon has thrown?" he asks, looking me up and down, confused.

I slip a pair of Valentino heels out from beneath my chair. "Yes."

"Like that?" he asks, his eyebrow quirked. I'm comfortable around Max, which I shouldn't be. It's frightening how easily I've adapted to his presence, as if my soul recognizes him now. Naïve bitch.

I take myself in in the mirror, running the palm of my hand down the black boudoir robe. Embroidery stitches are woven into the cuffs, the rest of the material transparent. A red lace bra lifts my tits up and tiny little red panties are holding together my inflamed ass cheeks.

Rolling my eyes, I shrug. "They've both pissed me off to epic proportions. Catch on, Max, this is how I make them hurt."

"This is how you get them back in line?" Max laughs, shaking his head. "Devon was right. You are going to kill us all."

Turning around, I pick up my martini glass and take a sip. "Is there something you know that I don't? If you want to earn my trust, it will start here."

Max runs his hand over his thick beard, standing to his ridiculous height. Now that I know he's my half-brother, I see the resemblance to my father. Not in a disturbing way, more in a way of God apologizing for my piece of shit dad and giving me Max instead. Maybe. I've been epically let down by almost every single person who is supposed to be my family.

Max seems to battle with his words, his face twisting in distress. Suddenly the lines around his eyes soften and he lets out a loud gasp of breath. "It's Bryant."

"What's Bryant?" I ask, tilting my head.

His eyes come to mine. "He's running for president."

SIXTEEN

Dreams aren't free. They cost you countless hours, blood, sweat, and tears.

-Isa

"He what?" I whisper, blinking. "What? He can't—he's—"

"—been building his campaign since before you came back." I think over Max's words, even though I know he has more to tell me. I'm partially annoyed because I would have liked to hear this from Bryant, and then wholly annoyed that he tried to keep yet another secret from me. The only thing that doesn't make sense to me right now is the fact that Devon is throwing a party.

Devon throwing a party isn't something that you want happening if you're running for president, and the other? Is the fact that I can't help but feel like there's something else Bryant isn't telling me.

Something big.

I'm going to kill him.

"Excuse me," I say, pushing past Max and heading for my bedroom door.

"Isa, wait!" Max calls out, and I halt, my fingers flexing around the cool door handle. "Listen, for what it's worth, he loves you."

"Love has never been our problem, Max." I try to smile, but it only comes out pained. "Trust has."

I push through the door and make my way down the hallway. Taking slow steps, my eyes catch Devon and Bryant talking at the bottom of the stairs. Bryant isn't in a suit tonight, choosing jeans that seem to have been put through the wash a few too many times, black boots, and a black shirt. Devon is wearing no shirt, dark jeans with the button undone, and no shoes. His hair is ruffled all over the place.

Finally both of them turn to face me.

"Partying without me? I'm hurt." I take a sip of my martini, already needing a top off. "Though I'm fascinated..." I say, coming closer to them. "How this is all going to work if you—" I bring my eyes to Bryant, who dammit, looks hot as sin. It's not right for someone to be this good looking. Every time I see him, I want to lick him. *You will not lick him. You are angry at him. For many reasons.* "Are running for president."

Bryant stills.

Devon chuckles. "So dead."

Before I can add anything more, Bryant's eyes are over my shoulder. "Knew you couldn't keep a secret."

Max must be walking up behind me because his voice is gaining volume. Closer and closer. "She's my sister. I'd like to at least start to build a relationship with her."

"You mean one that doesn't count having your tongue down her throat? It is a nice throat, I will admit, bu—"

I reach forward and grab Devon between the legs. He freezes, his eyes popping out of their sockets briefly before a slow manic smirk crawls across his mouth. "If you don't shut the fuck up about that, I'm going to cut this off, and now you and I both know that it won't be hard for me to get anywhere near it." I squeeze his thickness harder to emphasize my point, but Devon only groans, his eyes rolling so far to the back of his head that the whites of his eyes are all that's visible.

"I've missed you too, baby." He winks at me once they're back where they should be.

Bryant is noticeably glaring at me. "You done? 'Cause I can go another round."

I shrug, sucking down a sip of my gin, only finding it empty. "Not even close."

"Isa..." Bryant calls out, but it's too late, I've already turned my back on him and am headed to where I hear the music playing from. It's not loud music. As if the walls and doors are closing off whatever is being shouted from the other side. I make my way down the long hallway, past Bryant's office and the theater room, until I get to the end of the house.

I've never been in this room.

The doors are always closed, and before the incident, we had only come to this house a few times.

Two black marble doors with sleek granite handles.

"Isa..." Bryant warns again from behind me.

I slightly turn my head over my shoulder until my eyes fall on all three of them.

The three men who mean more to me than I even care to admit.

I turn away from them and open the door.

SEVENTEEN

Bryant

Sex is a lethal drug. It can be the trigger to your new obsession.
-Bryant

"Fuck," I grunt, watching as Isa disappears through the doors into Devon's Den.

"Well, to be fair, she sort of asked for it..." Devon purrs from beside me.

I glare at him, running my hands through my hair. "I swear to fucking god, she is going to be the death of me."

"Bullshit." Devon shoves me with his shoulder. "You fucking love it."

I snort, my eyes coming to Max. "Usually I hate snitches. But I respect what you're doing."

"If it was harmful, I wouldn't have said anything to her, but I don't think she didn't have to not know."

"Mmm," I answer, studying his facial features. I see zero resemblance to Isa. Which is a very fucking good thing, because it makes hating him that much easier. I can already see her getting attached to him, though, which could be a problem.

Maybe.

Depending on my final verdict on him.

I start walking down the hallway with Devon with Max following close behind me.

"I have to ask," Devon says, gesturing to Max. "Have you ever been with a man?"

I roll my eyes. "Devon, leave the straight men alone."

Max ignores him, pushing the door open and we all step through.

Now, there're two things you should know about my current living arrangements. The first thing, is there are no arrangements. I own houses, and people stay with me. That brings me to the second thing, Devon is the people that stay with me. When he moved into this house, I gave him free rein to the back of the house since I never used it.

What he has done with the place is questionable for even the slightly disturbed, but I'd be lying if I didn't enjoy it at times.

When you lose your daughter and your wife within a span of hours, you reach for anything and everything in an attempt to fill the void that they left inside of you. But nothing sticks, because when it comes to love, and I'm talking real fucking love, there is nothing strong enough to replace it.

The room is white, with intricate paintings lined impeccably across the wall. Everything is perfectly aligned.

Because that's Devon.

This room, also known as the sitting room, is decked out with leather sofas, three stripper poles, curved red booths, a tendered bar, dim, sensual lighting, and a corner we all know is where Devon racks up his coke. This is supposed to be his lounge room, with his bedroom and kitchen leading off the back, but he gave it his own Devon touch.

"She's right, you know," Max says, coming up beside me and handing me a glass of what better be fucking vodka and not water.

"About what part?" I ask, lifting the glass to my mouth.

"About how you have to get rid of all of this."

I chuckle, shaking my head. "This here. What do you see when you look around?" I don't know why I ask him. I don't even like this kid.

"I see a lot of wealthy men and the hottest strippers I've ever seen."

I shake my head. "No, you're seeing what we want you to see. This place isn't open to just anyone. These people in here? Are some of the most powerful men in the United States. No one, and I mean no one, who isn't supposed to know about The Den, knows about The Den."

"So it's like a gentleman's club?"

I smirk around the rim of my glass, cracking my neck. I find myself watching my fucking wife, who has found a rather comfortable spot on a curved leather chair that sits right at the front of the room. Her legs are crossed, her drink dangling between her fingers and her robe slightly open at the front. She's watching a couple who are about three seconds away from fucking on one of the sofas. I watch her watch them. It takes me back to the first time I met her, and how sexual she was. Like a feral, untamed wild cat, she needed to be fucked into place.

She still is.

"Yeah." I clear my throat. "Something like that."

Max follows my line of sight. "I care about her, man. A lot."

I pat him on the back, taking a sip of my drink. "Good for you. Maybe you can stick around." I leave Max to whatever he wants to do and make my way to Isa. She still hasn't taken her eyes off the couple when I lean against the chair beside her.

"You know, I will never understand it."

"Understand what?" I ask, thinking she's going to say something about the couple and their vanilla sex.

Her eyes come up to mine. She sinks her drink in one go and swipes the residue off her plump lips. "Why you can never completely trust me."

I pause. I didn't expect her to show emotion. Not in this kind of atmosphere. Isa is like the ice queen who builds walls upon walls until they're so thick that it takes twice as long to melt them.

It's worth it, though. She is worth it.

The colder the ice, the more fire in the heart.

Makes no sense at all.

Isa swings her legs over mine to turn sideways. "Why?"

I clear my throat, resting my hand on her upper thigh. "I trust you."

"Liar," she argues, her eyes widening but voice soft.

"Am not."

"Are so."

I roll my eyes and she gasps. "Did you just roll your eyes?"

Before I can fight it, an easy smirk crawls over the corner of my mouth.

"In all seriousness..." she whispers, turning away from me while looking out to the crowd of people. Damn, she's real emotional tonight.

I bring my hand to her chin and yank her face back to

mine. "In all seriousness, Isa, I'd trust you with my fucking life."

"I don't want your life in my hands, Bryant." Her tongue sneaks out and dampens her bottom lip. "I break everything I touch."

I bite her bottom lip into my mouth, tasting the familiar poison of her blood. "The fuck you do." I breathe in and out. "I set up the video at your father's ball, yes." Her thumb continues to caress my cheek. "I saw an opportunity and I jumped on it. When you first came back, I was shocked. I thought you had escaped and I would have to go through the pain of putting you back in that room and go through the healing process all over again."

Her body stiffens, pulling her hand away from me. Ah, this is Isa realizing those walls are thawing. She turns into fucking Elsa, throwing up more ice to stop them from lique-fying, but what happens when you put ice in the Devil's hand? It melts. "Don't fucking turn away from me, baby, because I'll be there. Right there wherever you turn. You can't escape me."

She leans up to climb off my lap, but I fling my arm around her waist and pin her down. I drag my lips over her ear. "When I found out what your father did, I wanted my revenge, yes, but I also saw the opportunity. We know that this is his final term, but it made me realize how much better this country needs. Deserves." I pause, sucking in a deep breath and waiting for her to turn back around to me. Slowly, she does. *Good girl.* "Are you with me?"

She licks her lips. "On one condition." Her eyes search

mine. "I will help you bring him down. But after that, I need you to do something for me."

"Anything," I say, searching her face. Her soft lips. Green eyes and the lashes that fan out around them. Everything shatters inside of me when the next words she says come out of her mouth.

"You have to let me go."

EIGHTEEN

I just can't.

I got a little drunk last night. I let myself go way more than I wanted to. After telling Bryant that my condition was for him to let me go, I drank more gin than what is humanly acceptable, and there may have been dancing on a table...

Alas, it's also my table, technically.

"What are you thinking?" Bryant asks, flicking his cigar between his fingers.

"I'm thinking how are you going to run for president when you can't even control Devon."

Bryant rolls his eyes, pushing off from his chair and making his way to the window in his office. "Because I handle you just fine, and your attitude is about the size of two Americas, three Canadas, and sixteen Australias."

There's a knock on the door and we both turn toward it. I was hoping to see Devon, or even Max, but neither of them walk through, instead I see long blonde hair and legs that go on for days.

"Stacey..." I murmur, my eyebrows raised before going back to Bryant. "Kind of thought you would disappear since we know your plan." I sink into my chair, massaging my temples.

Stacey offers me a small smile before walking straight to Bryant. She's wearing a pencil skirt and heels high enough to send my ass tumbling to the ground. They begin talking under their breath.

"Well, am I intruding? Because I can leave," I snap, annoyed at their rudeness.

Bryant looks up at me from under hooded eyes. "Sit your ass down, Isa."

I hate when he makes me feel like a scolded teenager.

Stacey leaves, but my eyes remain on Bryant. "Why is she still here? Are you marrying her?"

"Depends," he challenges, squaring his shoulders. "Are you still leaving?"

I snap my mouth closed. "You're an asshole."

He chuckles, inhaling a cloud of smoke before exhaling. "You already knew that, baby."

When I don't answer, he clears his throat. "Stacey is my executive assistant, Isa. She always has been."

Anger simmers beneath the surface. I clench my jaw so tight I can almost feel my teeth snap in my mouth. "Can we get this over with?"

Because I want to fucking leave.

The door swings open behind me again and this time Devon walks in, his face pale and his fists clenched. "I have to say. This election is going to be the death of me."

"So you want to remove him from office? Why don't you just wait it out?"

Bryant takes a seat on his office chair. "I don't need to remove him. I just want him to hurt."

"We could just kill him." Devon shrugs, taking a seat on

the chair beside me, as someone else enters and kicks the office door closed behind him.

"You can't kill him," Max says to Devon. "It'll cause too much commotion and James Taylor is just as bad if not worse than Johnson."

I sigh, squeezing my eyes shut. Their voices die out in the darkness of my brain. Fatigue wraps itself around my bones. "I'm tired." I've tried to continue with this same song and dance that plays on repeat in the background, but the more I dance, the weaker I get. I can feel myself slowly slipping into a territory that I shouldn't be in.

I know what I have to do. As much as I wanted to see this through, to see my father suffer because of all of the suffering he put me through, I know that I can't.

I have to go.

My eyes open. I stand from my chair, curling my lips between my teeth. I make my way to the window that over-looks the driveway. "The old me would want revenge. I'd want my father to bleed, die for his sins. But—" I turn to face them. "I don't have the energy. I've lost too much."

Before I can stop myself, my feet begin taking me toward the door. My fingers flex over the handle. "You guys can do what you have to do, but I'm done."

I slam the door closed and run down to my bedroom, dashing inside in a frenzy. It takes a few minutes to calm my erratic heartbeat.

I take four breaths while pulling my phone off the charger beside my bed. I hit dial.

The phone rings.

"Hey."

"Hi," I whisper. "I'm coming."

"What?" she bites out through a whisper. I hear doors closing in the background of wherever she is. "Are you sure it's safe?"

I hold my breath. My eyes water. "Jess. I need this. I need to be away."

"Wait..." Jess pauses. "You mean you're not telling Bryant?"

"I have to go. I'll see you soon and will call you when I land."

"Isa..." Jess warns. "I love my brother, but this isn't a good idea. He—"

"—Jessica!" I snap, and then feel instantly guilty. Jess has done more for me than I could have ever expected from anyone. She is my saving grace. I owe her my life.

I sigh. "I have to get out of here. There's so much uncertainty and lies. I feel like I'm suffocating."

Pause. "You know that's not what I'm talking about."

I lick my lips, chewing on the bottom one nervously. "I know."

I hang up the phone quickly. Before I can cross my bedroom to make my way to my closet, Bryant pushes open my bedroom door. "What are you doing, Isa?" His voice is soft, but the waves in his frequency are strong enough to drown me.

I rub the tears from my eyes. "I've got to go."

"Go where?" he tests. I find myself casing him out. Strong build, tanned skin, dark eyes and messy hair. Bryant is everything I ever wanted wrapped in everything that I can't handle.

He might kill me for what I'm about to do, but it's a risk that I'm willing to take. "Leaving."

He finally enters my bedroom, kicking the door closed while shoving his hands into his pockets. I continue with the task of tearing down clothes and tossing them into my suitcase. He watches carefully. I almost think he's not going to say anything at all until he breaks the silence with his iron fist.

"That wasn't part of the deal."

I sigh, zipping up the bag and turning to face him.

I take two steps. And then another. Until his shiny shoes are up against my bare feet.

I lick my lips and bring my eyes up to his. "I have to." I'm stuck. Confused. Agitated. *Confused.*

"Baby," he murmurs, his arm wrapping behind my back to pull me closer into his chest. His lips fall over mine and my stomach drops to the ground. "I need you." The words that wrap around his tongue so expertly fly out and punch me straight in the chest.

I squeeze my eyes closed. "I don't think I'm strong enough."

I feel his palm against my cheek before I realize tears are falling down my face. "Look at me."

Slowly, I peel my eyes open until ours are connected. Every fleck of color that lines his irises. Every thick lash that frames his lids. I see it all. My heart thunders in my chest. "You don't have to be strong. Not with me. Not ever."

I feel that crack slowly split open in my chest.

"I will always do everything and anything I can to support you, Isa. I fucked up by not digging into why you were left in that asylum." He breathes out over my mouth. "I will not fucking do that again."

Slowly, I let out a deep breath of air.

I want to tell him.

He deserves to know.

But I know if I tell him now, it will distract him. *Or will it help him focus?* Before I can stop myself, I fall to the ground, bringing my knees up to my chest. *I feel horrible.* Betrayal caves in around me, cutting off any light. Why is everything suddenly falling onto me at once?

"Hey!" He kneels down in front of me, his fingers wrapping around my chin. "Two more weeks. Two weeks of campaigning and you don't even have to be part of it. I'm just asking you to be here for it when I take the one thing your father ever cared about. More than his family."

Breathing in and out, I slowly rein in my breathing. My muscles relax and my shoulders drop as I lean against the bed. "I'm sorry." The words leave me before I can stop them.

"For what?" Bryant asks, searching my face. I want to say. I need to say. But I won't. Not right now.

My mouth tips up in a soft smile. "Okay. I'll stay for two weeks."

He drops down to the ground, stretching one leg out and leaning against his elbow. "Ready to be my wife?"

My eyes snap to his, but when I see the smirk that's sprawled over his soft lips, I relax. "Not even close."

The next day, I keep myself busy. I need to keep distracted if these two weeks are going to go by fast. Or even at a normal speed. People were going in and out of the house on a daily basis. Cars, camera crews, and the phone never. Fucking. Stopped. It feels as though Bryant had halted the chaos until this morning, and now it's suddenly blowing up.

I'm flipping pancakes in the kitchen when Jer and Ashley walk in, smiling.

"How are you feeling today, Isa?" Ashley asks, clipping her hair up into a cute little knot on the top of her head while smiling shyly at Jer.

I pause, placing my hand on my hip and narrowing my eyes at the both of them. "What's happening here?" I gesture to the two of them with my spatula. Ashley lives in the guest house and Jer lives in the south wing. Ashley is vibrant and young, and Jer is a middle-aged ex-marine. It wouldn't be absurd for anything to happen between the two of them nor would it be unheard of, which is why I'm questioning it.

Jer clears his throat. "I will be back this afternoon, trouble. I've got to drive Bryant into town."

"You want a pancake for the road?" I ask, lifting one in the air. "They're good—"

"—I have a question," Stacey's voice cuts in from the other side of the kitchen.

I ignore her, going back to my pancake. I flip it onto a plate, scoop up some butter and watch as it slowly melts on the griddle. "—Are you or are you not going to appear as Bryant's wife? Because people know that he's married to you."

Flipping off the griddle, I slide the plate of pancakes over to Ash and Jer silently, before shoving past Stacey and making my way to my room, already annoyed with this day and the fact that she has ruined my pancakes. I don't know how much longer I can tolerate being around her.

My phone rings on the bedside table as I enter, and I reach for it, answering after seeing Jess' name flash over the screen.

"Change of plans." It's the first thing I say even though she is the one who called me. I put it on speaker and toss my phone onto the bed.

"What's happening?"

Clearing my throat, I massage my temples and begin pacing up and down the end of my bed. *Fucking Stacey.* She's getting into my head. "I think we might need to change how we're doing this."

"Okay?" Jess whispers. "But what do you mean?"

I'm about to open my mouth and answer when Devon walks through the door. His eyes fall to my phone, and then to me. I panic.

"Don't say another word and I'll call you back!" Just before I dive onto my bed to hang up, Jess yells.

"—wait! Isa!"

Devon freezes.

I stiffen. *Fuuuuucccckkkkkkkk!*

Panic surges through my veins as I finally hang up on her. Maybe he didn't recognize her voice? Maybe he—

"What the fuck are you up to and why was Jess on the phone? We haven't seen her since your wedding."

I reach for words that I don't think I can mentally grasp. "I—I—" Shit. I was a much better liar when I never gave a shit about anything or anyone. Devon always made it hard to lie to him.

"Isa..." he warns, his footsteps breaking through the silence as the click of the door vibrates. "What have you done, baby?"

I squeeze my eyes shut and drop down onto the bed, the soft covers folding around my body. "I can't tell you, Devon."

"Why?" he asks, and before I know it, he's sitting right beside me, his hand on my thigh. I study it. His soft skin against mine. Perfectly manicured fingernails on hands that have ended lives. Fucking pretty boy.

"Because Bryant can't know right now, Devon, and as much as I know you love me..." I pause, bringing my eyes up to his while chewing on my bottom lip nervously. "I know you love him just that little bit more." There's a long pull of silence before he takes his hand away from my thigh and rubs it over his mouth.

"Isa, love has nothing to do with loyalty, baby girl. I love you more than I could ever love anyone, Bryant included, but loyalty?" He shakes his head before standing back to his feet. I search his eyes as he studies me closely. "You're right. Don't tell me. I will tell him. But Isa..." Devon's blond brows curve in. "Be careful, okay? Bryant is still the beast that you should fear, even though his teeth appear to be blunt when it comes to you."

I squeeze the covers in my hands before nodding. "You're right."

I have to remember who Bryant is and what he's capable of. It slips my mind sometimes, during my recklessness. Devon leaves after that, and I slip into the bath, scrubbing up. It's not until I'm rolling around in my covers later that night when my door opens and the scent of whiskey rolls in in heavy waves.

"Bryant," I whisper out into the darkness.

He doesn't say a word, but I feel the mattress sink where he takes a seat beside me. I wish I could see him to be able to see what mood he's in.

"Don't talk," he growls out softly. "I've failed you way too much, Isa."

I keep my mouth closed because I'm afraid that if I say anything, one word, it will break him out of whatever he's about to say. "I don't deserve you."

I reach out for him until his warm arm connects with the palm of my hand and I squeeze around it like a vise. "Shhh. Come here."

"I did something."

I pause. Thoughts flash through my mind at what that could mean, and honestly, with it being Bryant, the border is vast. But none of that matters.

He clears his throat, and I have to fight the urge to crawl up out of bed and make my way onto his lap. "You can leave tomorrow, baby. I won't stop you."

I still, my fingers flexing over his thick arms. Pulling the cover of my sheet off my body, my feet blindly find the floor. "Why are you saying this?" I whisper, until I've rounded the bed. My knees connect with his legs and my heart thunders in my chest. "Why the change of heart?"

A dark chuckle reverberates around the room, sending

shivers down my spine and right to my toes. "I don't have a heart."

My hands come to his thighs. I feel him tense beneath the palm of my hand as I lean forward, skimming my lips over his. Warmth. Comfort. *Home.* "Why are you saying this?" I repeat.

His hands cover mine and he squeezes but doesn't kiss me back. I ignore the sting it causes in my chest. I shouldn't. It's what I've always wanted, isn't it? "I have to show a united front, Isa. I need a wife, and if you can't—" he breathes out. "I love you, Isa. It will always fucking be you. Above every-fucking-thing there will always be you, with your smart-ass mouth and your sexy smirk, but I can't."

My smile falls and realization comes crashing into me.

"I'm going to win this election, baby. I know you don't want me, you've made it painfully obvious how much you want to leave, so I'm telling you that you can leave tomorrow. I'll have PR cover it, while giving it a respectable amount of time before announcing my engagement to Stacey."

I rear back as if I've been slapped across the face. Hot tears sting the corners of my eyes. "What?"

"This is what you wanted, I'm only fast-tracking it so you don't have to wait two weeks."

I want to scream at him, but the words are stuck in my throat, caged by the pain his have caused.

"I—" I pause, breathing in and out. "You want me to leave?"

Silence. I hate that we can't see each other, so I step backward in search of the light switch, only the light I hit on is the bathroom. It will do, giving me enough to view his face. "You want me to leave?"

Bryant is sitting on my bed shirtless with his slacks unbuckled. I tilt my head at the way his abs tense beneath the intricate art of his tattoos. It's the first time I've seen Bryant somewhat unhinged. His hair is disheveled all over his head, his cheeks flushed and his neck straining with veins, but his eyes? His eyes are a mix of frantic and defeated.

"Bryant..." I whisper, taking small steps until I'm directly in front of him. My fingers come to his chin. "I don't want it to be like this."

He laughs sarcastically. "What the fuck do you mean, Isa?" He glares at me from beneath his lashes. "This is exactly what you wanted. You made it known to begin with, and guess what?" He stands, and I watch as his tongue slicks over his bottom lip and his eyes come straight to mine.

I recognize the shift in him.

You don't marry a man like Bryant without recognizing his energy shift.

"I fucked Stacey tonight." He leans down to my ear. "And it felt fucking good." He barges past me, leaving my mouth open and my heart in tatters on the ground.

NINETEEN

You can hate life, but you need to live it anyway.
-Isa

Pain. The searing hot emotion is pulsing through my veins and slashing in my eardrums. I haven't slept at all. My eyes weak and heavy. I know that I need to get up and get ready, but I can't get last night out of my head.

It's not that he fucked Stacey.

It's that for the first time ever, he's given up on me.

My plan has suddenly been thrown into a blender and been chopped, sliced, diced, and turned to puree.

Nothing. Matters.

There's a knock on the door but I don't answer.

"Isa..." Max says from the other side. "I'm coming in."

"Really needed a lock in this room," I mumble when the door opens and closes behind him.

"Are you okay?"

He takes a seat on the chair beside me, his hand coming

up to my hair. "I came down to check on you last night when I heard part of that conversation."

"I'm not okay, Max." When I bring my eyes up to Max, it's when I realize one thing.

Trust.

I can trust Max. Through all of my ups and downs since I've come back, he has shown me that under it all, he has my best interest at heart. I am to Max what Bryant is to Devon.

"If I tell you something, promise not to judge me?" I ask, gazing out the window behind him at the rising sun.

"I tried to kiss you. Pretty sure I won't judge you."

If I wasn't so sad, I'd laugh. "I've been keeping a big secret. One that could get me killed."

Max stills, leaning forward until his elbows are resting on his knees. "Talk to me."

I run my tongue over my lips and exhale.

I'm stuck. Between what's right and wrong and left with a lingering emotion of not being wanted. Between Bryant leaving last night and all the sleep I didn't get, I decided that I wouldn't be me if I made this easy on Bryant. A better woman would leave with her tail between her legs and defeat marring her face. Not me. If Bryant wants a war, I'll give him something worth fighting for.

The house is busy, busier than what I'm used to and I don't particularly like it. I've just finished my morning run when I hear someone enter into the kitchen behind me.

"I thought daddy said you had to go?" Devon enters the kitchen and jumps up onto the counter beside me. He's shirtless and wearing loose gray sweats.

I wrap my lips around my protein shaker and take a long gulp. "Mmm, only, when have I ever listened to what daddy says?" I cock a brow.

Devon chuckles, kicking off the counter and landing on his feet. "Ah, how about when he has you gagged and tied up to his bed?"

I roll my eyes, emptying my shake down the sink and rinsing the shaker. "I'm not leaving, Devon."

"Oh, I knew you wouldn't." His hand comes to my hip, his thumb circling my skin. "But the question is, our little pet, just how much chaos are you willing to shower him with?"

I want to say none. Because I don't want to do this same song and dance that Bryant and I have been moving to since we met each other. I want to scream and say that there's so much I have to tell him. But I don't. Removing my shirt so I'm in nothing but my sports bra and yoga pants, I shrug. "Just enough to make him hurt." I'm heading out of the kitchen when Devon stops me with his words.

"You know he had sex with Stacey last night..."

The words are like sharp razors, skating over my skin.

I turn back around to face him. "I know. Why?"

Devon's eyes glare into mine. Like a magnetic force that he's tapping into, I feel what he wants. What he needs. His eyes weaken as he licks his bottom lip. "Feeling reckless? Need a revenge fuck?"

I could easily sleep with Devon. I could easily make Bryant's life painful. An eye for an eye. "How about throwing one of your parties tonight?"

His eyes drop down my body before coming back up. "Done."

Reaching my bedroom, I kick my door closed and slip under the spray of the shower, scrubbing off my sweat. Times like this is when I wish I was a simple girl with a simple brain. I wish I functioned with normality, then maybe I would see things differently, maybe have different circumstances. Bryant assumes that he has been my biggest warfare, but he's wrong.

My soul is the most complicated war I've ever had to battle against.

———

I spend the rest of the day sorting through all of my old belongings, when I find my wedding dress. Removing it from the flat box, I lift it up against my body in the mirror.

"Did I even eat?" Running my hand over the small sequins, memories flash through my head of our wedding day. *So fake*. Everything from the vows to the feelings. Everything in my life is there as a consequence of something else. I don't own any of my memories. Tossing the heavy gown into the closet, I keep going through all of the things that I want to keep and the things I want to toss, when my phone starts dancing on the bedside table. I rush toward it, sliding it unlocked when I see Jess' name.

"Everything okay?"

Silence. "Someone is chasing us. They know."

I freeze, squeezing the phone in my hand. "What do you mean? You need to—"

"—I know! Listen, we're about to board our flight. We will stay somewhere close to Bryant's." She sighs.

"Jess..."

"Isa, I promised you. I will keep it. I will call you when we've checked into our hotel."

I breathe in, count to ten, and then exhale. "Okay."

Hanging up and tossing my phone onto my bed, I feel my heart pounding in my chest, all of my blood rushing from my head to the very tips of my toes.

It's five-thirty by the time I finish sorting through the last few boxes. *Shit, that went fast.* There's a knock on my door just as I'm going through my selection for Devon's party that I recklessly told him to throw.

"Come in!"

"Sorry, Isa, I was just checking to see if you needed any help?" Ash says, her frown and somber eyes a dead giveaway that she found out about Bryant's and my fight.

"Ah, so you've heard about Bryant kicking me out?"

She tucks her hair behind her ear. "I did. I can't believe it."

"Don't worry," I say, finally finding the perfect two-piece black dress. I'll match it with fishnet tights that have little diamantes scattered throughout the stitching and some black-red bottom thigh-high boots.

I'm not fucking around tonight.

I toss them onto my bed before turning to face Ashley, who's still standing at the threshold, looking confused. "Say, Ash…"

She brings her blue eyes to mine.

"Ever been to one of Devon's parties?"

Her fingers twist together. "Oh, no. I don't think Bryant would like that."

"Fuck Bryant. You're coming."

She nibbles on her lip nervously. "I don't know…"

"Ash." I walk toward her, grabbing her by the arms. "You're what? Twenty-four? You need this. You should be partying." I don't know Ashley's story, but I know that Devon knows it. Something about Bryant saving her when she was a rogue teenager living on the wrong side of the law. Or Devon making him save her.

"I am finished for the day." She turns over her shoulder quickly. "But I don't have any clothes in the house."

I tilt my head to my closet. "You could fit mine."

Ashley shuts the door behind herself. "Done."

I gesture to the closet. "What's mine is yours."

As she loses herself inside, rummaging through my clothes, I begin removing mine, slipping on my silk robe.

"You know, I really needed this." Ashley sounds out from the closet where she's still trying to find something to wear. She comes out holding a green dress with thin spaghetti straps. It's tight and short and will complement her blonde hair. "You really don't think Bryant will mind?"

I snort, applying my foundation. "Trust me, he will be too busy being pissed at me for still being here. He probably won't even notice."

"True," Ash says.

She slips on the dress and I get busy with my makeup. Once I'm done, I work on Ash's face as she tells me about college. She's studying to become a veterinarian. I didn't even know that she was in college. She had said that Bryant put her through as part of her keeping the pool house and her job. The deal was that she was to go to college in order to continue to live and work for him. She seems happy, even though she's older than everyone at college. Jer drops her off and picks her up. I tried asking about her and Jer, considering he's eleven years her senior, but she closed up and didn't want to talk about him. She is adamant that there isn't anything romantic going on between them and that he's more like a father figure in her life. A hot father, if that. Not sure I buy it.

"Let's get drinks. Bryant has a very expensive alcohol cabinet that I feel like raiding."

We make our way into the sitting room, where shelves of the finest whiskey and vodka are lined, glistening down at me. It's like the heavens have opened and I'm about to choose my angel.

"Are you sure he's not going to be home?" Ash asks nervously from behind me.

Rushing into the kitchen, I bring a bar stool into the lounge and line it up to the bottle of scotch I want. In hindsight, it doesn't make sense why I would do this, considering Devon has a bar inside his den, but this is all pure revenge. It's all part of my plan. A plan that I clearly do not have. Once my hands are secure around a glass bottle that has the words *Macallan* and the number 52 over it—whatever the fuck that means—I bring it down with me and begin tugging at the gold casing over the lid, before finally flicking it to the other side of the room.

Taking a swig, my muscles relax as the smooth liquid slides down the back of my throat. I hand it to Ash. "Treat it mean, keep it keen."

Ash's eyes flick from me to the bottle. "That looks really expensive, and Bryant doesn't drink cheap alcohol on a bad day..." I shove it into her chest. She takes it off me and brings it to her lips. "Ah, well..."

Pushing open the doors that lead into Devon's Den, music pours out, smacking me right in the face. A remix version of "Last Resort" by Papa Roach licks through the otherwise mellow atmosphere. Ash and I have taken a few shots of the whiskey to calm our nerves, but I need something in my hand now. She was right, it did look expensive, so I put it back where it belonged. Hopefully Bryant doesn't notice.

The purple lilac lighting sets the perfect tone. There are groups of people scattered around the room, but as soon as Ash and I enter, people stop.

Pause.

We're the only women in the room who aren't stripping on a pole or being paid to be here to fuck entitled rich men while their wives are tucked in bed at home. Fuck that. I will never be that wife. I wasn't created to be a trophy, I'm the product of the fucking prize.

"Vodka on the rocks," I say to the bartender who wears a royal blue and white suit to perfection.

He nods, sliding a glass across the counter, just as arms wrap around my waist.

I take a sip, turning to face Devon.

He chuckles devilishly, his lips skimming mine. "You're in so much trouble."

"I am?" I ask innocently, tilting my head.

His eyes fall down my body, pausing every two seconds. "So much *fucking* trouble."

"Hmmm, guess there's no point behaving then if I'm already in trouble." I shoot back the rest of my drink before pushing Devon away from the center of his chest. Moving through the swarm of people, I find my chair. The same chair I sat on not long ago with Bryant underneath me.

Tonight he's not here.

Last night, he put his dick inside someone who wasn't his.

And tomorrow, he would probably announce to the world that he's remarrying.

A waiter passes by, and I bring my hands out to her. She's young. Probably Ash's age. "I need you to bring me a bottle of Cristal."

The young brunette nods her head. "Okay, Mrs. Royal. Be right back." Before I can ask her how she knows who I am, she's gone.

"Fuck my life." I lean back on the chair, just as Devon makes his way to me, shirtless with jeans on. "Double fuck."

He grins down at me. "Are you just going to sit there and be bitter?" He nudges his head up to a corner in the room, before leaning in closer, his lips against my ear. "Or are you going to put on a show for your soon-to-be-ex-husband?"

Just as he leans back, the waiter is back with my bottle of Cristal. I bring the rim to my lips, sucking down the bubbly liquid while keeping my eyes locked on Devon. I can feel the alcohol pulsing through my veins, releasing all of my worries.

Standing, I run the palm of my hand over Devon's chest, and then down, until I'm at his crotch.

I squeeze. "One, me fucking you will be what Bryant expects me to do, and I don't much like being predictable, and two?" I release him and step backward. "Your music sucks. Where's the DJ?"

Devon flinches at my words. He's hurt. Good. As far as I see it, he and Bryant are a package deal. He pledged his loyalty to Bryant while vowing his love for me. All that did was make him look inconsistent.

Before he can answer, I'm pushing my way through bodies as I make my way to the small DJ booth on the other side of the room.

The young guy behind the deck sees me and grins.

I lean over his turntable. "Play some other shit. This isn't Devon's party..." I smirk, running my finger down his velvet cheek, before scraping my nail over the rim of his lips. He's hot. He's young, but his boyish features and soft baby skin is doing things to me right now and who am I to turn down a feeling other than depression.

I push the finger that wears my wedding ring into his mouth while pulling out my phone. "The Mystic" by Adam Jensen starts playing as I hit the red button. I record my wedding finger between his supple lips, the multi-million-dollar diamond glistening against the flashlight. I slip my finger out and flip the camera to forward-facing, sucking the same finger into my mouth all while flipping him off.

I open up a message to Bryant and upload the video with a caption:

Fuck you.

"Better?" the young DJ yells, leaning into me.

I shrug. "It'll do." Spinning around, with the room circling with me, I make my way onto the dance floor. Squeezing my eyes closed, I try to keep down emotions that threaten to pour out of me. When I open them again, I find Ash in the DJ booth talking to the young guy and waving at me with a cheesy smile. She's dripping in sweat with a big smile stretched over her face. She's having fun. Not a problem in the world. To live amongst the mundane and not know about all the things that go bump in the night.

The song remixes into "Rodeo" by Kane Brown and I flip my hair in a circle, lost in the music. The soft tune, seductive and hopeful. I roll my body against the empty space in the room, trapped in my own thoughts and world. Lost in the mystic feel of the party. The strippers dancing against the poles, couples having sex in the corners, famous people snorting coke in the back.

I can feel his eyes on me before I see him, but I ignore it. I ignore him as I move around the room wildly. When the chorus kicks in, my eyes are on Bryant's. We'd find each other with or without the help of light.

His jaw is set in an angry angle, his eyes on mine.

I chuckle. "Asshole." Even though I know he can't hear me. When the song ends after I've danced out the rest, he finally takes the steps toward me.

His arm snaps around my back, his lips to my ear. "Outside. Now."

Rolling my eyes, my hips sashay as I drift out of the room. The doors slam behind me, cutting off the music and replacing the sensual energy with electrifying tension.

Scary.

"What the fuck are you playing at, Isa?" He growls, squeezing my hand and dragging me down the hallway.

I pull out of his grip as we reach the front door. "Me? What the fuck is your problem! Kicking me out? Are you fucking serious?"

"You fucking wanted to leave, I simply gave you an out!"

"An out?" I laugh hysterically, my arms may be doing that

crazy thing they do when I'm mad too. "My god, you are fucking delusional, Bryant! I said that I would help you!"

He laughs, his head tipping back and his white teeth flashing. It's a little scary seeing him laugh. He barely smiles. I know this isn't good. In one movement, he flies forward, backing me up against the front door. My hand squeezes the handle from behind.

"What are you going to do, Bryant? Hurt me?"

Both of his hands are pressed against the doors, caging me in. He pins me to the wall with his waist. This would usually turn me on, being pushed up against the wall with his cock between my legs, but he fucked someone else last night while I slept down the damn hall.

His perfect features begin to morph into defeat. "I don't want to fucking hurt you, Isa."

Realization sinks into my pores and shoots into my veins. I've been forcing his hand for too long. My place in his life. For all I know, he moved on while I was in the asylum and I just didn't know it.

I lick my lips, the cracks in my heart threatening to expose my vulnerability. "Don't you love me anymore?" The words come out as a whisper, and before I can force them back into my mouth and swallow them, they're out there in the wild.

"What?" He growls. "What the fuck—" The door opens and I'm falling backward, the dark sky peering down at me after I land on my back with a thud.

"Br—" Hands wrap around my throat and pull me to my feet.

"Isa!" Bryant yells. I reach for him, but I'm being pulled back, farther and farther away. Gunshots blare out and I watch as Bryant falls to the ground.

"No!" I scream. Kicking backward, I break free from my captor and jolt forward to Bryant laying on the ground, but before I can reach him, I'm being lifted again with a cloth covering my mouth.

Silence stretches out through the room, my head tilted to the side. The first thing I notice is my arms tied to something behind me. The second is my legs tied. There's a single light dangling over my head and the distinct sound of a dripping tap. My head pounds, and my vision is hazy as I slowly open my eyes.

My father sits in front of me, his suit buttoned, and his face marred in controlled anger. "You're awake. Good. This won't take long."

"What the fuck are you doing?" I growl, tugging on the restraints that are latched around my wrists and ankles.

My father, or I should say, Peter, clears his throat. "I think it's about time we clear the air, don't you?" He pauses. "—Your husband is a very powerful man, Isa, but he forgets what I'm also capable of."

How did I get here, to be tossed between my husband and my father? I don't question if Bryant is a powerful man, because I know that he is.

"Isa, it's no secret that you and I do not see eye to eye and never will. In fact, when you were born, I didn't want you."

I chuckle. "Are you fucking kidding me? You're a disgusting human."

Even with his blatant repugnance of me, I can't help the hurt that cuts me open inside. His words yet again leave me feeling dirty and unlovable. All I'm good for is a quick fuck and to be thrown around. People talk about how powerful the word love is, but neglect to mention the potency of being unloved. It's crippling to your mental health and leaves stains as dark as an ember on your soul. When my parent, someone who was put here to love me unconditionally, can't find it in himself to love me, then what makes me think someone who isn't obliged to, will?

"You tried to have me killed at sixteen! You locked me away in a damn asylum for half a year, thinking I was crazy! To say we don't see eye to eye is a severe understatement."

Peter leans forward, resting his elbows on his knees. "I never wanted you. You were a mistake that I should have discarded."

"Why didn't you!" I snap, once again tugging on the ties. "Just do it now and get it over with."

He stands from his chair and shuffles closer to me, his eyes flying over my shoulder. "Oh, I am. This day that should have happened a long time ago. You have done nothing but bring shame on my name, and to make it worse." He pauses, unbuttoning his shirt. I already know that this is it. I'm going to die by the hands that should have protected me. "I didn't need you after all. I could have killed you a long time ago. You were always like this, Isa. Rebellious. Destructive and toxic. I'm just glad you never bled those parts of yourself onto your sister, which by the way, have you heard from her?" His lips kick up in an ugly snarl. "Of course you haven't, because not even she wants to know you. You're disposable, Isa. Bryant moving onto Stacey only further proves that."

I don't react. It takes all of my will to not retort, but I don't. I'm used to it. Peter has always been a master with his words, a skill that very few own. Only he uses it for bad, not good. "Just do it. Why am I still fucking alive! What, you can't do it? You're going to make one of your bum boys do the dirty deed for you? See, that's the difference between you and Bryant, Father, is that he won't utilize his power to end your life, he'll use his bare hands for straight-up pleasure. I hate you."

"Oh, I'm merely not wasting my energy on you. Don't flatter yourself." His eyes once again go over my shoulder.

"So why did you take me?" I snap. I should want to give up on everything. On Peter, Devon, Bryant. If I didn't have something to live for, I would die for nothing. But I do. I have something to fight for.

"Because." Peter leans forward again, reaching into his pocket and bringing his hands up to gesture to someone behind me. "You were a mere distraction. Ever wonder if your husband is even still alive, Isa?" A large man dressed in black with a ski mask covering his face appears beside me.

Peter nods his head, his eyes coming back to me. "Good-bye, Isa." He stands and makes his way to the door, reaching for the handle. He pauses. "The only thing you gave me in life, is hate." He slams the door behind himself and I blink through the tears.

I always knew the reason to him hating me so much came from his sheer obsession with perfection. I was the antonym of everything he stood for, I would never be able to exist in his dictionary. Humans can be as evil as any demon, as ugly as any entity. The human race is not exempt from evil. Evil lives within the soul, and Peter S. Johnson is one of the worst.

I bring my eyes up to the black statue standing in front of me. He leans down, pulling out a knife from his back pocket. He's wearing black jeans, a black hoodie under a leather jacket and a black beanie over the ski mask. His hands are also covered in leather strapped gloves. There's not an inch of flesh visible.

"I will make this easy for you."

He leans down and I squeeze my eyes closed. Tears drip over my face and fall down the front of my chest. They say that in the final moments before your death, that your life flashes before your eyes. If that was true, then I lived a life of regret. The apologies that I owe Bryant lay heavy on my chest, and if I don't at least spew them out now, I know for a fact that they'll be weighing my casket down. Providing I get a casket. Depending on where or what this person does to me.

"I'm sorry," I whisper out the words through my strained throat. I swallow, but it stings. The emotional turmoil wreaking havoc inside me physically fucking stings.

"Who are you talking to?" the statue asks, leaning forward. His voice is robotic. He's using a voice enhancer.

I don't open my eyes. I don't owe him an explanation or an answer. I just need to make my peace. I need to make my peace even though I will never see Bryant again.

"I'm sorry I failed you. I'm sorry that you fell in love with a girl who was so brutally broken that she could never love you back the way that you deserved to be loved. You were a monster and a very bad man, but you loved me with everything that you had to give. I'm sorry you couldn't fix me. They say love conquers all, but it couldn't stand against my demons. I'm sorry I wasn't pretty enough, even though you always made me feel like the most beautiful girl in the room, but it didn't matter, because I was broken. I was never going to be sophisticated or savvy enough for you either. I'm sorry I was a mess, that I was just another mistake that came barreling into your life." My voice cracks. "I wish I could see you one more time so I could tell you the biggest thing I'm sorry for..." Pain digs its long claws into my chest and rips me wide open, spilling my secrets all over the ground. A sob chokes the words as they leave my lips. "I'm sorry that your daughter is still alive and that I kept her from you."

A hand flies to my throat, instantly cutting off my airway. Shocked at the brutality, my eyes pop open and there, standing in front of me with the ski mask removed, is Bryant.

TWENTY

Ever died multiple times? Just love the wrong man.
- Isa

Confusion wraps itself around all of the particles in my brain. "Bryant?"

He releases me, stumbling back against the wall. I watch as he slowly slides down, dragging his knees up to his chest. "What the fuck did you just say?"

"I—" I pause. "It's you?"

He brings his cold, emotionless eyes to mine. "Yes, the fuck it's *me*."

"You were going to kill me?" I gasp, a new wave of pain washing over me. My trust for Bryant will be broken forever after this. There will be no repairing it. He tried to kill me while I was most vulnerable. He sided with my father. *He didn't get shot.*

He gestures down to my feet. "No. I was freeing you. Now tell me." He glares at me, and I blink past the tears, the pain slowly disappearing when I see that one of my legs is free. "Is. It. True." Amongst that, I didn't consider what Bryant might feel for me once he finds out the truth. I have to tell him, though, I can't keep it from him anymore.

"I never wanted to hurt you." Shit way to start, but it was the first thing that came out.

"Really?" He glares at me. I watch as the corners of his jaw tense and release. "Could have fucking fooled me."

Breathing in and out, I sigh in defeat. "Harper is alive. She wasn't hurt, Bryant. Brianna was, that's where the blood came from." I swallow again, in an attempt to calm myself, or at the very least stop the tears from pouring down my cheeks. "Jess's date who was there that day was a surgeon. He checked her over thoroughly at his private practice. It wasn't our plan to keep her from you, but I saw it that day. The chaos that I existed in. Our daughter was caught in the crossfire of our own creation, I didn't want that for her. Not ever." I pause, and I shouldn't have.

"That wasn't your fucking decision to make, Isa."

I can't even look at him. Like a coward, I find a spot on the wall to train my eyes on.

"When my father carried me into the limo, before trans-porting me to the asylum, I called Jess and told her to run and take Harper with her while creating a plan to deflect you from the fact that she wasn't dead. But you didn't make it hard, because you wanted her cremated." I finally bring my eyes to his. "I know you will never forgive me for this, but I was going to tell you. As soon as I left the cabin, I was going to tell you immediately, but then I was once again reminded about the dangers that surround your life."

He hasn't blinked. Hasn't moved. Not an inch.

"You live a dangerous life, Bryant. We almost lost her."

He sneers at me, kicking his legs out in front of him. "You

know what's fucking funny about this whole fucking thing, Isa?" he snaps, and I watch as his lip curls up in a nasty grin. He stands back to his feet, the atmosphere charging to life as he leans down, placing both hands on either side of my chair. "Is I fucking knew all along."

TWENTY-ONE

You can't love the pain out of someone, but you can love them despite it.
-Bryant

I watch as a range of emotions sprawl over her face.

From shock.

To relief.

To... fear. Good. She fucking should fear me. For months, I have been going backward and forward with Jessica on Harper. I shouldn't have let it drag out this long, but when we all thought she was certifiably crazy, Jessica reached out to me.

"Wait, what?" she asks. "So you—" I watch as what I assume a memory comes into her head. "I saw you with Harper one time."

"Yeah. You did. But you were going through your Brooke phase."

Leaning down, I cut off the rest of her ties. She stands to

her feet, massaging her wrists. "Why? Why would you keep this up? For what purpose."

I pause, studying her closely. "Simple, really." There's a beat of silence. "Trust." I start walking out the door when she reaches for my arm.

I pull away from her. "Bryant, you can't hold that against me."

"What? Are you fucking crazy? Actually, don't fucking answer that. It took you this long to tell me. How long, huh?" I start backing her up against the wall. She's quick to run away from me, which was always one of the reasons why she was smart, despite the way her brain worked.

"How long what?" Her eyes fling between mine.

When her back is pressed against the wall, I bring my hands up and rest them on either side of her head. "How long until you were going to tell me that my daughter was fucking alive."

"I—I don't. Now! I was going to tell you any day!"

Rage and anger swim inside of me. I know there's a part of me that's being irrational, considering I've known about Harper since day one, but the other half is still furious that she continued to lie to my face about it.

I gave her outs. More than once I asked her if she had anything to tell me, but she constantly said no. She always complained that I was the secret keeper when she fucking held the heaviest load. I didn't hide Harper from her, she hid her from me, I was just fortunate that Jess made the right decision and came clean.

I lean down until our lips touch. "Not fucking good enough." Then I push off the wall and head for the door. I don't know if she's following, and I don't fucking care. Going through the long corridor of the abandoned prison, I make my way to the end and push open the doors. Devon and Jer stand beside a bound and cuffed Peter.

A naked Peter.

My eyes fly to Devon. "What the fuck did you do? I was gone for twenty minutes. How did you manage to get him naked, bound, and bleeding in that time?"

Devon grins, licking blood off his military knife. "I only need two."

Shaking my head, I squeeze Peter's chin, tilting his head up to mine. When I finally hear Isa's footsteps patter behind me, I chuckle out. "You gonna tell her, or should I?"

Peter's eyes stay on mine. Even in the face of death, he remains headstrong.

He's either dumb or brave. I'll go for the former.

Isa doesn't speak.

"He encouraged Brooke. Brooke was daddy's little toy, wasn't she?"

"What?" Isa finally cracks, coming up beside me. Devon and Jer both tense.

I turn to face Isa, not wanting to be anywhere near Peter. Aside from my being upset with her about keeping this lie going for the time she has been back, I knew she came from a good place. She never did anything maliciously and would die to protect our daughter. I couldn't fault her or be upset with her for protecting what's ours. I would've done the same if I thought she was under threat too. Which is why I decide to leave the anger here. "He and Brooke were together two weeks before the wedding. Jer has photos back at the house, but we have enough reason to think that he filled her head with all sorts of shit, only pushing her to breaking point on that day."

Isa closes her eyes, inhales and exhales, before opening them. "Let him go."

"What?" Devon snaps.

I don't answer. I partly knew she was going to do this.

Leaning down in front of her father, she removes the ties

around his mouth. "Are you going to hurt me or my family in the future?" she asks, and I watch as her energy turns placid, calm. I don't know what the fuck she's playing at because he just ordered a kill on her. He's dying today whether she fucking agrees or not—period.

Peter spits blood onto the ground and sneers up at her. "I won't rest until you're all dead."

"Hmm, I don't like that," she mutters calmly. Too calm.

I shoot a look at Devon, who is already smirking. Squeezing his shoulders, she leans forward, placing a gentle kiss on his head while taking Devon's blade out of his hands. "You inflicted irreversible damage on my soul all of my life. But it stops now."

Before she removes her lips from his head, I watch as she slowly sinks the knife into the back of his neck.

"I really didn't want your blood on my hands, Father, but better your blood on mine than my family's on yours."

Blood spills from his mouth and pours down her shirt front. He opens his mouth and gargles incoherent speech that's muffled between the warm liquid of blood. He grips her shirt and pulls her closer into him and all of us jerk into motion.

He whispers with a snarl, bright red blood smeared over his teeth. "She's alive, and she's going to kill you."

We all stiffen, and I cut a glare to Devon.

Devon shrugs that he doesn't know.

Isa stands once Peter stops breathing and is hunched over with blood slithering out of his mouth. "Who is he talking about?" She turns to face me. "I know it's not Brooke. She's definitely dead."

You smell it instantly. The stench of metal. "No, it's not Brooke, we cut her into tiny little pieces and scattered her body all over the golf course." I shuffle back, unease gripping my throat. He could be bluffing.

I take a step forward, ready to pull her back when she leans farther into him, bringing her face to his. She jerks the knife down his spine, enough to where she can reach. "See you in Hell." Finally, she pushes his dead corpse away, where it hits the concrete with a splatter.

Silence. "Did you fucking teach her that shit?" I glare at Devon. I know it wouldn't be Jer, that's not his style of kill.

Devon readjusts himself. "Yeah, every girl should know how to sever a man's spine. Teach them not to break their hearts, but now my dick is hard." She ignores him as her fingers shake and the bloody knife she's holding drops to the ground.

Jer shakes his head, turning around to head out the exit. "I'll call in the crew."

"Devon, wait outside," I say, my eyes on Isa's.

Once Devon is out and it's just Isa and I standing in the room, I tear off the beanie and the ski mask. When he shot at me—thankfully fucking missing—Jer was already on his ass and following him. It took Devon thirty-two seconds to throw his emergency bag into my R8 and another twenty seconds for us to kill the two guards he had at the front of the abandoned building, including who was going to kill Isa. "Tell me what you're thinking."

She blinks passed the tears, bringing her hand up to her cheek to swipe them away, only she leaves blood marks over her face. "I'm thinking I'm free."

My hand finds hers, and I pull her into my chest, swiping her hair away from her face. "All that shit that you said in there when you didn't know it was me." She looks away, shame flashing over her cheeks. "Hey!" I snap at her, my fingers flexing around the back of her neck so she can't look away. "Don't fucking pull away from me, Isa. That, all of what you said, doesn't mean fucking shit to me, baby. No one is perfect, some are just good at hiding their flaws instead of airing them out as warrior flags like you do." I press my thumb over her bottom lip. "I could kill him all over again for the pain he instilled into you, baby. I can promise you that you'll never feel that way ever again, and I'll do my damn best to help eradicate it." I press a kiss onto her lips, and she doesn't move.

"You fucked Stacey..." I can hear the crack in her voice and I hate the way I went about trying to let her go.

"Please, you fucking know I didn't. My dick only wants you."

Her lashes fan out over her cheeks as she blinks up at me. "I'm sorry for lying to you. I thought I was doing the right thing."

Running my thumb over her bottom lip, I slip it into her mouth and then pull it back out. "Are you done?"

"Done what?" she asks, her warm breath falling against the palm of my hand.

"Done running from me?"

She leans her head into my hand. "Yes."

Wrapping my hands around her thighs, I lift her off the ground. "I've tried to distract myself from the fact that you're wearing this sexy as fuck little outfit, but it's time to pay up." I walk her backward until she's up against a wall. I slip my finger beneath her skirt and tear a hole into the fishnet tights. Sliding the tip of my finger over her panties, I inhale into the side of her neck. "Death makes you wet, baby. You're definitely going to Hell."

"Maybe," she moans, squeezing her legs around my waist. "But you're coming with me."

I crash my lips onto hers as my finger slips inside her. She contracts around my finger tightly.

"Pull them to the side and fuck me. Right now."

I chuckle, biting down on her bottom lip and tugging it roughly. "Always so fucking eager." I massage my dick with the hand that was just inside of her while unzipping my pants. Pulling them down until my cock lands heavily in the palm of my hand. I pump myself slowly.

"Agh, Bryant!" Her eyes fly open and snap to mine. "Now!"

Lining her up, I slam inside of her roughly and her head collides with the wall. "Fuck, this isn't over. We're finishing this shit at home." I withdraw and drive back in. Pumping her hard and fast until I feel her cum drip down my balls and her legs shake around my waist. I lick the blood from her cheek and grind against her. "You're lucky I don't hurt you."

"Am I?" she teases, leaning over and kissing me. "Or do I like it when you do?" She pushes against my chest until I stumble backward, getting the hint that she wants to ride. I tug on her hand and lay down as she crawls over my lap until she's straddling me. Her pussy swallows my cock whole and I watch as her body rolls over mine, her hips grinding over me. She flips her head back and my balls tense up.

"Bryant," she moans, and I'm momentarily lost in the way her hips circle over my cock, the grip she has around my cock about the same as my grip around her throat. I drop my hands to her hips and squeeze, guiding her over me.

Biting down on my lower lip, I reach forward and squeeze her nipple through her dress. She falls down on top of me, her lips coming to mine. I bring my hand to the back of her head to keep her there. Her tongue dives into my mouth possessively, her body snatching and owning my dick like it's her most prized possession. She moans into my mouth, but I don't let her up. When she throbs around my dick and I'm losing myself, spilling inside of her, I still don't let her up. Finally, she pushes off my chest and stands, pulling her little two-piece bottoms up with her.

Shaking her head, she flashes a half smile. "Why are we like this?"

"Don't know," I grunt, zipping up my pants and standing

to my feet. The blood from her father slowly spreads closer to us. "But I'm not fucking sorry."

TWENTY-TWO

In the end, all that matters is who made it with you.
-Isa

I don't know how long I slept for last night, considering I can't remember what time we got home. I remember the cleanup crew, as Jer had called them, coming in as we were leaving, and I remember falling asleep on Bryant's lap in the back of the limo. Jer and Devon stayed behind. We had a lot to talk through, and although my father was our main threat in our life, I still needed reassurance that it was safe for Harper to come home. His final words continue to play on repeat, as if a never-ending threat. Between everything, Bryant running for the presidency and Stacey, I wasn't so sure right now was a good time for her to come home to us.

"You're up?" Bryant jogs down the steps in sweat shorts and a basketball singlet. Not his usual style, but adds to his youth.

"I am." Last night was also the first night that I stayed in his room and today, we're moving all of my things up. I wasn't surprised when I walked in last night to find the walls as obscure as the midnight sky and furnishings as polished as the finest gold. A double king bed ate up a quarter of the space of the room, while the modern bathroom and twin closet took up another quarter. There was a large window with a patio driving off to the side of the bed, an open fireplace against the wall opposite the bed, and one large black and white abstract art piece which hung on the wall above the headboard. It was surprisingly cozy for someone so cold.

He reaches for the coffee pot and turns to face me. His eyes are hard, his stubble longer as if he hasn't shaved in a couple days. "We need to talk. A real talk."

I nod, blowing into my hot mug of coffee. "I know. Now?"

Bryant runs his hand through his hair, shoving it back off his face. "In my office."

I watch from the corner of my eye as he enters his office space and takes a seat on the chair that's hidden beneath his desk. I've always liked his office. It's the one room in the house that I feel represents Bryant in a way that articulates all sides of him. From the classical novels lined on his floor to ceiling bookshelves, to his heavy mahogany table that has leather stitched into the top. The décor is seductive and intellectual. Bryant isn't shallow, he's layered thicker than cement. His soul is deeper than any ocean, and anyone who dares try to reach the bottom of that ocean would run out of oxygen before even having the pleasure of scratching the surface. He likes it that way. I was built from ice, and he was made from the waters of the Atlantic, but essentially, that same ocean that created Bryant was the very same that I built my ice walls with.

"No more secrets," I whisper, leaning back against the chair.

"Mmmm, Isa, no more secrets." I didn't miss his tone. It was a warning, yet said in jest.

"Why did you make me think that I had gotten away with keeping Harper safe?"

"A lot of reasons." My eyes found his, and I watch as he turns in his chair to face me. Giving me his undivided attention. "At first, it was because I didn't trust you. I believed you had gone. I thought you were gone forever, and that your other personality was here for good. I couldn't continue to see you in that way, so I stopped visiting. I'd call and get updates, but I was always fed the same story, that they hadn't seen you since after the wedding."

I believed him, there was no reason for him to lie to me now.

"It still hurts."

"What does?" he asks, and it's the first time that I've felt a dark cloud slightly shift from me. There was always an ulterior motive to whatever conversation we would have, and I would put my hand on my heart to say that I don't think anyone has a love story that they've had to fight this hard to get, but I believed him. His intentions. He has no reason to lie to me.

"The fact that you didn't fight for me." There's a long stretch of silence before I hear him move from his chair.

I bring my hand up, stopping him. "No. You stay there and I'll be over here. It's the only way we can drain out all of each other's information without it leading to sex."

He stops before finally peddling backward and flopping back down onto his seat.

"And then after?" I ask. "Why didn't you tell me you knew she was alive after you knew I wasn't crazy?"

He clears his throat. "I had to figure out if you remembered. Then when I figured you did, I wanted to know why you were so eager to keep her from me. I found that out obviously last night."

Running my hands over my face, I shake my head. "I'm sorry. I—I thought I was doing the right thing, keeping her away until all of this was figured out. She was safe with Jess."

"I don't hate you for that, Isa. You did what you had to do, and it showed your humanity."

"So why the back and forth with me, then? Why was it all I want you, no I don't, yes I do, no I don't..." I breathe out, tilting my head to the side until I'm pinning him with my glare. "We had already gone through all of that, why put me through it again?"

He got up from his chair but before I could stop him this time, he took the few steps to me and dropped down opposite. "Look at me."

I did. It was truth time and I wanted truth. "Why?"

His eyes softened. Fucking softened. Never seen them like that in my life—except when it came to Harper. "Losing you that first time was fucking unbearable. I couldn't—" He swallows roughly, and I watch as his Adam's apple swells when he swallows. "I couldn't go through falling in love with you all over again just to lose you all over again. Fuck, baby." This time his finger is beneath my chin and he's tilting my face up, bringing me level with him. "I fought hard when you got back. I wanted you. Needed you. Having you walk around me like that damn near killed me, you hear? I was terrified that if I let my guard down with you again, that you'd only raise your weapons."

A single tear fell from my eye.

He swiped it with his finger. "Loving you is a constant battle, but it's a war I'm willing to die for."

A sob liberates out of me, my head falling onto his shoulder as waves of defeat wash over me. He curls his arm around my back. "I love you, Bryant. That never stopped."

He kisses me on the top of my head. "I know, baby. I love you too, and god fucking help anyone who interferes with that."

"Think my father is an example of that." I chuckle, swiping the tears from my eyes and leaning backward. "Speaking of, what are you doing with his body?" I haven't given much thought to Lydia or Brianna since I've been back, and that's not because I've given up caring—well yes to Lydia —but no to Brianna, for now. It's more because I've been so fixated on making sure Bryant and I are okay. I've never been able to focus on multiple things at a time. It confuses my overactive brain.

"Well, fuck." Bryant grins, running his hand over his scruff. "That's up to you, baby. Pig farm or Hart Island?"

"You still own that pig farm?" I ask, shocked. "I thought you were joking about that?"

"Why would I joke about owning a pig farm?" he asks with complete sincerity, cocking his head back.

Jesus Christ.

"I don't know." My arms fly up into the air. "To scare me!"

"Pssh." Bryant smirks, tapping my leg. "Please. You give yourself way too much fucking credit. Pig farm it is." He stands from the bench seat that sits across the window, but I reach for his hand, stopping him.

"Wait."

He looks down at me.

I shake my head. "Hart Island. I don't—" I swallow.

"I get it, baby. You still want the stupid fuck to be buried. Deadbeat motherfucker."

"Correct."

"Too much humanity," he grunts, taking a seat back on his chair. "Next issue. Max." He runs his index finger over his lip, obviously gauging my reaction.

"What do you mean?" I ask, my hostility fragrant. "Max has been there for me through everything."

Bryant leans forward. "Isa, he worked for your father. Something doesn't add up."

I huff, folding my arms in front of myself. "I refuse to believe that."

Bryant shrugs. "Don't give a fuck, babe. What I say goes, and all things considered, I would say I'm a more credible source." He grins. "Don't you?"

I fight the urge to stand up and punch him straight in his pretty face. I flip him off instead. "Fine. We can figure that out as we go, but for now?"

Bryant grins. "She's already here."

TWENTY-THREE

A mother's love is infinite, and if it's not, then God fucked up and gave you the wrong one.

-Isa

"I'm nervous." I grab at Bryant's hand as we head downstairs and into the main foyer. "What if she doesn't like me? If she thinks that I abandoned her?"

"Baby, she's seven months old, not seventeen. She won't even remember this when she's older."

My anxious footsteps clink on the marble as we descend. "What if something happens?"

He stops me, shoving me against the wall and pinning my hands above my head by my wrists. "Stop talking shit to yourself. This house is guarded and armed. So tight, in fact, that not even your incestuous brother is allowed through the gates. She is going to be safest here, with us."

I still don't think he's right, and I blatantly ignore the jab at Max. "I've been nervous about this since the day I woke in that cabin, Bryant! That's not going to turn off just because you wave your power around in my face." I pull out of his grasp.

He growls, so low that I would have missed it had it not been directly over my collarbone. I bite down on my tongue to remind myself to remain in control. He may be my husband, my life, and the person I trust more than anything, but he is not my controller. At least not when sex isn't involved.

"I'm trusting you, Bryant. If this fails and something happens, I will never forgive you."

He gestures down the staircase, pushing up from the wall. "Deal."

Rounding the bottom, I clutch the railing in my hands, take two breaths, and turn to see Jess standing there, holding Harper in her arms.

My chest throbs with emotion, my heart screaming in my chest. "Holy crap."

Jess smiles, bringing her eyes from Harper to me. "That's Mama, Harper."

I make my way to the both of them, as Bryant hangs back behind me. "Hey, princess."

Harper reaches up with her little hand and clutches my hair, bringing it back to her tiny cupid shaped mouth and sucking on it. Jess hands her over to me and I take her, the heaviness of not just Harper's weight but my own guilt pressing down on me.

I missed so many milestones in her life. I will never miss another.

Her hair is light chestnut brown, her eyes the color of warm hot chocolate, and when she smiles, I see—"Of course you look like your daddy."

Jess chuckles. "I tell her that a lot."

Finally, my focus locks on Jess. "I can't thank you enough for all that you have done."

"Oh please." Jess waves me off. "I should be apologizing to you for you know, being an obvious little sister..."

I roll my eyes. "I'm not hurt by that or honestly surprised. It's a testament to how close you and Bryant are and for that alone, I am thankful."

"We do need to talk, though," Jess says, removing her jacket and placing it on top of her suitcase. "All of us. Is Devon here?"

I'm still smiling down at Harper when I shake my head. "He's not. We can talk over dinner."

"That sounds really good." She jumps onto Bryant, who lifts her off the ground. "I take it I have a room here, right? Got any new hot security guys I can play with? It's been a while. Safe to say, Gary didn't last."

Bryant laughs. "You'll have to take that up with Devon. He's occupied the entire wing, and no. I don't hire anyone younger than forty now."

"Hey, I'm all for the silver fox thing." She stands back to her feet. "Devon took an entire wing? That mother—"

Bryant glares at Jess.

"Fusher." She leans into Harper and squeezes her little cheek. "We won't tell Daddy how many swear words Auntie Jess shared with you, pumpkin."

————

"I love family dinners," Devon murmurs around a mouthful of steak.

Jess pours herself another wine while fixing her anger on Devon. "We need to talk about me taking one of those rooms after this. I prefer ground level."

"Actually." Bryant glowers at both of them. "Neither of you need to live here. It's not like you can't afford to be somewhere else. You choose to be here. You can both move out."

"What! But you just got me back!" Jess argues, but I see the hint of a smile on her face.

"You have a condo in Brooklyn," Bryant counters, stabbing his steak knife in her direction.

"True." Jess shrugs. "Fine, but I'll be here every day."

Devon snickers. "Sleeping with what security?" Their bickering dies out behind me because I'm still trapped in Harper.

"Hey! You okay?" Bryant kicks me from beneath the table.

I flash him a genuine smile, one that bares all of my teeth. "Yeah, really good."

"Okay, anyway, so the reason why I wanted to have this chat with you all here is that while Harper and I were living our best life in Florida, someone sent this to me." She slides a photo across the table. Bryant picks it up, scanning it and then sliding it over to me. I place my fork on the table and pick it up.

I pause. "That's Fate."

"What—what?" Jess asks, leaning forward. "What do you mean Fate?"

"That's Fate, the cabin in Washington where Max took me after he broke me out."

There's a pause, and while they're collecting their thoughts, I study the photo. It looks recent. Too recent. Squinting my eyes at the window, recognition soon swims through my body. I look ghastly, scared. Shocked. I'm standing, staring out the window, my eyes on God knows what. I'm still wearing my white robe, and my hair is matted with sweat against my face.

I throw the photo onto the table as if it sent a wave of shocks through me. "Who took that?"

Jess stares at me, setting her glass down onto the table. "I don't know. It was dropped at our door in a yellow envelope. No name attached and no reason why."

"When?" I ask, fighting down the terror that's about a second away from seizing my bones. "When did they drop that off?"

Jess watches me carefully. "The day I called to say that we were coming back. Why?"

My brows cross in confusion. "That makes. No sense..." I stand from my chair and begin pacing back and forward. "That photo. It is possible that it is old, right?" I glare at her.

Jess shrugs, her eyes flying between me and Devon. "I mean, sure! But Isa, what's going on?"

I lick my lips, bringing my attention to Bryant. "I remember. Max was right, when the drugs were detoxed out of my system, memories came back to me in waves. Some stronger, others not so much, but eventually, after a few days, they all came back."

"And your point?" Bryant waves his hand.

I lean down, my hands pressed against the table. "My point is, is that *that* is not me."

"What?" Bryant's face alters to confusion, his head tipping back. "What do you mean that's not you. That is clearly you."

"I'm missing something." I continue pacing up and down. Up and down. I need a drink. I need answers. "We're missing something, Bryant. Something big."

"No, baby. You've been through a lot." He stands and makes his way to me. "Maybe the memory just hasn't come back to you yet."

Frustratingly, I look to Devon for back up. He's already watching me carefully. "Hmmm."

"What is *hmmm*. You know I hate when you do that, Devon!" My arms are flying around. I can't seem to think straight or rationally, because I know deep down, that whoever that girl is in that photo—it is not me. And I don't say that as in that's Brooke. I mean that is not me—at all. "I remember *everything.* Have for a long time, as soon as the drugs were out. *That* is not me."

Devon leans back in his chair. "I'm thinking out loud, you know that's what that means."

I drop back down into my chair.

"So, what about your brother, Max? He obviously will know something."

Harper's soft cry cuts through our chat and I instantly turn to her aid, removing her from her highchair.

Before I can console her, Bryant is there, his arms around her little body. "I got her."

I relax, going back to Jess. "He will, but I don't think we can trust him. Right?" I look to Devon and Bryant, since they're the ones who were so forceful with putting the idea in my head that I couldn't trust Max.

"Right," Bryant snaps, rocking Harper in his arms. His suit shirt is rolled at the sleeves, showcasing all of his tattoos and muscles. His wedding band back on his finger. I'm paralyzed by the sight, seeing Bryant holding our daughter like I always dreamed. Love can soften even the roughest, all it needs is time. Bryant shakes his head. "I've never trusted him. I tolerated him around Isa because I knew where she was all along."

I think over his words, tilting my head. "Wait, is that why you made me stay here?"

Bryant shrugs, taking a seat back at the head of the table with a happy Harper balancing on his knee. "Yes. There was no way you were leaving with Max that day—or any after. I would kill him before I'd allow him to take you away where I can't see."

"You really need to work on your control issues..." I mutter. "Considering who was occupying your bed while this was happening."

"Isa, Stacey isn't part of the problem, and she was never in my fucking bed."

"Bryant," I parrot in his exact tone. "She was his wife!"

"Wait! What the fuck did I miss?" Jess interrupts our back and forth. "Fill me in. Right now, before continuing with your fight."

Devon begins yapping off to Jess, while my eyes remain on Bryant. I need to ask the question I've been needing to ask. Wanting to ask. But just as my mouth opens, Jer is rushing into the kitchen.

"You guys might want to come check this out..." We all stand and follow him through the foyer and into the living room, where the fire is dimly lit. Candles are scattered around the large comfortable U-lounge sofa.

"Yes, sad news coming in today that unfortunately Peter S. Johnson has been murdered. He has led our country through many trials, and though he may not have been a favorite, he was here for two terms. His body was found at his home where he shared a life with his wife Lydia. There has been an arrest already made, sixty-five-year-old Jason Grant, who has no connection to Mr. Johnson himself, but police are assuming he was hired by someone who is involved with black market pharmaceutical drugs."

"That's right, Amber. After the scandal at his ball where it was revealed that he had been attempting to create his own drug, and worse than that, using it to abuse his daughter, it was only a matter of time before someone wanted the secrets to go to the grave with him." They share a few sad looks between them before continuing. *"Lydia herself has asked for privacy during this time while she deals with the loss of her husband, which I understand. It is unfortunate timing as the elections start this week. How's Bryant Royal looking? I have my money on him."* That was Amber. Of course. *"Your money isn't something he needs. And I think we can both agree that women all over America will be giving him their vote...."*

I lean against the doorframe. "How did you pull that off?"

Blinking past the tears that threaten to take hold, I keep my eyes fixed on the TV, though anything that they're talking about now isn't being processed.

"Ahhh, my sweet one. We're men of many tricks." My teeth clamp closed, my jaw set. I don't know if they notice my mood shift, but everyone falls silent.

I turn to face Bryant, who's just passed Harper to Jess. "James Taylor will be acting president now."

Sighing, I massage my temples. "At least it's just acting."

"I'll go give her a bath so you can both work through this." Jess disappears, with Jer and Devon close behind them.

Bryant cracks his neck, popping off the first few buttons of his shirt and drops down onto the sofa. "Spit it out, Isa. So we can fight, put our kid to bed, then I wouldn't mind fucking you into the a.m., so speak now."

Sometimes it scares me how easily Bryant reads me.

"I've always been around this life, Bryant. The campaigns, the fake faces, the importance of it all." I move across the room and take a seat on the coffee table in front of him. "They tried to train me like a monkey to comply to their rules. To do this and that and not that and this. Do—" I suck in a deep breath. I need to swallow some of my anger if I want to articulate this in a way that won't have me screaming at Bryant. Why can't he understand without me saying anything at all? "Bryant. This world, the one that you're so willingly able to step into, took so much from me growing up. It owned my life just so that it could be the thing to destroy it—and it did. I'm twenty-six years old and I still haven't grabbed back my life after they trampled all over it. And I get it. You don't think it was a president problem, it was a dad problem, but—" I lean forward, bringing my hands to his knees. "This is one big trigger for my nightmares. I see these campaign posters around the house." I hike my thumb over my shoulder. "And I don't feel the pride that a first lady should feel, you know what I feel?" He doesn't answer, so I carry on. "Anguish, bitterness, rage, predisposed bullshit for our daughter." I shake my head, swiping the tears that are falling down my cheek.

Talking about this with Bryant is like pouring salt on an open wound. When you carry all of your past demons as a scar bared on your flesh, talking about those demons again is very much the same as taking to that scar with a scalpel and slicing it right back open.

"What do you want from me, Isa?" he whispers, his blue to my green.

I exhale, defeated. "I want to not have to need to have this conversation with you."

Leaning forward, he brings his palm to the side of my cheek. "Baby—"

"—sorry! I don't mean to interfere..." At the sound of her voice, I want to scream. My internal organs are being doused in gasoline and the only way I can put out the pain is if I set them on fire. *Touché*.

I'm on my feet in a flash, turning to face her. "What the fuck are you doing here?"

It's just like the first time I saw her. She ignores me. As if I'm irrelevant and she only bows to her master. Who just so happens to be my goddamn husband.

"Isa..." Bryant warns from behind me, and I snap.

Spinning around, I shove him in his chest. He doesn't move, but my intention was made clear. I wanted to hurt him. "Fuck you. This isn't even about Stacey anymore. You want this life, Bryant? You want to be president? Then you can't have me."

When he doesn't answer, his lashes flicking over his flaw-less skin, I'm annoyed when I feel the tears spill down my cheeks again. "Right. Of course not."

"Isa, wait!" Bryant reaches for me, but I yank my hand out of his grip.

Once I reach Stacey, I stare down at her, which is easy considering she's a few inches shorter than me—even with heels.

"You come anywhere near my daughter, bitch, and I will gut you alive. You hear me?"

Her eyes settle on me. "Whatever is going on between you, Bryant, and Max, I have no part in, Isa." She holds my stare and I have to hold my patience not to hit her. "Do you really think Bryant would keep me around if I was? I mean you and your daughter no harm. I don't know what Max got into." She pauses, and I watch as a tear slides down the side of her face. "All I know is that I was lucky I got out when I did." She swipes it away smoothly, collects her composure, and then turns back to Bryant. "Can we have a word? It won't take up much of your time."

In that moment, I hate her. I hate that she can compose and control her anger. I hate that she is pretty and seems to have some sort of bond with Bryant. But more importantly, I hate that I believe her.

"Yeah, my office." Bryant gestures down the hallway and I watch through blurred vision as she disappears down the foyer, her designer shoes clicking across the marble floor. "Isa, this conversation isn't over. But you have to stop this with Stacey. I'll explain later."

I bite down on my tongue to stop myself from screaming. I want to say so many things. I want to throw a tantrum and demand to know why he is so protective over her. *Why her!* But I don't.

I storm up the stairs and find my lifeline.

Harper.

TWENTY-FOUR

Bryant

You don't have to know someone to understand pain.
- Bryant

Past

"You can't do that..." I say, gesturing down to the chessboard. "This isn't Drafts. It's Chess." I leaned back in the pool chair, the sun hitting my skin. My parents were away this weekend, so we had the house to ourselves. Hated that they were coming back tonight though. I loved my mom, but fuck I loved throwing parties and doing whatever the fuck I wanted.

"This game is boring. I'd rather get naked..." I turn my head toward her at the mention of her getting naked.

"Stace, I'm all for it, but if your dad finds out that we're fucking around, I don't know how my dad will feel about it. Considering they run a business together."

Stacey had been a part of my life for as long as I could remember. She was a couple years younger than me, which I know sounds creepy as fuck considering I fuck her every night of the week—but there has *just always been her. We'd date other people, sure, but we'd still fuck each other whenever she and her family would travel here or us there.*

"B, they already know. You're tripping." She climbed off her chair and straddled my lap, her knees on either side. "And anyway, they've been fighting so much lately that I'm almost certain they're going to get a divorce."

"Nah." I grabbed onto her hips and ground her pussy over my cock. "They're just too rich."

Stacey looked up at our mansion, sitting perfectly behind the pool. My parents bought this place in Connecticut. It was perfect for Dad to go back and forth to New York as well as mine and my sister's schooling. My brother wasn't worth shit when it came to school. "This house is more than a mansion."

"It's haunted." I grinned against the curve of her soft neck, lifting her from beneath her thighs and throwing her into the ice blue pool. She surfaces with a laugh, rubbing the water off her face.

"You never fight fair, Royal."

I tilted my head, leaning down. "When have I ever?"

She reached forward and grabbed my hand. Before I could stop what she was about to do, she yanked me into the depths of the pool. I swam up to the surface, rubbing the water from my eyes.

Her legs wrapped around my waist, her mouth to my ear. "Neither do I."

It was true. Stacey was my match in every way. We would never need each other, but being in each other's life sure made shit interesting.

"Sounds like they're home..." she whispered against my lips.

"Oh, come on, you two! Not in my pool, I just got it cleaned!" my mom scolded us from the patio, a hand shading her eyes and her other on her hip. Both our fathers stood beside her, shaking their heads.

"Told ya." Stacey grinned, sucking my lip into her mouth. "They already knew."

. . .

I squeeze the bridge of my nose as Stace takes a seat on the other side. "She hates me and she doesn't even know the worst of it." My eyes are still squeezed closed when I feel her hand on my arm. "Migraines again? You haven't had those in a while."

I move away from her, tucking my hand under the table. "Yeah, and about Isa, she won't know. Not right now, at least."

"Bryant..." Stacey murmurs. "I don't think that's a good idea. More secrets from her is exactly what she seems to hate."

"She does," I agree, pinning Stace with the coolness of my tone. She has aged well. Real fucking well. Like Isa, they age naturally. Unlike my mother or Stacey's mother, for that fact. "But she is fragile right now. She's already insecure having you around. I think telling her how much we really know each other will only infuriate her further."

"Are you back with her?" Stacey asks, and I know why she's asking. It's not so she can steal me, it's Stacey addressing how she needs to proceed. It's what she does. She plans months, years ahead of herself and hates any sudden change that she wasn't prepared for.

She's impossible to deal with—in short.

"Stace, as long as she and I are both alive, we will always be together."

"I see it..." she whispers, and when she looks down to her lap, her shoulder-length blonde hair curtains around her petite face. She looks up at me from beneath her lashes. "I wish—you're very lucky."

"Max was a piece of shit. You'll find someone else."

Stace laughs, but it's a laugh that hides sorrow. There're underlying battles that are screaming behind that chuckle. I know her enough to know that. "I don't know. I think I'm ready to be single for the rest of my life." Stacey trusts me. Completely trusts me more than she trusts anyone.

. . .

"I found a guy."

Stacey walked into my hotel room while I secured the final tie around my neck. Moving to the other side of the room, I poured amber liquid into a crystal glass, the sound of cold ice clinking with the whiskey cracking through the small silence.

"Count your blessings it ain't me... unlike the bride who I'll be waiting for at the end of the aisle in about... twenty minutes."

She glared at me. "Very funny, B. Very fucking funny." Moving closer to me, she took my glass off me. "She's lucky, B. Anyone would be lucky to be able to see the side you keep so hidden." She swallowed my drink and gave it back to me. "I know this is your day, and Isa Johnson is a total babe, but can we talk about me for a few seconds, please?"

I gesture for her to hurry up with a flick of my wrist. Typical Stace, I'm about to marry the first woman I've ever fucking married and she wants to talk about her train wreck of a life. If I didn't fucking care about her, I'd snap her neck and put myself out of the misery.

"There's one problem about this guy that I just met."

"To be fair, I take full credit for your shit taste in men, since my dick was the first you ever had down your throat. I set you up to fail."

She glared at me, flicking her long blonde hair over her slender shoulder and tapping her thigh-high leather boot against the tiled floor. "I'm serious, Bryant! I'm worried and I need to vent. Can I tell you why I'm worried?"

"Hmmm, why is that, princess?" I liked to call Stacey princess whenever she was being a brat. Which was, admittedly, more times than I called her Stace. The fact that she's bringing this up on my fucking wedding day only solidified that.

"I don't know him, Bryant. What if I like him a lot, and then he turns out to be a fucking psycho," she whispered harshly so the conver-

sation didn't travel to the dining room, where both our parents and siblings were currently seated.

"He won't be like your dad, Stace. God didn't have the energy to make two of him. Not that I think he's fucking bad to begin with." Stace always preferred my dad over hers. "Anyway, have fun. You are not fated to marry for love. That's what happens when you're the daughter of a bank owner and the master money launderer."

She sighed, running her hands through her hair. "He's coming for dinner."

"Really? When?"

"Tonight. Like after your wedding!"

"He's fucking keen..." I raised an eyebrow at her, leaning against the desk in my room.

"Right? It's weird. But I don't care because he's pretty!"

I rolled my eyes. "Your pussy is too easy to fuck, that's your problem."

"If there's something you need to say, do it." I shuffle in my chair, reaching for the humidor and taking out a cigar.

"I don't think we should be keeping our connection a secret. It might help her, I don't know, understand why we're close?" Stace mutters, and I watch as a range of emotions soar through her face in waves.

I roll the cigar around in my mouth, allowing the tang of tobacco to linger on the tip of my tongue. "Let me tell you what Isa will do if she finds out that you and I used to fuck, suck, and lick each other since way before we even went through puberty." I blow out a cloud of gray smoke. "She'll kill you out of sheer jealousy, and then either me or Devon will have to figure out yet another plan to hide a murder. Because that's what we will always do for her. We're the soldiers that linger behind her."

Stacey sighs. "Bryant, what the fuck has all of this really got to do with Max? Something is not adding up."

I clench my jaw, simmering the rage that's threatening to rise to the top. "Oh, I'm well aware that the coincidence is way too fucking obvious, but I've run checks on this kid. He's fucking clean. Foster homes after foster homes, and then dead end."

"Huh," Stacey says, and I don't miss the look of challenge that flies over her face. "I was married to him for twelve months. He was perfect at first, but then shit started to get weird. That cabin, the psych ward, the obvious secrecy whenever I'd ask about anything. He kept so much away while keeping me in close."

"We'll get to the end of it, and I doubt he'll be walking away with his life."

TWENTY-FIVE

The excuses you create are just dressed up lies.
-Isa

I have two options. I can wear white or black. My head swings between the two dresses.

"I think you should go for black." Jess gestures to the black lace dress with her margarita glass. "You always look good in black."

Ash shakes her head. "But that's it. It's expected of you to wear the black. I say go white. It's so not you." Their small bickering dies off in the background as I internally go back and forth between what dress I'm wearing to this damn event. This is it. I know that whatever happens tonight will be the deciding factor in Bryant's and my future. Having a child with someone doesn't give them immunity to hurt you.

My fingers flex over the white silk gown. Strapless and tailored to fit my curves like a glove, Giorgio Armani did well with this one.

"Want a drink?" Jess asks as she's diving behind my bedroom door.

I shake my head. "No, thanks. I need all of my wits tonight."

Ash drops down onto my bed when Jess disappears. She takes my hand in hers. "I'll take good care of little Harper tonight. I'm actually really excited. I've always loved kids and babies."

I chuckle. "You say that because you didn't have any siblings. But yes, she's special."

"I've got all these games lined up that I want to play with her." I don't have the heart to tell Ash that Harper is too young to play anything, so I let her yap off into the background as I slip into my dress and busy myself with the rest of my preparation.

My hair is done, soft curls trail down my back, and my makeup is completed. It's natural, without looking natural. Low effort. When I make my way into the tent that's set up in the back yard, I scratch at the palms of my hands agitatedly. There's so much uncertainty that surrounds me and it's making me feel unhinged. My father's death didn't lessen it, if anything, it made me more nervous.

"Well damn." Devon's fingers flex over my hip as he pulls me into his side. I'm paralyzed by how quickly they managed to turn Bryant's boring back yard into one of festivities, but I dig it.

"Thanks," I grumble, still not happy with Devon. I do my best to ignore him, people-watching as couple after couple enter the tent through the large doors. Security guards are posted everywhere, with one at the entryway.

"You're still mad at me?" Devon sulks. "Come on."

"Nope," I answer, bored. "I don't care anymore. Have a good night, Devon."

I go to walk away from him when his hand comes to mine. "Isa, there's something you need to know."

I snap, finally turning to face him. "And what's that, Devon? What now?"

Devon's lips roll under his teeth. "Max is here with someone."

I yank my hand out of his grip. "Leave me the fuck alone."

I turn and enter into the tent, bypassing the guards who only have to look at me once to know who I am. Circular tables are elegantly placed around the room with white and black centerpieces anchored in the middle. A candle on each table flickers, lighting the already dim setting. There's a makeshift stage, speakers, a bar, and catering staff that are moving and swimming through the sea of people with silver platters holding all sorts of appetizers and desserts. I still haven't found Bryant.

"This way." Jess leads me to the front of the room, where she gestures to my name decoratively drawn onto a little white card that's placed above a plate with gold trimmings.

"Where's your brother?" I ask, taking a seat on the chair. My feet automatically thank me by throbbing as soon as they don't have the pressure of my weight. I should have broken my shoes in yesterday. Or even this morning.

Jess places her gold clutch onto the table. "I don't know. I haven't been able to find him. I guess we will know when he enters the room." I hate all of this. It's all too familiar to my life prior to being married. "I did see Max. He was with a woman. I can't see her face because she's wearing her mask." Jess takes out a cigarette and places it into her mouth.

"My kid pushed you to start smoking?" I ask, eyebrow quirked.

"No," Jess answers, exhaling through bright red lips. "Your husband did."

"Her husband did what?" Bryant comes up behind me, his hand on my shoulder and his lips on my neck. "You okay?"

Without even blinking, a smile stretches on my face and I pat his hand. Everything is for show, and it's a show that I've been performing in since my father first ran for office. It's a show that needs to end.

"We're about to start. I put Max and his plus-one opposite you so we can figure him out."

I want to protest, but I can't. The words are stuck in my throat, held there by the turmoil of what I am to do and not to do. When I was a kid growing up, I'd rebel. Everyone knew that. But could I do that to Bryant? No. I couldn't.

I tap at his hand. "Got it."

Bryant leaves, mingling with people he needs to mingle with. I spin around to follow him, realizing I'm doing a shit job at being his wife when I see Stacey's body standing beside him. A red dress stuck to her with an equally red mask.

Anger brews inside of me, anger that I have every right to feel. "God, I hate her."

Jess turns over my shoulder. "Who?" I watch as her eyes turn to slits behind her mask. "When the fuck did that happen?"

"Did what happen?" I ask, suddenly second-guessing my idea to be sober tonight. I need vodka. On ice.

"Stacey Humphries. When did she come back into Bryant's life? Damn, I missed a whole fucking lot."

"You were gone six—wait!" I saw it. The moment Jess realized she had said something she shouldn't have. Her shoulders turned rigid and her eyes froze on the spot. "What do you mean *back* into Bryant's life?"

"Shit." Jess turns back around and swallows the rest of her champagne. "Isa, you might need to—" She pauses, leans over when a waiter is about to pass her and swipes up another flute. "Actually. No." She sinks the entire second glass of champagne in one go and cranks her body to face me. Her hands come to mine. "Stacey Humphries has been a part of our lives since we were kids. That?" Jess hikes her head over her shoulder. "Is natural selection. They have always been all over each other. It was honestly disgusting considering she *was* my friend. When you said Stacey, I didn't think it was that Stacey."

One.

Two.

This is fine. I don't have a say in who he was friends with as a child or who he had sex with before he met me. *Only he was engaged to her before I came back in the picture.* "What? How? Why?"

Jess leans back in her chair, deflated. I understand her exhaustion. "What? I've already answered. How? Her father and our father went to college together, and why? Well, that's something I don't know." Jess shakes her hands. "Wait! Was she the one married to Max, as in your half-brother?"

I nod my head, squeezing my fists so tight little crescent moons indent into the palms of my hands. "Yes."

I watch as the skin around Jess' lips turns purple. "Something isn't right about this." Her eyes begin flying around the room. "Too much coincidence and I know these men. Nothing is fate. They *are* fate." I pause. Thinking over her words.

They are fate.

Nothing makes sense. I'm reaching for memories that I know aren't there.

Sagging back in my chair, and barely holding myself together after finding out just how deep Bryant and Stacey's connection really goes, I huff out a breath of air.

"She means nothing to him, you know that, right?" Jess interrupts my thoughts.

But it's too late. I'm already swimming in the deep end where alligators and monsters live. "They were just young fools playing around. My brother isn't that same idiot. He's scary now. Stacey would get eaten alive."

"Hmm." I offer a smile, pouring sparkling water into my glass and bringing it to my lips. Before I can take a long enough sip, Max is standing on the opposite side of the table, with sure enough, a girl in his arms. She's wearing a black dress with a basic black lace mask. The opposite of what I'm wearing.

Interesting. Not so much, since the theme tonight is black, white, and red.

"Isa," Max says, nodding his head.

I don't know how to act. As far as Max knows, we, us, our dynamic shouldn't have changed. "Hi." My eyes shift to the girl standing beside him as they both sink into their chairs.

"Pearl, this is Isa. Isa, this is Pearl."

I smile at the young girl, seemingly upset that I can't see any of her face. The mask she opted to wear isn't the usual masquerade style. Hers covers her entire face, with only her small lips and the depth of her hazel eyes showing.

Pearl bows her head, before reaching for the water and pouring some into her glass.

"Where have you been?" I ask Max, to distract myself from the goose bumps that have appeared on the back of my neck.

"I was giving you space with Harper." He brings his glass of whiskey to his mouth. "How is she?"

"Good," I whisper, my eyelashes fanning out over my cheeks. "Real good."

Max smiles softly. "Can we talk?"

"After, yes." Busying myself with gulping enough water to

distract me, I pray tonight goes faster than it already has. I need to put distance between myself and my thoughts.

Bryant takes the stage after being introduced by a dark woman in an elegant white gown. Her smile was infectious and despite the fact that I was in no mood to flash my pearly whites, I couldn't help but give her a chuckle at her commentary. He strolls across the stage with an air of confidence that only someone with his level of swagger could pull off. Wherever he is, people watch. Whenever he enters, people stop what they're doing. I can see him being the president, and I think that's what frightens me the most. I lost my life to this, I don't want to lose him too.

Bryant proceeds to announce the long lineup of auctions. I'm momentarily zoned out when his next words catch me off guard.

"All proceeds will be spread between the lower-class mental health institutes throughout the United States of America." His eyes come to mine. My throat tightens and I can feel the tears build up behind them. Jess squeezes my leg from beneath the table. "It's something that has over time become very important to my wife and me, and our family." He raises his glass. "For those who don't have a voice, we must be it. The first auction tonight will be for my beach house in The Hamptons." His voice dies out and I shake my head.

"I can't believe he did that."

"I can," Stacey says, taking a seat beside me. I freeze. I don't want to give her the satisfaction of gaining my attention. "Because under the monster is humanity. I thought you of all people would know that."

I snatch Jess' wine glass straight out of her hands. If anyone is going to make me drink, it's this bitch. "You don't know what I know about Bryant, Stacey."

"True." We both lock eyes and I feel as though everyone

in the room dissolves at my feet, it's just her and I and our pussy flashing contest.

"Because if you did know him the way I do, Isa... you wouldn't need to force him to give up his office over something that you're so insecure about from another man."

I glare at her, gritting my teeth. Jess whispers something beside me but nothing. Matters. "You're one to fucking talk. You were married to my fucking brother."

Stacey briefly bats an eye at Max before coming back to me. "Tsk, tsk, don't go talking about a subject that you're not ready or educated enough to talk about."

"How so?" I growl, managing to keep my voice at a low, respectable level.

"Well, for one." She clears her throat. "He is not who you think he is." Her voice is just above a whisper, barely audible. The crowd begins clapping, tugging me out of my thoughts. "But I have a feeling that you're about to find that out."

Bryant sits between Stacey and I, his arm wrapping around the top of my chair. I know that he wants me to be more involved. I know that I should at least try to be, but I've grown up believing all I had to bring is shame. At these events, I always felt inferior, unwelcome, and like I was the dirty secret Peter had to try to hide. It's hard to slip out of one habit and into another.

My phone dings and I reach inside my clutch, taking it out.

Tell me Max isn't there.

It's Devon, and he's once again being cryptic.

He is and he's opposite me.

There's a long pause and Bryant leans into my ear. "Who is it?"

"Devon," I answer, just as my phone vibrates in my hand. I open his next text.

Is he alone?

I roll my eyes, just as Bryant's fly to the woman sitting beside Max. He must pick up something from Devon's text that I haven't.

No. He's with a girl. Help Ash and stop harassing me.

My phone starts ringing but I silence it, turning the screen flat on the table. I can't deal with Devon's constant issues while distributing my thoughts over everything else that's going on in front of me. The atmosphere is busy.

The rest of the dinner moves quickly, Max and I share awkward stares from across the table, and when Bryant leaves the table, I finally gesture to Max. "Can we talk outside?"

Max nods, tossing his napkin onto the table before following me out the side exit. The cool air whisks through the strands of my hair, cooling the sweat that is forming on my lower back.

I spin around. "What is this?" I flash the photo in front of his face.

He looks at it, then comes back to me. "It's you."

I shove him in the chest, only he doesn't move. "No, it isn't. I would remember. My brain is clear now, I remember everything that did happen. Everything that I created inside of my head doesn't even exist upstairs anymore. So, who the fuck is this?"

Max opens his mouth, but when the words fly out, it's not in his voice.

"It's me." The woman he was sitting with steps out of the shadows, taking Max's hand while slowly removing her mask.

My breathing stops.

Shock shoves me backward as the building and trees sway in the distance. Slowly, I recollect my thoughts. "What the fuck?" When you look into a mirror, you see the reflection of yourself. Everything is you, only flipped around. But it's fine, because you know it's you. Pearl is everything like looking into a mirror, only this is not fine.

Because this is not me.

This is Pearl.

"Isa..." Max warns, coming closer to me. "What are you thinking?"

"I'm thinking what the fuck is going on?"

A car pulls up behind me, over the crunching of rubber tires and loose gravel.

Max tilts his head and I see it. The exact moment his eyes flash and his true colors present themselves.

"You're not on my side, are you, Max?" I say the words, but car doors are opening behind me and my heart is beating loudly in my chest. I'm suddenly aware of the fact that we're down the side alley of the hotel. Why didn't I leave through the front doors?

Max slowly shakes his head, his finger pressed to his lips. "No, Isa."

"Why?"

Max leans in. "You and Brianna took everything from us. You were both the golden children."

I laugh so loud that Pearl jolts beside him. I square my shoulders. "Are you fucking serious, Max? My father tried to kill me, you stupid fuck!"

"Guess he didn't succeed a second time, huh?" Pearl says, and every time I look at her, an eerie feeling washes over me. "Get in the car, Isa, and don't make a scene."

"Or what!" I spit, disgusted in Max. Ashamed of myself for allowing emotions and for thinking that once again, I could trust someone that I shouldn't.

"Or my precious little niece—"

"Nah, uh, uh." I hear Devon's voice boom off in the background. Chills break out over my spine at the eerie sound of hearing Devon's voice so calm.

Slowly, I turn over my shoulder to see not only a black city car behind me but also a dark limo that's caging us all in, parked sideways. The door is open, and Devon is walking stealthily toward us. He's not the Devon I recognize; this is The Reaper.

"You see, I don't particularly like hearing my niece's name being threatened."

The exit door flies open, and Bryant is standing breathless, his eyes on mine. He quickly checks over my body before slowly turning his head to Max and Pearl. "What the fuck is going on?"

"Seems you were right about Max. Isn't that right, Max?" I say, twisting back toward the city car that he was expecting I get into and seeing it empty. No driver. No other passengers.

"Oh, is that right?" Bryant says calmly while unbuttoning the first couple buttons of his shirt.

"Yep! And, there was also the part where they tried to get Isa into their car and used harming Harper as a way to make that happen—" Devon's words were cut short by the sound of bone cracking. Blood splatters over the side of my face as Bryant relentlessly lays into Max.

"Bryant!" I yell, tapping his shoulder. "Get off, we need to get answers."

He doesn't stop punching, and when I turn to Devon for help, he merely shrugs and grins.

"Bryant!" I growl. "Now! Get off!" Bryant's fist stops midair before he slowly climbs off him, swiping his mouth with the back of his bloody hand.

When they're both at a distance from each other, Max spits to the ground and looks up at me from swollen eyes.

"Devon?"

"Hmmm?" he answers.

"Is the area secure?"

"No one is watching, baby girl."

I bring my eyes to Pearl, who to her credit, doesn't look fazed. "Who are you?"

"I'm your twin sister that wasn't good enough."

"Not good enough for what? Abuse?"

Pearl tsked, bending down and helping Max to his feet. "You got a shot at life, Isa."

"Again, are you fucking joking? My life? I would have chosen your life over mine!"

"You know nothing about my life," Pearl answers, her eyelashes fanning out over her cheeks. "Who do you think he was testing on before you, Isa?"

"What do you mean?" I say, stepping forward. Bryant's hand flies to my palm, stopping me from going any farther. "What do you mean?" I repeat.

"Isa…" a voice I haven't heard in a long time cries out from the city car. My head turns, and before Bryant can stop me, I launch forward, searching inside.

It's empty.

"Isa, is that you?" the voice asks again.

"Am I going fucking crazy again?" I say under my breath.

"Let me out!" she screams, and I quickly fly out of the back seat, rounding the trunk. I point. "Fucking open it, Max!"

Max steps backward, arms up as he slowly leans down into the car and pulls on the lever. The trunk pops open and I throw it up, gasping.

"Oh my god!" Tears well in my eyes. "Brianna?"

Brianna's eyes fly between all of us, her hands tied behind her back. "Help me."

After the initial shock of her being tied up, I help her out of the trunk and turn my gaze on Max. "Tell me now."

Max shakes his head as Devon ducks behind Brianna and helps with her ties. "I have to admit, knowing that you killed Peter is satisfying, considering you thought you killed him because you assumed he was your only threat."

"Why?" I tilt my head, rummaging through all of the memories and words inside my head to construct the right ones that I want to spew out. But there's nothing. Nothing that I feel will hold enough force to annihilate him once and for all. At least not right now.

Max staggers backward, half of his face swollen already. He leans against the city car. "Simple. Rewrite life..."

My eyebrows cross.

Pearl falls beside Max until they're side-by-side. "We were going to replace you with me. Max was supposed to kill you in the cabin, and then I was going to take your place."

"But what happened?" I ask, my eyes narrowed. "Why the sudden change of fucking heart?"

"Well," Max says, swiping the blood residue off his chin. "We knew that Bryant would pick up something was off with Pearl, so we were trying to figure out another plan. For as long as Bryant and Devon were around, there was no way we could have convinced everyone she was Isa."

I throw my hands up. "I don't understand! Why would my parents get rid of you?" I snap to Pearl.

"One parent," a voice said from somewhere in the shadows. It wasn't one I recognized. Not off the bat anyway. When I zoned into the shadows in the corner and saw a woman step out, my brain short-circuited.

I recognized her instantly, as if every motherly bone in her body was still connected to mine.

"You died," was all I could say. After years and years of not seeing her, that was the first thing I could say.

"What?" Brianna screeches from beside me, her hand coming to mine. It was almost a protective gesture that warmed a side of my heart that hadn't been touched by Brianna before. Ever the cold older sister.

"Daddy dearest was going to lose everything he had and it would have all been because of me, but you had to take that from me too."

"But you didn't exist..." I say, pointing to Pearl. I look to Brianna for backup. "Did she?" Brianna was a couple years older than me, but I'm sure she would remember something. Anything.

Brianna shakes her head, her short blonde hair skating over her slender shoulders. "No. I don't remember."

"He gave her away." My mother comes into view, and it's the first time we see her in what little light we have. There's a subtle beauty about her, much like Brianna and I, I guess, but something else. There's something about the way her lips move and her eyes never remain in the same place for too long. *There's something I'm missing.* "What are you thinking, Isa?" Her lips move, but I'm paralyzed by the energy she's exuding. I recognize it. Warmth.

"I'm thinking you've been to that asylum..." I whisper, my eyes narrowing. I'm talking on straight instincts. Nothing more. "I'm thinking my fucked-up father had one weakness." I breathe in and out. "When I first met Max, he mentioned—probably unintentionally because he's about as dumb as he looks—that there was a reason as to why my father was trying to find a cure for insanity and schizophrenia." I raise my brows and I feel the air once again shift around us. My lip curls at the edges. "I'm not wrong."

"Baby, speak in a way that we can understand." Bryant's hand is on my lower back.

I suck in a deep breath. "Isabel—that's your name, right?" I don't wait for her to answer before I carry on. "Is sick beyond help. My father was trying to find the cure for her, to help her." I pause, thinking around all of the different scenarios in my head. Why me, why Pearl, why did he use us to trial the drugs on? Realization skims over my flesh like a sharp blade. "Because genetics," I whisper my answer out loud, merely testing it on the tip of my tongue.

"Oh, holy shit!" Devon chuckles, shaking his head. "She's fucking right, isn't she?"

I don't need anyone to answer me, because I already know that I am. This whole time, he needed it for my mother, because even Lucifer needed a woman.

"Schizophrenia can be genetic, and all mental illnesses can be hereditary." I'm still whispering out loud.

"But why not me?" Brianna asks. "Or even Max?"

I shake my head. "No, the question is *why* you? You were the perfect child. The staple of what made our family look like the perfect family. There's no way he would have touched you when he had a fuck up like me or the lost daughter like Pearl to play with. Max had his role in it all, he was the doctor. Dad needed him for his brains—or lack thereof." I exhale, shaking my head. "How did you get out?" I point to Isabel.

Schizophrenics are not bad people, and neither are those who are clinically insane. If she is truly with Max and Pearl in all of this, it will have nothing to do with the illness and everything to do with the human. Bad people are just that—bad people. You can't categorize them and slap a label on them. They're just rotten. There's a high chance that she has been manipulated by my father, though, so until I'm convinced otherwise, I will treat her accordingly. I have a feeling that she's not the bad person in this, she's a victim as much as I am. Having so many strong personalities around me is draining. I wonder if she is the same. Or maybe I'm being naïve.

Isabel's shoulders hunch forward, her head bowing. "Max and Pearl. I—" Her eyes squeeze closed as if she's struggling to form the words. Before I can think twice, I'm moving toward her.

"Jesus Christ," Devon calls. "Bryant! Stop her before she ends up hurt again!"

"Leave her," Bryant snaps at Devon. *Does he notice it too?*

With the strength from Bryant, my hands come to her arms. Frail and skinny, like tiny bones hidden beneath a cloak. "Isabel, I am not like him, or them. I—" I pause when the smell hits me. I would recognize it anywhere. Bleach and poison. "When did they get you?"

"Tonight," she whispers, finally lifting her head up with her eyes on mine. "I'm sorry. I never wanted this." Her eyes close as she stumbles to the ground, and I catch her, helping her down gently until she's curled up in a ball and leaning against the car door.

Pure, undiluted rage pulses through me as I slowly stand to my height.

I spin around to face Pearl and Max. "How fucking dare you!"

"He stole me," Pearl interrupts in a panic, clearly reaching for my sympathy. "Stole me and locked me in that damn asylum for *five* years. Mom was here to help get you into the car."

"I will kill you," I whisper softly, tears threatening the corners of my eyes. "That is a promise."

Pearl shakes her head, fear flashing over her face. She's frantic, obsessed. "He took me away from my girlfriend. You know her, right? Brooke?"

Everything freezes.

I have whiplash from the revelations, everything hurts.

"Not true, she was sleeping with Dad."

I can't believe I enjoyed throwing that in her face. The adrenaline is only heating my skin, sweat pouring out of my pores. I need to run, exercise, eat, something other than stand here with my feet aching in a five-thousand-dollar dress.

Pearl snickers, her eyes going to Max. I could see the admiration she showed for him. "He wanted to find a way to force a psychotic break. He wanted to make someone psychotic, Isa. He used me as a test dummy for *five fucking years*. What you put up with for six months, I endured for sixty." She clears her throat, her shoulders squaring. As if she cracked and showed a shimmer of weakness and had to quickly compose herself. "Max finally came into the asylum and he and father agreed that I would take your place and he would continue on you until he found a cure to help Mom, and get props for finding the first cure for a mental illness. When the wedding happened, Max seemed to convince Father that you were ready to bring in to do the switch, only when you came in, you fought the drugs that they were feeding you. You compartmentalized half of yourself into my Brooke, and the other into Isa. They needed you to be all *Brooke* so they could finally work on trying to cure you. Father never wanted to hurt Mom. Ever. She was to remain intact until the drug was absolute. But you, Isa Royal, you fought the hardest. So, they kept us both there, until Max set up the plan with Father. When Dad noticed that you were, in fact, not going to come to with the drugs, he allowed Max to break you out. To get close to you. Gain your trust." Pearl steps forward. I didn't realize I was crying until tears drip from the curve of my jawline and onto my sternum.

"Come a step closer, bitch and I'll rip all that pretty hair out," Brianna growls, her grip around my hand tightening. I couldn't relish in the protectiveness of my sister, because I was still trying to wrap my head around all of the truths that were spilling out.

All of them this time.

I was played a puppet. All this time, I rebelled, defied against normality, only to be controlled all along. They're the winners here, not me. They were controlling me without me even realizing it.

Pearl stops a few steps ahead of me, and it's then that I feel the strong presence behind me. No doubt Devon and Bryant. A war is about to rip out between us, and I don't want the residue of it to land on Bryant's hands. "Gain your trust. Kill you and place me in your life." Her eyes darken, enough for me to see beneath the shadows of the streetlights. *Pearl and Brooke.* I can't move past that piece of information.

"And what do you mean you and Brooke?" Everything else she had said was what she had already said, only with different words.

"She was my fiancée," Pearl whispers, her shoulders sagging in defeat.

If I was a lesser woman, I'd attack her while she was down. But I'm not. I prefer a challenge.

"Who, by the way, you also took from me. You were her only mission in the plan, and you even managed to have her sucked in. So I snapped. When Max updated me on her falling for you and screwing everything that walks—including our father—I told him that I didn't want her. She turned to hate me, resent me, and in turn, took it out on you." Memories flash through my head of the final words Brooke spoke to me. *"She can't have everything."* Pearl runs her fingers through her hair. "She knew I was going to leave her behind because of it, and because she couldn't gain access to me in the asylum, she figured she'd kill you, since doing that would eliminate me gaining my freedom under your name. Kill you, and Isa is dead. I couldn't replace a dead person. I lose, you lose, she wins."

Information is heavy in my brain, though now everything makes sense. Brooke makes sense. Her insane instability makes sense.

"You could have never pulled that off. Replacing me."

"Oh, I could. Easily." Her eyes swing to Bryant, dropping low down his body and coming back up. "In bed with your husband, playing mommy with your daughter..."

I fly forward, and my hand is on her throat before her tongue can even curl around the first syllable of her next word. Slamming her body up against the car, I squeeze roughly until the tiny bones and fragile muscles in her throat crack beneath the palm of my hand.

I smirk. "That would have never worked."

"Really?" Pearl tilts her head. "I would have been the trophy daughter your father would have always wanted, the wife Bryant always needed, and the mom that wouldn't have put Harper in harm's way with her shit decisions for friends!"

My left arm rears back before my fist collides with her cheek.

"You don't know shit about me, my husband, or my daughter. You don't know shit about my *family*. And you are both deluded if any of you thought you could replace me." I cut my stare to my mother, unlatching my grip around Pearl's throat. "What was in it for you, Isabel? What did they say that you gained with helping them?"

"Oh we didn't tell her anything about hurting you. She wouldn't get in the fucking car if we did. We said we were helping you." Pearl laughs, mock frowning. "She's weak. Don't know what Father saw in her. She kept rambling like a crazy person about how much she can't wait to see her daughters, all while not thinking about how *I was* right in front of her."

Amongst her blubbering, a thought enters my mind and I can't get it out unless I say it. "So you knew we were siblings?" I turn to Max, trying to wipe the disgust off my brain, but fail.

He smirks. "I did."

Bryant growls behind me. I can feel his energy hovering over me like a demonic entity, just waiting for his moment.

"Bad," Isabel interrupts, shaking her head furiously. "She is bad, bad, bad. Not sick, just bad."

The final cloud of uncertainty moves away and the light shines in. My mom isn't bad. She's a good person that was left with bad people. A fierce force of protective energy surges through me and I know that without a doubt, I would kill and be killed for this woman. The woman who I also recognize to be the woman in the photo I found when I was in my father's office all those years ago.

"Lydia was going to be next too." Pearl runs her slick tongue over her teeth, and I have to fight the urge to knock them all out.

Brianna steps forward now. "Lydia stepped up the best she could when father stood down. It's why they call them stepparents. Lydia is none of your concern."

"Enough!" Bryant hollers behind me, and the silence that shifts into the air is chilling. "I've heard enough."

His hand finds mine, and he twists my fingers with his, turning me around to face him. I inhale his scent, burying my face into the crook of his neck. "Mom comes home with us."

He kisses the top of my head as I slowly gather my composure. "Yeah, baby, she is. We will take care of her." I appreciate him hiding my vulnerability, taking control of the situation by doing so.

His arms tighten around me, but his words are for Pearl. "I would have never bought it if you switched places with Isa."

"True," Max says, and my jaw snaps closed. "Which is why the switch didn't happen. Though I was convinced right up until that first night at your place." He pauses. "Fate? The cabin was your father's. It was his and Brooke's fuck house. Even had portraits of her hanging around the place until Pearl redid them, smudging out her face." I shiver at the realization that I had been wearing Brooke's clothes and not Stacey's.

"Stacey..." I whisper. Even though it's muffled into Bryant's suit, Max hears it.

"Was a plant all along. I knew her connection to Bryant from the day I met her. It was all part of it. Though when she suspected I was hiding things, she left me. She didn't know exactly what she suspected, which is the only reason why she is still breathing right now..."

I feel Bryant tense.

I should feel jealous that he's protective over someone else that's not me, but I find myself not going there. If anything, it has made me realize how much heart he does hide beneath the elusive surface and lavish suits. There's a peace that is washing through me. All this time, I thought I was crazy. Unbalanced. A recluse. But it wasn't me at all. It was the forces around me.

"Shut the fuck up..." Bryant growls. "You're lucky you're still breathing right now."

Max chuckles.

Bryant ignores him, bending down and tucking his index finger beneath my chin to tilt my face up to his. "I'll ask you one thing."

I blink, following the hard edges of his high cheekbones and scruffy jawline.

He bends down until his lips touch my earlobe. "Hart Island, or pig farm?"

They deserve murder. They deserve pain. Suffering. Torture.

But I don't want to shower Bryant with more sins, I want to wash the ones that are already stained on his hands clean. It will take years, but I'm confident.

I shake my head.

"Baby, we can't let them go. Harper will never be safe. They could come back and plot more bullshit. We will be constantly looking over our shoulders."

"He's right." Brianna breaks her silence, and I slowly turn my face toward her. Her arm is over our mom protectively, as she rests against her chest. Her otherwise perfectly prim attire and stature is bent, crooked, and dark. It's the most real I've ever seen her, and I love it. "Isa, think about it. I have a kid too. I won't feel—" She shakes her head.

Devon clears his throat. "It will take under two minutes."

My lips curl beneath my teeth.

"We can come to an agreement, Isa..." the woman who should have been called sister says. "You don't have to do this."

"You." Devon points. "Shut your fucking mouth before I bury my cock in it."

"Thought it'd take you two minutes," she tries to answer back.

"Oh, it would. Who said you'd be alive?"

Oh god.

"I don't want more death..." I find myself saying, my voice breaking on the edge. I squeeze my eyes shut.

"How about this..." Bryant whispers into my ear. "How about you, Brianna, and Isabel let us handle it, and we promise you that they will never be a problem for you again."

"And you won't kill them?" I say, blinking up at Bryant. I don't know why the sudden change. I *should* want them dead. I do want them dead. I just don't want to have to live with their ghosts for the rest of my life.

His eyes narrow before he smiles. "Sure."

I'm not sure I believe him.

I nod, swiping my nose with the back of my hand. "Okay."

I turn to face the two of them. The people who by blood, were meant to be family to Brianna, Isabel and I, but only wanted ours spilled.

Devon points down to the inside of the building. "The

three of you get back inside. I'll make sure Isabel gets home safely too, Isa. You can trust me."

That fucking word again. *Trust.* Do we ever really trust anyone? Or are we just let down when they lie.

"Bryant!" Devon says. "You have a speech to make."

"He's right." Bryant exhales, loosening the tie on his suit. "I do. Shit."

Just as Devon smirks, three other men step out from the shadows, wearing dark suits. They must be with Devon.

Devon winks. "We got this."

"Devon, I said no—"

He puts his finger up to his mouth, instantly shutting mine. "Shhh, my little rock star. As we agreed. You will know nothing."

"Isa!" Max calls out, as Pearl starts swearing against one of the other men. "You don't want to do this."

"Do what?" Devon chuckles. "She's not doing anything. That's the whole point."

Bryant takes my arm, gesturing us down to the end of the street where the limo Devon came from sits. "You can take Brianna and Pearl back to the house. I'll be home straight after I say my withdrawal speech."

I stop, just as we're short of the car. Bryant pulls the door open and Jer is already sitting in the driver's seat. "Your what?"

Bryant moves the stray hair away from my face and tucks it behind my ear. "I'm not doing this. I can't be the product of your trigger, baby."

I think over who this man is. Everything that he makes me feel. How much of a great father he is to Harper. If he even put a smidge of himself into being a president like he does into being a husband or a father, then I know that America will be well looked after. I had reservations. I had triggers. But after everything coming to light tonight, I've found that it didn't matter. It didn't matter that my father was the president. I would never have been good enough for him anyway. Ever. It was a him problem, not a president problem. Stacey, I'm still not sure how I feel about, but I again feel that peace washing through me. Like this is it. It's over.

"Did you hear me?" Bryant asks, searching my eyes. "I have to go in, baby. We've been out here for forty minutes and the auctions are finishing up."

"No," I rush out, my hand coming to his.

"No you didn't hear me? I figured." Bryant rolls his eyes, tapping on the top of the car as Brianna slips inside.

"No as in I don't want you to withdraw."

He pauses, slowly coming back to standing. He searches my face. "What?"

I reach for his hand and study how contrastingly different we are. His tattoos against my spotless flesh. I can't help but think over my thoughts just minutes earlier about washing away his sins. "Bryant. You're my husband. I trust you. I'm not perfect, and I won't be good at this life. I don't know a thing about censorship or even being able to string a sentence together without an F-bomb. But I'll be here to support you. I can't promise I'll be perfect, but I'll do my best."

"Baby..." he whispers, placing a soft kiss on my forehead. He looks back down at me. "Go home."

I smile, for the first time in a long time, I feel the edges of my lips curve over my teeth at full extension. "Do what you feel is right. Okay? And I'll be here for you."

"I won't let anything happen to you or Harper."

"I know," I whisper, nodding my head.

"You can always be whoever the fuck you want to be and people can deal with it."

I grin. "I also know this."

"I love you." His eyes soften around the edges.

I bring the palm of my hand up to his cheek. "I love you too."

A voice clears behind us. "Um, sorry, Bryant."

Bryant tenses, his eyes widening on me. He's probably expecting me to snap and be hostile like I have been to Stacey, but after everything tonight, I feel like I may have overreacted. I trust Bryant, and that's the bottom line. It has to be.

"Sorry, you're up!"

Bryant kisses me again. "I'll see you tonight. In our room. In my bed." He leans down and bites on my ear. "With your legs spread and tied to *our* bed."

I flush beet red as I watch him turn and head toward Stacey. Just before they disappear through the front door, Stacey turns to face me.

"Oh, and Isa?" she calls out, as I'm halfway into the car.

I bring my eyes to hers.

She smiles genuinely. "In case he didn't tell you, I haven't fucked this idiot since I had pimples on my cheeks."

Bryant laughs so loud that the only thing that cuts it off is the doors closing behind them.

"Motherfucker," I snap under my breath, getting into the car and slamming the door closed behind me.

We arrived home forty minutes ago, both had showers and then helped put Mom to bed in Devon's quarters. She's so demure and frail, and every time I look at her, I want to kill Peter all over again. How could he claim to love her the way he obviously did but treat her like this? Ash is cooking us up waffles in the kitchen as Jess, Brianna, and I are sipping hot cocoa at the dining room table.

"Are you fucking kidding me?" Jess whispers, shocked. We just filled her in from start to finish on all that has happened.

"All along? This was the play? People were hurt because of this? I mean, damn." Jess gestures to Brianna. "Your sister got shot, stopped talking to you because of it, and Harper was in danger—with us literally on the road."

"Jess," I snap. "I know. I know how it all unfolded." I massage my temples before picking up my mug.

"I never hated you because of me getting shot," Brianna finally says, after keeping quiet the whole time. "Well, it was that, but it was more that you were always so reckless. I guess I just felt more anger toward you because of it." She exhales, looking into her hot cocoa. "I didn't know where you were. Dad said you were getting better and it made sense, you know? I mean, you did some crazy shit."

I snort. "That's putting it lightly."

Brianna almost smiles. "I believed him when even in my gut I knew that something was off. It was all too convenient to have you away getting better. But then I thought Harper had been hurt. There was so much blood, that it could have been hers, only it was obviously all mine." Brianna swipes her tears. "I'm sorry, Isa. I should have fought harder for you as a kid, through this, and I should have been a better sister."

I brought my hand to hers and squeezed. "You don't need to say anything." And she didn't. I knew. I knew where she was coming from and I also knew that now, when she smiled at me, that it was genuine.

"Right! I have pancakes!" Ash comes laughing into the room, carrying a stack of the best fucking pancakes I would ever have the pleasure of eating.

Later that night, I'm wrapped up in Bryant's sheets, sweat licking off my body and the bright moonlight peeking in through his floor to ceiling windows. His room is a minimalist dream.

Harper's crib is now tucked in the corner in the room, though, with Bryant refusing to allow her even a footstep away from him.

"Are you ever going to tell me what Devon has done to Pearl and Max?" I murmur.

Bryant chuckles, so deep the muscles on his stomach shake my face. "No. I won't."

"But how am I going to wash your sins clean if you don't allow me to see them?" I run the tip of my finger over the cut lines of his stomach, over his tattoos.

"Simple," he whispers. "You don't. But you continue to love me anyway."

"How did your speech go tonight?" I ask, my throat swollen.

"Good," he grumbles. "I think despite the fact that you can't stand him, James Taylor will probably make a great president."

I freeze, pushing up from his chest while tucking my hair behind my ear. "You stepped away?"

Bryant nods, his finger brushing over his bottom lip. "Fucking yes I did. Isa, none of that matters to me. I don't need it. I have you and Harper, that's all I'll ever need."

I lean down and press my lips to his, crawling over his lap and rubbing myself over his thickness.

He chuckles into my mouth, biting down on my bottom lip. "Take it you're happy."

"Yes." I press another soft kiss onto his lips. "So fucking happy."

Bryant told me that Stacey had also found out that Max's connection with me had to be much more than just him getting back at her for leaving him, which is what she thought the first time Max and I came to Bryant's for dinner. Bryant convinced her to go along with it and to pretend like nothing was happening. At first, Stacey was there to sit at Bryant's side when he knew he was going to run for presidency, but of course, that all changed the second I came back. I think over time, I will warm to her, but for now, I still don't like her.

Bryant and I, our road to love wasn't an easy one. It was hurdled with tricks, games, lies, and death. People who shouldn't have, deceived both of us, but we got there in the end. To the end.

My lesson wasn't easy to get to, but is simple enough to explain. If you feel crazy, make sure you check the people around you before self-diagnosing yourself with insanity. The people you invite into your life don't always wipe their feet at the door before entering your mind. My father may have failed me, but my mother didn't. All this time, she was my saving grace, and I eventually was hers.

TWENTY-SIX

Bonnie and Clyde ain't got shit on us.
-Bryant

Christmas Day

"Bryant! Bring the food into the sitting room!" my mother orders from the lounge, sipping her glass of wine. Tinsel and Christmas lights decorate the entirety of my parents' tradi-tional plantation-style home as the smell of crispy roasted meat and fluffy crusted potatoes fill the space. I never would have thought in a million fucking years that our Christmas this year would be filled with all of the people who are in the room today. Isa, Harper, Mom, Dad, Devon, Jess, Jer, Ash, Stacey and her new flavor for the week, and Isabel.

Isa bought a psychiatric hospital in Connecticut close to our home and named it *Sane*. There was no way we could have Isabel in our home because of the severity of her symptoms, so we did the next best thing and bought a whole institute. One where we knew not just Isabel, but all of our patients would always be treated with respect and safety. We hired the best of the best in this business and redecorated it to look more like a home and less like an actual hospital. Stacey and Isa have turned into best fucking friends. I knew they would. They're too similar in some ways to not find common ground. Now Harper calls her auntie and her and Jess fight over who is the favorite. Brianna just laughs at them all, knowing it's probably really her.

Mom and Dad don't know a thing that happened between all of us, and they don't need to know. They found out about Isa's father and what he did to her, but that's about as far as the extent of their knowledge goes. James Taylor ran for presidency and won. I didn't know him personally, but Isa is quite passionate about how much she can't stand him. I think it has more to do with the fact that he reminds her of her father and less to do with him as a person. I didn't give up on Isa. Not once. But you should never stop trying, even after you've won, because the person who lost to you won't be far behind.

All of the family's chatter dies out behind me because all I see is her.

Nothing but her.

The girl who took everything inside of me and replaced it with parts of herself. She bled for me, would die for me, and carry me to the fucking ends of the earth. The woman who drove me goddamn wild for the second half of my life, only to finally sit her stubborn ass down and allow me to take care of her.

My queen who wears her broken soul proudly, just so other women don't have to feel like they need to conceal or fix theirs. She's a fucking soldier. A product of resilience. It doesn't matter if you knock her down, she'll always come back up swinging, and you better fucking run when she does.

Isa is right. I will never tell her what Devon did to Max and Pearl. But as I bring my glass of whiskey to my lips, I smirk smugly with the knowledge that they will never be able to lay another finger on my family.

Isa smiles up at me as Harper bounces on her knee opening her presents. My mom has her phone, recording, Stacey is kissing her new lover, Jess is sitting eagerly, waiting for Harper to open her present, Jer is wearing a bright Christmas sweater that Isa bought him, Devon has his arm around Isa, and Isabel smiles off to the distance, her hair tied up in a clean top knot, her eyes bright and filled with love.

Everything is as it should be. Max and Pearl will never hurt my girls again.

Why, you ask? Because dead people stay dead.

EPILOGUE

Twenty-one years later

Harper's engagement to Dylan, someone she met in college, wasn't a shock to me. It was to Bryant. I had to hide all of the guns in our house, and Devon's house, for the first six months that she was dating him. Bryant hated him.

Bryant still hates him.

"My baby girl!" Bryant stretches his big, muscular arms wide, wrapping them around Harper. He wears his salt and pepper hair short on the sides and slicked back on the top. His tattoos are as clean as they were the day I met him, and he's every bit the same asshole too.

"Hey, Daddy! Are you ready?" Harper drives home once a month so she and he can go on their father-daughter dates. It was part of the requirement from Bryant for allowing her to date Dylan.

As I said.

He still hates him.

"Hi, sweetie." I give her a hug before pulling Dylan in for

his own. I, on the other hand, adore Dylan. He takes care of her in the way that Bryant did me. He's just too stubborn to see it right now.

"Hi, Mrs. Royal." Dylan walks in, shaking off the snow on his hat and hanging it on the stand.

"Dylan," Bryant grunts, his eyes narrowing. "Did I ever tell you about Heart Island?"

I shove Bryant out the door with Harper. "Get out. Now. Leave Dylan alone." They both leave, and I lean against the doorframe just as they're sliding into the back seat, with Jer popping out of the driver's side.

Jer waves at me from a distance.

I wave back. Jer has helped immensely over the years with my building of Sane, my psychiatric hospital. We now have four clinics over America and are looking at opening another in Australia. My mom is still here, and she and Harper share a strong bond that frightens me on the best of days. Harper's personality is infectious, sweet, and unique. I'm not sure what Bryant and I did to deserve her.

The sun sets in the background as the limo drives off into the sunset, and I sigh, resting my head against the doorframe and inhaling the leftover oxygen of the day.

We made it.

And we will keep making it.

One step at a time, but the steps will always be taken together.

My husband.
My kids.
My mum, sisters, and brothers.
Sarah Sentz - AKA Momager AKA Kris Jenner AKA KJ.
My team of editors.
My Amy Haltz.
My Wolf Pack.
My Street Queens.
My Master Bloggers.
My author buds.
All the strong women who inspire us to be better, do better,
and treat everyone better.
My dog, Raze.
My BFFS Gin & Wine.

My sanity. RIP.

Finally, I acknowledge all this who deal with their struggles
internally. The ones who don't involve people in our dark
times because we're too afraid that our darkness will stain
their hands. Your struggles can be a lonely place, and the load
can be heavy, but you're not alone. You're a warrior.

Printed in Great Britain
by Amazon

46909538R00151